NEVER BEEN TRACED

A Tomas O'Malley Story

KENNETH S. KAPPELMANN

Black Rose Writing | Texas

ISBN: 978-1-68433-342-4
PUBLISHED BY BLACK ROSE WRITING
www.blackrosewriting.com

Printed in the United States of America
Suggested Retail Price (SRP) $18.95

Never Been Traced is printed in Gentium Premier Pro

This book is dedicated to the 7 students from one school district who took their own lives

over the 4 years my children were in high school in Kansas.

They will never be forgotten by their family, friends, and loved ones

Teenage suicide is critically important in today's society. With the increase in social media, bullying has taken on new levels which often are never recognized by parents or friends. If you are being bullied or threatened through social media, please get help immediately. If you are thinking about suicide, are worried about a friend or loved one, or would like emotional support, the Lifeline Network is available 24/7 across the United States.

National Suicide Prevention Lifeline: 800-273-8255

Although this book is fiction, situations do exist that can lead to extreme depression, anger, and loss. Do not be afraid to get the help you need.

NEVER BEEN TRACED

1 I CROUCHED IN the bushes with a bead of sweat sliding off my pale, cold nose. It was chilly outside, common for March in Chicago. However, wrapped in a black Tyvek suit from head to toe did not allow for any body heat to escape. If it had been daylight and anyone had seen me, they would have thought I looked like an astronaut, only instead of NASA's white suits with red and blue letters, this suit was solid black. I special ordered it from a pharmaceutical supply company out of California. The suit provided the necessary barrier to ensure, as a Boy Scout would say, "no sign left behind."

My heart was racing. Although it seemed well planned out, I had only been working on this for a few weeks. I did not know this area well which made it hard to plan it right, but it had to be done.

"Come on," I whispered. "Don't be late today. There's no time." My voice cracked slightly and I wasn't even sure if I was speaking out loud or just thinking the words as there was nobody in the area to hear.

As if by clockwork, the front door opened and the young, junior cheerleader came bounding out. The temperature was actually above freezing, another fear I had. If it was too warm, it wouldn't work. The cheerleader carried a backpack that had a Swiss Gear label on it. I did not know why I looked at it or acknowledged the brand of backpack, but I did. My legs tensed up and the nerves seemed to fire making the pain of the crouched position even stronger. The girl ran to the driver's side of her car, which was literally only five to six feet from the bushes where I sat silently watching. She opened the back door and threw her backpack on the seat, and then, shutting the door quietly so as not to wake the neighbors or more importantly her parents, she moved to the front. She reached her hand out to grab the handle and then heard a stick crack. She turned and stared directly toward me. I froze.

"Inky, is that you?"

A black cat with a white patch under its chin leaped from the bushes passing a few feet from where I crouched. I wanted to scream but remained motionless and quiet.

"You scared me, silly cat," she said, reaching her hand out.

The cat let out a soft meow, rubbed her side against the girl's leg a few times, and then bounded toward the garage and into a small cat door at the base.

"Well, good morning to you too," she said with attitude only a teenage girl can muster on demand. She turned, opened the car door, and climbed inside.

Here it goes, I thought. *Now or never. What are you going to do, little girl?*

The girl started the car, messed with some of the controls on the dash, and as quickly as possible, jumped back out of the car leaving it running in the driveway. Within moments, she was back inside the house and out of sight.

I took a deep breath and lowered my head because the realization that this was actually going to happen suddenly was thrust upon me. I closed my eyes and again felt the aches and pains throughout my lower body. My legs were stiff. They had been bent down in a crouched position for hours. My feet hurt. The new shoes I just purchased the day before were not comfortable and not broken in. My muscles were tight, possibly from the tense nature of my whole body or possibly from my unusual position. But despite all these factors, it was now or never.

I stood slowly, checked the area for any unplanned witnesses, and when I saw nothing, I darted to the car. Quietly I opened the door making even less noise than the cheerleader had previously. I slipped into the car, put it in gear, and backed out of the driveway. In only seconds, I was gone.

Now it was all timing. I had a mile to go. The same mile I had walked several hours ago from my car. I drove the speed limit as the last thing I wanted was to be picked up for speeding wearing an all-black Tyvek jumpsuit in a stolen car. I knew one thing and one thing only—this all depended on timing. If I got there too late, it was all for nothing. If I got there too early and there was a delay, the car would come up missing and become a target for the police. Everything had to be perfect.

I drove by my parked car on the road and knew I was close. The keys were in my car so it would be a quick getaway if all went as planned. *As planned*, I thought to myself. In my mind, I really started to wonder if I could even go through with it... If I could go through with it a second time. But this time it was not an adult, it was a kid, a teenager. Then I remembered why I was there, why this teenager, and why this had to happen. I had to do it.

I reached my location and turned the lights off but left the car idling. I was a few hundred yards from my car, which was out of sight, not just because of the darkness of the morning, but my car was over the crest of a hill. It was a perfect location not tied at all to the house in front of me. I looked ahead. A streetlight several houses down provided just enough light to see the Mustang in the driveway. *That fucking Mustang*, I thought. *Of course he drives a Mustang. I'm surprised the rich boy doesn't have a Corvette or Mercedes.* The bitterness in my thoughts was clear. This punk was an entitled ass who needed to be brought down a notch.

Just then the porch light came on. It appeared to be motion-detected because the previously unnoticed teenage boy was already bounding down the steps. His hair appeared unkempt and it looked like he was wearing sunglasses. It was before 7:00 AM, still before sunrise, and he was wearing sunglasses. Enough said.

He ran to the passenger side of the front seat and threw his backpack in. He swung his head like he was a model at a photo shoot as he turned to switch to the driver's side. For a moment, it appeared he was going to slide across the hood like Bo Duke used to on the General Lee.

When he came around the front of the Mustang, I saw it: a letter jacket. *What was this, the 1960s?* But the thought ended quickly because it was time. Sweat now streaked down both sides of my face. Perhaps it was from the Tyvek suit, but more likely, it was immense stress for what was about to happen. As the young man passed the front of the car, I shifted my stolen car into drive and floored the gas. The boy made it to the Mustang's driver's side door when he must have realized the engine sound was too loud for the normal morning traffic noise, and way too loud for this very residential street. He turned in time to see the headlights come on, but he had no time to move. The car was bearing down on him. The front bumper hit his knees square and they actually bent ninety degrees under the car. The hood ornament punctured directly through his navel and his head slammed into the hood and then bounced up like a ball. To me, there was no sound. To the environment, it sounded as if a bomb had gone off. The airbag exploded, sending my head back against the seat. *Stay conscious,* I thought. I had to stay conscious or this would all be for nothing. I had more to do. I had to stay conscious and get out.

Though dazed, I pushed open the door. It stuck a little. The impact of the car had pushed the frame back, but I was able to force it open—an issue I had not taken into account while planning this out. Regardless, I climbed out of the car and took a quick glance at the boy who laid limp on the hood of the cheerleader's car with a pool of blood forming around him. I quickly grabbed an envelope I had stashed inside my Tyvek suit and tossed it next to him. With a quick glance toward the house, I saw a series of lights coming on. With that, the sprint was on.

I had to remember every critical step of the plan. I first took a quick step in the pool of blood to create a few footprints on the concrete driveway. I then was careful to step hard in the turned-up dirt from the skidding car leaving another indentation there, then at a full sprint, I was headed right back to the parked car just over the hill. From any direction with the black Tyvek suit, black shoes, and black gloves, I knew I was completely invisible. I knew I would not be seen except for maybe at the car. I had to get into the car, start it, and get out without drawing attention. Behind me, I could hear the commotion of the accident—voices and screams from those in the house who ran out to witness the gruesome remains of what was left of their son, or brother, or whoever came out first. The loudest scream came from who had to be the mother, but I didn't care. *The mother should have raised a better son*, I thought.

I arrived at the car, kicked off my bloody shoe, and placed it in a bag I had left attached to the door handle. I glanced around and saw nobody. I climbed in the unlocked door, turned the key which was already in the ignition, and calmly drove away. My heart was racing and I knew I was not out of the woods yet. I was driving away from a murder scene dressed in full Tyvek with a bloody shoe in a bag in a neighborhood that I had no business being in. Finding a safe place to undress and dispose of the only evidence left was critical. I believed there was no trace left behind that would tie back to me. I had been very careful. It is the one thing I planned for certain. Leave only the evidence I meant to leave.

As the sun rose over the normally quiet neighborhood just off downtown Chicago, one car slowly made its way out of this small residential suburb, and one family's life was quickly turned upside-down.

2 "YOU GET A CALL already this morning, Tommy?" Tammi asked me as she went to grab her robe.

"Yep," I replied. "Let me just clean up a bit, and I'll be out of your way. Some high school kid was run down in his own driveway. Sounds pretty messy. Franky is going to meet me there."

"Okay," she replied, her tone showing just a hint of disappointment. She appeared like she was going to elaborate, then held her thought.

I stopped, recognizing the change. I was a twenty-plus-year Chicago homicide detective. I had moved up the ladder at a normal pace but stalled out at detective. It was not for lack of ability in solving cases. In fact, I had cleared more cases than any other detective in the department. It was more a lack of political savvy. I got along well with my sometimes partner Frank Sullivan, another long-term detective. There were maybe half a dozen other detectives that I considered *good people.* My boss, Sergeant Craig Carter, was basically a hard-ass, but solid nonetheless, and everyone else pretty much didn't give a shit what happened to me, as long as it didn't come back to bite them.

I took a deep breath allowing my voice to be less hurried and show a genuine level of caring. "What is it, Tammi?" Simple and to the point, just like I always was.

"I was hoping we could talk this morning," she replied.

That stopped me in my tracks. The dreaded "we need to talk" can be directly translated from woman speech to man speech as, "it's not you, it's me," followed by, "I think we need some space." I had a crime scene to get to, but I was not going to simply let this one hang out there. "What do we need to talk about, Tammi?" Instantly I noticed that my voice was not as strong as it typically was. It was almost as if I was saying the words gingerly to make her less apt to return with anything I didn't want to hear.

She smiled which put me a little more at ease, but that ended quickly. "No, Tommy, I don't want to be rushed. We will talk tonight, but please set aside some time." She turned, went into the bathroom, and shut the door.

That did not make me feel any better, plus I needed the bathroom to get ready to go. "Fuck it," I said out loud though nobody was there to hear me. I threw on my sports coat and ran my hand through my hair looking in the mirror as I did so. I issued a disappointing grunt, then left the room even pulling the door shut a little harder than I should have just to send the message, *I don't want to talk later. If you're going to dump my butt, let's talk now.*

We had been dating for only a handful of months. She was out of my league when we started and she was out of my league now. Further, after one date, or should I say one *night* together, she was kidnapped and tortured by one of the most powerful crime bosses in Chicago. Ross Moretti orchestrated a frame-up of his rival boss, Joey Polino, which left Polino, two undercover officers, and a mess of prostitutes dead and my new would-be girlfriend beaten and left in a cage. Somehow though, she let me back into her life and since that time, we had been together. Moretti and his hired henchman Marco Filini walked away clean with all charges on Moretti being officially dropped last week. Now suddenly my longest standing relationship since my marriage was looking like it was going to suffer the same fate as Moretti's charges.

Tammi was, and still is, the assistant manager at a top-of-the-line steak house in the heart of downtown Chicago. The case led me to that restaurant and from there she and I fell in love. Fell in love is relative to your point of view. When you are out of your league, you are in love. When you are the leader in the league, you are hanging out enjoying your time. Things had been going very well since those first few hard weeks after the kidnapping. We had worked through it and I had even tried to up my game for her. She migrated from a drawer, to part of the closet, to essentially being completely moved into my place by the end of January. From my perspective, things were good. From her perspective, we needed to talk.

I headed directly out of the house without stopping to grab anything to eat or drink. I arrived at my 1974 shit-brown Camaro with the rebuilt 350 Chevy small block, and yes, just by saying it I know everyone thinks, *boy, that guy is super cool.* I fired up the beast and the tires may have even squealed a bit as I started. I felt like I was in high school and I had just walked into a party and seen my girlfriend kissing my best friend. That woman knows how to get under my skin. She is the true puppet master, and I am some lame string puppet tied to her fingers. That is what happens when you date out of your league. I had no business being with her and I knew it.

It was about a twenty-minute drive to where the accident was. I knew Franky had a slightly longer drive and the medical examiner, Dr. Elise Gerstenberger or Dr. G as everyone called her, would be driving from North Chicago, which means I had time. Most people try to go to Starbucks, Caribou Coffee, or even White Hen Pantry in the morning in Chicago. Me, I go to Mr. J's, and I don't order coffee. I order a

Dagwood, AKA the greasiest, fat-induced burger you will ever find, and by far the best burger in the country. I entered the fine dining establishment at 7:45 and to my surprise, Frank Sullivan was already inside ordering.

"I picked you up a Dagwood, Tommy. I hope that was all right." Franky was smiling, already knowing the answer. His tone changed slightly when he saw my face. "What's the matter? I know you wanted one or you wouldn't be here."

"No," I said changing my expression immediately. "It's not that. I couldn't be more pleased with a Dagwood—loaded I assume."

"Of course," he replied.

"It is Tammi," I added more softly. "She *wants to talk*." As I said the statement, I placed air quotes around the end of the sentence and then realized how stupid that looked and pulled my hands down.

"Uh oh," he replied lifting an eyebrow. "I thought things were going well?" The tone of the comment made it a question.

I sighed. "I did too. It's been a long time since I thought something had a chance. Ever since you-know-who left me for the f'ing lawyer, I really hadn't given anyone the time of day."

"How is Stephanie?" Frank asked smiling.

Stephanie O'Malley, now Stephanie Bascom, was my first wife. We had two beautiful kids, both in college. I was not estranged from my kids. We talked on the phone and saw each other at one or two holidays a year at least for a day or so, but since their mother had remarried and moved out to the burbs, our paths just did not cross as much as they should.

I looked back at Franky and clearly saw that my momentary stupor with my thoughts about my kids had made him slightly uneasy. "What was that?" I asked. "I was thinking about something else," I added, buying time.

"I asked about Stephanie. How is she?"

"Still a bitch, but since her income with her hubby greatly exceeds my own and both kids have scholarships, all seems much better than a few years ago."

Franky recognized my lost thoughts and let the small talk drop. Besides, the Dagwoods had arrived. "Want to eat here or in the car?" asked Franky.

"I say let's chow them down here. We are going to beat Dr. G there regardless."

"Agreed," Franky added, stretching his arm outward as he spoke.

"The gun shot still hurting?" I asked.

"What?" He replied. "I can't lift my arm one time and have you not ask about it?"

"Forget it," I added in return, my tone clear.

Franky had been shot in the line of duty several months ago. It was a big case that brought us both a lot of notoriety, and pain. It was the first time he had been shot, and he hoped it would be the last. He said it was not nearly as romantic as he always thought it would be, and kept him at his desk for more than six weeks. We sat at a nearby table without further talk until I took my first bite.

"Oh my God!" I exclaimed. "In some ways, this is better than sex."

"Jesus, you guys are having problems then," he answered, smiling slightly. "These are good, but not even close to sex-worthy."

"Fair enough," I replied. "You are welcome to your opinion."

We didn't speak much more for the next two or three minutes. The grease from the burger was hot and leaked in spots across the table, but for the most part, we left the place clean. We knew we had a crime scene to get to and although the Dagwood was a nice diversion, that diversion did have a limited time and the crime scene did not. Franky's phone vibrated. He picked it up and glanced at his text. "Carter wants to see us after we finish at the accident."

"What about?" I asked.

"Doesn't say. Just he wants to see us."

I shook my head trying to answer his unasked question. "I didn't do anything so don't ask."

"Damnit, Tommy. Every time you say you didn't do anything, how come every time it ends up you did?"

Again I protested. "But this time I didn't."

"Whatever." Franky's tone clearly showed he did not believe me. I really did not have a response. History had shown he was right, but this time, I truly did not have any idea why we needed to meet our sergeant.

We headed out, looked at each other, and without speaking, collectively decided to take Frank's car. The Camaro would be fine waiting for me at Mr. J's. More than likely, I would be back.

• • • • • •

We pulled into the residential area and there were more people than there should be on the sidewalk on such a brisk day. It was not what anyone in Chicago would call cold, but it was not morning walking weather either. Obviously, they were walking toward something—something that was drawing their attention.

This was one of the small residential outcroppings that grew out of a revitalizing project by the city of Chicago. In the horizon, most of these houses still overlooked downtown. Another four to five miles in any direction and you were in low-income housing, but in these pockets, you could find some very nice single-family homes. The school district was still inner city. Most of these kids went private, or at least that's what I had seen in the past. Crime did touch these neighborhoods, but at a much less rate than the adjacent areas. This particular neighborhood had been nearly fully developed for about seven years. In that time, I probably had been here due to cases at least ten times, but it was reduced every year. The process was working, so my first thought was, *what happened today to change all that?*

As we approached the address that had been sent to us, we knew well in advance we had found the right house. There was a crowd around a driveway. There were groups of people. It seemed like six to eight people per group was the magic number. There were at least four groups that size with occasional participants moving from one to another.

Franky looked to me. "What the hell happened?"

I did not answer. The car was barely crawling forward. There were people crossing the street and some of the small groups had set up their campsite in the center of the road. "We need to get some crowd control. Every family in the closest thirty houses has decided to come and contaminate the crime scene." I paused and pointed. "Holy shit! Check out the Mustang."

In the driveway was a Mustang. It had been T-boned right where it was parked. The damage on the car would have captured anyone's attention, but this one had taken it one step further. On the hood looked to be a teenager, most likely male, but to be honest, I wasn't sure. It appeared the boy had been pinned between the car in the driveway and the car that did the T-boning. His legs, though still attached, were no longer correctly connected to his torso. However, the most upsetting piece of this picture was most of his brains and blood appeared to be across the car. I could tell even from this distance the speed of the car hitting him was significant, to say the least.

"We need this crowd backed off," broke in Franky. "And we need everyone interviewed."

I nodded. "Nobody kills a kid and gets away with it."

"Nobody," added Franky.

●　　●　　●　　●　　●

We parked the car in front of 908 Keystone Place, one house south of the accident, and jumped out walking toward one of the groups. A uniformed female officer turned and smiled as if she knew me, but I had no idea who she was and with that, was not interested in talking. She had already failed in my mind. There was no control in the area and with each passing person coming within fifteen feet of the car, my crime scene was being contaminated.

"Detective O'Malley," she said, loud, not loud enough to be called a shout, but loud enough for me to hear.

I ignored the call. "Let's get some crime tape up." I was talking to another uniformed officer who was holding tape in his hand but not actually doing anything with it. "Move everyone back across the street. This road is going to be completely closed all the way back to the intersection to the south and about the same distance north. I don't want one person to set even one toe on the concrete."

The officer nodded and to my surprise, aggressively put the words into action. "Detective O'Malley?" the woman's voice said again, this time more quiet and questioning. "I was told to ask for you when I got…"

I walked toward the Mustang without acknowledging the female officer's voice. I already knew who she was, not her personally, but the type. She was either recently promoted and trying to assert some officer authority over the scene or recently transferred and trying to do the same. Most likely both. Bottom line, I did not have time for someone who thought so highly of herself.

"Detective O'Malley," she stated louder again.

I stopped, let out a long sigh, and turned back toward the sound of the voice, which to my surprise came from a woman who was now only a few feet behind me. She was in a street uniform with her hair pulled up neatly under her hat but I imagined that it was longer than typical regulations. Although she did appear attractive, that did not soften my response.

"Listen, Officer…" I gave a long enough pause to let her know I was not going to read her name badge and she should fill in the blank.

"Halterman. Patricia Halterman, and I'm a—"

I cut her off with my raised hand. "Tell me, Officer Halterman, what do you see here?" I motioned with my hand spanning the scene. "Do you see a situation that is under control? Do you see organization and leadership?" I believe she was about to answer but I did not give her the chance. "No, you don't. Why is that?"

Again she was going to answer, but I raised my hand directly in front of her face. "Because when my partner and I arrived here, nobody had done anything to control the scene. Nobody had kept the onlookers away. Nobody had set up a perimeter. Nobody had done their job."

I decided I would let her say a few words before I cut her off again. To my surprise, she had honed in on only one comment. In a questioning voice, she replied, "You have a partner?"

Frank and I had been on the job longer than anyone else at our level. Pretty much everyone knew we worked together more than fifty percent of the time. But new officers on the job would not know that. Instantly my detective mind started sifting through all the faces from the past and although I was sure I did not know this woman, she definitely knew me. The thought came to me to say, *Listen, sugar lips, why don't you go and get me and my not real partner some coffee and we will do your job for you*, but something inside me told me to keep my trap shut and simply control the crime scene.

"Listen, Officer Halterman. I don't mean any disrespect, but when I drive up and see an entire neighborhood walking through what most likely is evidence, I get a little worked up. I need you and your team to expand the perimeter and get these people off the street. We have a dead boy here and I can guarantee you the graphic nature of this accident is only causing more pain for the family and friends. We need every single person who even heard a bird chirp documented and interviewed. The medical examiner and her team will be here shortly and I want the area clear. If there is a clue left here, we are going to find it this morning."

She acted as if she was going to say more, but instead she turned and started dishing out direction. Something seemed a bit off with her, like she felt she was above this, but from my perspective, she was wearing the uniform and she could do what I told her without further comment. I didn't have time now anyway. When I met with Carter I would ask if he knew this Halterman and see what the story was. Until then, I had much more important things to do than worry about a street cop with delusions of grandeur.

"Franky!" I hollered.

"Yeah, Tommy, over here."

I looked toward the wreckage and saw him bending over the hood of the car. As I approached, I pointed to another officer and directed him to assist Halterman. "What do you see, Franky?" I asked as I drew near, the site actually turning my stomach.

"I see a kid who turned just in time to see a car split him in half. We are running the plates now. The kid had to be dead on impact. It looks like his head hit so hard on the hood of the car his brain almost exploded. The parents are inside. I haven't spoken to them yet. There's an envelope on the hood, and if you look, there's blood splatter all across the car hood and window, but the envelope is clean. I believe it was put there after impact."

"Jesus," I said. "A calling card? What do we have here, Franky?"

"I don't know for sure, Tommy, but I don't think this was an accident. There are no skid marks. No signs of braking. If anything, the car was accelerating when it drew nearer. The kid's phone must have been in his hand because it was launched about twenty-five feet over the car." He pointed to where I saw an evidence flag marking the location as well as several footprints identified on both the pavement in blood and in the lawn.

"What else do you have?" I asked.

"Nothing that you're going to be touching or talking about until I'm through with it," answered a voice I knew well.

"Elise, good to see you. Long drive in today?"

Dr. Elise Gerstenberger was the Cook County Medical Examiner. She had been the ME almost as long as I had been a cop—not a detective, but a cop. She was not the typical medical examiner. When I hear the title, I think of an old crotchety gray-haired man who talks with a low, grumbling voice and treats cops like crap. No, Dr. G, as everyone called her, was in her fifties and looked twenty-five. She ran every day, including the Chicago Marathon, and took extreme care of her body. To say she was pretty would not do her justice. However, none of that mattered because she was the best damned medical examiner I had ever met, and everyone knew it.

She placed her hand on my shoulder before answering. "Traffic was just starting to get bad. I was already headed in when I got the call. How are you doing, Tommy? This one looks bad."

Franky stepped over from where he had been inspecting the impact. "This is your scene, Doc. There's evidence all over the place. Footprints, the car itself, blood. I don't think the perpetrator was trying to hide anything."

"Maybe a crime of opportunity or passion," Elise replied. "But I guess we should let the evidence tell us that. Now please, remove yourself from my scene before I find some evidence linking you to the case."

"No problem," I replied. "There is an envelope on the hood of the Mustang. We think it was left from the driver of this car. I would like to know..."

"Again, gentlemen, last time I checked, you are not on my team. My team collects the evidence, you decide what to do with it. That envelope may or may not be important. You will find that answer in my report, and you will get my report when I am done. Not before. I do not speculate."

"That's the doctor I know and love. We're going to talk to the family."

"That would be a mighty fine idea for you to do," she replied, tilting her head slightly.

Anyone else I would probably call a bitch. Not Dr. G. No way.

Franky and I turned to walk up the driveway, careful to not step in anything that could possibly be evidence. I glanced back to Elise who was already working with her team to photograph the entire area before getting to the body. Officer Halterman, to her credit, had already cleared the entire area. Not only had she moved the onlookers across the street and another thirty feet or so off the road, she had organized them into lines and appeared to be setting up interviews. No, this did not improve my thoughts about her in the least. It basically only meant she went from not doing her job to doing the minimal amount of it. Nothing to be thought of as special.

"How do you want to do this?" asked Franky pulling me from my thoughts.

"Let's go in and see what we are walking into. For all we know, they already know who ran their son down and why." As a detective, sometimes you need to chase the evidence and pull information from every person around every corner. Sometimes all the information was readily available and handed to us on a silver platter. I was hoping this would be the case here. Boy, was I wrong.

• • • • •

We walked in the house, and it was exactly what I would expect. A small group of people, probably family or friends, around a table, one officer I didn't know, and a man and a woman. The man, I was guessing the father, wore a solemn look. His face was red and it was clear he had been crying, though he was not at this point in time. The woman, who I assume was the mother, was still in tears and through those tears came cries of "why," similar to Nancy Kerrigan after she had been hit with a police baton by Jeff Gillooli, the Tanya Harding-linked accomplice. I'm not sure why that reference came to my mind so vividly, but it must be sound recognition because this woman sounded exactly as I remembered Kerrigan. I don't know how I would have sounded if it were me in that situation, but I don't think I would be screaming "why" at the top of my lungs.

This momentary stupor ended when Franky said, "Hey folks. I can't even begin to understand the pain you're feeling at this moment, but I also want to stress, the best thing my partner and I can do for you is to find who did this. To do that, we need some of your time. Is there any way we can speak to you for a bit?"

Franky had a way of getting directly to the point, but doing it in such a fashion that included empathy and a softness that often brought the people involved very present to the discussion. The person I believed to be the mother looked up and then put her head back in her hands without speaking. The father figure placed his hand on her shoulder and then replied, "I am Mark's father, Michael Schulman, but you can call me Mike, and this is his mother, Runae."

That is why I am considered the best detective in the country. Picked out the mother and father with no help.

Mike Schulman continued. "What is it you want to know, Officer?"

Franky nodded and replied with a deep and caring tone still present in his speech, "It's Detective, actually. Detective Sullivan. Frank Sullivan. And this is Detective Tomas O'Malley. We have been assigned to the accident and would like to ask you a few questions about your son, Mark."

At the sound of his name Runae Schulman again broke into tears. Her voice was stressed and drawn out through the tears, but the words were clear. "What accident?" she said snidely. "That bitch drove her car right into my son."

Instantly that caught both Frank's and my attention. "You know the car that hit your son?" Franky asked.

"Know it..." she replied. "It's that bitch's car that seduced my son and then accused him of rape." Her voice flattened and she turned to stare at both of us. "I would know that car anywhere."

"Do you mind if we sit down?" I asked. "And perhaps we can have some privacy?" That second statement was meant for the others in the room. I didn't know them but there were several people there. I turned to acknowledge the others. "We will need statements from everyone, but it is critical we get key information now from the parents and we can't have your statements adjusted because you listen to what they say." Everyone seemed to understand. The officer who had been quiet since we appeared took the hint and began directing everyone out of the room, and I assume taking down their information. The only ones left sitting around the table were two grieving parents and two awesome and good-looking detectives (not really necessary descriptions but still accurate).

I took the lead now. "So, you know the owner of the car? Can we start with that?"

Mike glanced to his wife and the unspoken message he received was, *I am done answering right now, you take over*. Softly he began. "The car looks identical to Leah Malecha's car. She lives a mile or so from here. My son and she dated a while."

"Are you certain it is hers, or does it just look like hers?" I asked.

Runae answered aggressively before Mike could speak. "It is hers. I know it is."

I softened my voice now and raised my hand slightly. "Now, now, don't worry. It still has the plates so we will be able to trace it for sure." I paused and let that set a bit. Anything I could do to help them understand that we would catch who was responsible for this and would help them calm down and be more open was the first step. "Now, you mentioned that your son and Leah dated. Can you tell me about that?"

Mike took over again. "She's a cheerleader and my son is a football player. It made sense. They dated for a while." He now paused and looked up as if calculating on an imaginary chalkboard in the sky. "Maybe two months or so. Then, the night of the Christmas dance, they broke up and Leah later filed a complaint with the school that she had been raped that night."

"She filed it with the school and not the police?" I asked.

"Yes. She went to the school first, and then those at the school offered to perform their full investigation first and determine if there was anything they could find to support her case. They didn't want her going through everything if it could not be proven. No evidence could be found to support the claim. No witnesses or physical evidence, so the school representatives convinced her to drop the case."

Without speaking, I glanced at Franky and we both had the same thought. That was more than just motive, that was *extreme* motive. It had been my experience in more than twenty years of police work that roughly 100% of the time when a woman claimed she was raped, they actually were. Only people wanting to keep it quiet kept the truth from coming out.

"What happened with their relationship after the allegations came out?" Franky asked.

"It ended," Mike said. "I believe Mark called several times trying to work things out, but she would never take his calls."

"What school do they attend?" asked Franky.

"Fenton Northwest. It's a private school just inside the city limits. Most of the kids around here go there."

"I know Fenton," I said. "Used to be just a boys' school but added girls about four years ago."

"Correct," Mike replied. "I think five years ago actually."

I wanted to ask if they believed their son raped this girl, but now was not the time. We needed to keep these parents on the receptive side of the conversation, not shut them down. "Let's just pretend that although the car looks like hers, that it's not, and she had nothing to do with it. Who else would want to hurt your son? Did he receive any threats? Had he been in any fights? How about football games? Did he take another boy's position?"

"No, none of that," Mike answered. "He was a four-year starter at defensive end. He wasn't a straight-A student, but around a 3.0 GPA. He had a full ride to play D2 ball at William Jewell in Missouri. Everyone loved him."

In twenty-plus years, I had never heard a parent tell me their kid was bad. I remembered Andrea Jackson whose daughter had been mixed up in murder, prostitution, and drugs. Everything she told me was positive about her daughter. What's the cliché—rose-colored glasses? I am sure they believed it, but that was an answer we needed to take with a grain of salt. Franky knew that too.

"Great. Really good to hear," Franky broke in. "But make sure you're thinking about every avenue. A teacher, a coach, is there anyone else out there who would want to hurt your son?"

"No," Mike repeated again. "Nobody. Mark really did not upset the applecart."

His tone was slightly more agitated this time but not at a level that would shut him down. I wanted to redirect him back to uncontroversial areas. I stood and softened my voice slightly. "How about social media? Does he use Facebook, Snapchat, and Twitter?"

Before I could add anymore, Runae interjected, "All of them. All kids do."

I did not expect her quick answer but I thought I would push for more. "Right, all kids do, and often all kids have issues with it. Kids will say things from a keyboard that they won't say in person. Did he participate in that? Were you part of his social media or did you simply trust him?"

"What do you mean, did we trust him? Of course we checked his accounts. We were linked to all his accounts." She now had a slight tone as well. Franky and I worked well together and now was the perfect time for him to take over again, but he did not have the chance.

Officer Halterman entered the room carrying an evidence bag with a cell phone inside. "Detectives, the medical examiner recovered this from the lawn. She took her required photos and fingerprints. She wanted to know if you would take it to the lab for the IT boys to break it down, but you need to keep the chain of evidence."

I took the bag and Halterman exited back to the scene outside. I began examining the phone through the bag liner. I turned back to Runae and Mike. "Do you mind if we scan through this a bit? It may help direct us to who did this."

"Of course," Mike replied. "Do whatever you need to."

I removed the phone from the evidence bag and determined it was already on. To my surprise, it was not password protected. Perhaps he did not have anything to hide, and they should trust their son. I went to his Instagram and Twitter pages and there was not much there. A few pictures of him at what looked to be parties, but in none of them was he even holding a beer or anything questionable for that matter. Further, nobody in the background of the pictures was either. What this meant to me was not the same thing it meant to Mark's parents.

"You see, Detective," broke in Runae who was watching the pictures as Franky and I scanned them. "He had nothing to hide."

I smiled but didn't answer. In my mind my reply was, *big red flag, this boy was simply careful.*

I then opened his Snapchat. I am by no means an expert in these applications, but because of my job and the number of times evidence is found in these areas, I had become comfortable with them. What I instantly found when I went to his accounts page was he had two Snapchat accounts. One without a password, and one with. "What is the password for this account?"

Runae's smile faded for only a second before she answered. "You must be mistaken. We do not allow him to have password-protected social media."

I turned the phone to her. "The account, MarcoQQQQBeetch, requires a password."

"That account is not his," she replied quickly and without hesitation.

Franky again used his soft, parental, understanding voice. "It is on his phone. Listen folks, it's nothing to be embarrassed about. You said yourself, all kids use these. All kids also do things their parents don't know about. Having hidden social media accounts allows them to talk to their friends about things their parents don't know about. Can you guess the password? We will be able to get into it, but it would be easier to get in now together."

Mike shook his head and didn't answer the password question as he seemed to be stuck like his wife in disbelief that their son would have done this. "What does it even mean, MarcoQQQQBeetch?"

Franky looked at me and I don't think he could even guess. I pressed my lips together and replied, "If you will excuse my language, I believe it means, 'Mark Will Fuck You Bitch.' The city had to stop allowing four Q's next to each other on personalized license plates because in the social media world it means 'fuck you' when you say it fast."

"Oh my God," exclaimed Runae. "It can't be." She again broke into tears.

Franky interjected. "Hey folks, we are getting off-track here. I still go back to what you already said—all kids do it. This is not a crime. His screen names are not a concern. What if someone in these communications within this account made some threats against him? Think hard. What could the password be?"

While he was talking, I had taken a second scan back to Facebook and Instagram and found secondary accounts in both of them as well, and both were password protected. Runae and Mike saw me do this and again looked as if they were balloons losing air. Franky and I were losing them. That was for sure.

Just then the kitchen door flew open leading to the garage and a teenage, pimple-faced kid emerged with tears streaming down his face. "Mr. and Mrs. Schulman, what happened to Mark?" His voice was distraught and loud and almost not understandable.

Runae opened her arms. "We don't know, Andy," she replied, now through flowing tears again as saying the words to someone brought the pain back to the surface. The two embraced.

"Excuse me, Andy was it?" I asked.

They broke and he turned to face me. The kid had to be 16-18 years old. Definitely not a football player. I would put him captain of the debate team, but who am I to judge.

"Yes, I am Andy. Andy Carpen."

Mike interjected. "Andy is also a senior, though still seventeen years old so he's slightly younger than Mark. But above all, he is Mark's best friend. He has been since they could walk. He lives five houses down."

I introduced myself and then Franky and motioned toward a chair. "Andy, do you mind grabbing a seat? You may be able to help us."

He seemed hesitant all of a sudden. Not suspiciously hesitant, just hesitant. He took a seat next to Mark's dad and Mike placed his hand on his shoulder in a comforting manner. I looked up to Franky and he took the hint without even a pause.

"You see, Andy," started Franky. "We need to figure out what happened and why. We are going to ask you a few questions, but we need to do that with your parents present because you're only seventeen, as Mr. Schulman mentioned. However, one thing we can ask you is if you know Mark's passwords to his secondary social media accounts? Not his main ones that everyone sees, but the MarcoQQQQBeetch accounts?"

Instantly Andy's face changed. To his credit, Mike Schulman calmly inserted, "It's okay, Andy, we know about them. They may help us find out if there is a potential person out there who would have wanted to hurt Mark. Do you know the password?" His voice was soft and comforting, somewhat out of character for how he had been to this point.

Andy's voice, however, was weak and even cracked. "I know what it's been in the past, but I don't know if he has changed it. We didn't share passwords all the time or anything."

I studied Andy as he spoke. I pride myself on not just listening to words from witnesses, friends, suspects, or anyone I'm obtaining information from, but I read their body language. I could tell Andy knew exactly what the password was, but he really didn't want to give it to us. As I was thinking about this, he continued. "You know, why don't you just look at his accounts while under my account? You can see his story and his posts."

"That's a good idea," I responded, "but we would rather get into his account. Then we can see everything. We can see the messages he did not send to you, or items that were directed just to him, and so forth." I paused, let that sink in, and then asked again, "So what is that old password you mentioned?"

Andy looked toward Runae and Mike and then to the ground. He spelled out the letter and number combination. "I T A K E B E E T C H E S 6 9".

By spelling it out slowly, I think he thought I would not recognize what it meant. "I take bitches sixty-nine?" I looked to Mike and Runae and knew they were in disbelief. "Interesting choice for a password."

Andy looked directly toward me and in a very defensive tone, added, "It didn't mean anything. It was just funny."

"Listen, Andy, that password may be a lot of things, but funny is not one of them." I was not pleased and did not feel like accepting any spin on this subject. This football playing, most likely rapist, seemed like he was really just a royal piece of crap, but no matter what, he didn't deserve to end up crushed between cars, so right now my only goal was to find the driver of that car.

"It worked," stated Franky. "At least for Instagram."

Just then Patricia Halterman reentered the room with a questioning glance in my direction. She lifted her head just enough to send me the message, *Hey, Detective who was a jerk earlier, can I talk to you outside?* I motioned to Franky to keep looking through the phone and then stated to the others around the table, "I'll be right back."

When I entered the garage, I saw a classic 1969 Camaro. My eyes instantly were drawn to the car as if it were calling to me from someplace I could only dream of going. I knew my '74 could not even be in the same room with this beauty.

"Detective O'Malley?"

I snapped from my trance and turned to Halterman. "What do you have?" I asked.

"I have the address for the owner of the car. It's in this neighborhood, less than a mile away."

I smiled. "Let me guess, the owner's last name is Malecha?"

She appeared surprised. "Yes, Peggy and Dan Malecha, but how did you know?"

"Because they don't call me the best damn detective in all of Chicago for nothing."

She smiled, which was the first time I had seen her do that. "I don't think anyone calls you that, Detective." She paused, then added, "Would you like the address?"

She caught me just for a second there, then I covered and don't think she noticed. "Yes, let me give you my phone number and you can text it to me."

She was raising her hand as I finished. "Sergeant Carter already gave me your number. I will text it to you and that way you can have mine."

If I covered the first time, I failed at covering then and she knew it. Without another word she walked out of the garage back toward the accident. My phone beeped with a new text from an unknown number that simply had an address, and a name—Detective Patricia Halterman.

"Shit!" I said to myself as I walked back into the kitchen.

Upon entering, I saw Franky still working on the phone. The boy's parents and best friend seemed to have left Franky to his business and began some softer conversation amongst themselves. I leaned into my partner's ear, "I have the address of the car owner. Do you want to come with me, or continue here?"

He immediately got up from the table telling me he had some information that he was not going to share for all to hear. He escorted me to what I assumed was the dining room and in a soft tone, answered my earlier question. "I think I need to stay here. This Mark Schulman looks like a Grade-A asshole. He has all kinds of posts that are simply breaking other players down for their play, their looks, or anything else he can poke fun at. He has a video of him peeing in a two liter of soda and telling a buddy he spiked it with alcohol and then the buddy drinking his pee and throwing up all over the place. He really is a jerk."

"Any of it worth killing him over?" I asked.

He shook his head. "Not that I have found yet, but I've only been at it for a few minutes and only Instagram. Facebook and Snapchat is where the action is. My problem with Snapchat is finding the old stuff."

I nodded agreement. "Okay, stay on it and keep talking to the parents and the friend. There is more here, especially with the kid. Andy knows more than he's saying, I can feel it."

"I think so too, partner," he replied.

We both went back into the kitchen. I let the group know I was following up on a lead but did not divulge that it was the car's owner, an owner they already knew. Instead I left that item open and as quickly as possible exited the house. I nodded to Detective Halterman as I passed. The scene was in very good order now and Dr. G's team was still busy. The body had not been moved and it still turned my stomach when I saw it. You never want to see anyone killed, but children cut very deep. *Who could have done this?* I thought. Maybe I would find out at my next stop.

3 I DROVE INTO the Malecha's driveway and was surprised to see a squad car already there. Why the hell would Halterman have informed the local police? She started as an idiot, I was fooled into thinking she might have a brain, and right away she's back to being an idiot. Great to come back to reality so quickly. Sometimes when I think to myself, I actually smile at my thoughts and people wonder what in the hell I'm doing. When I was a kid, I did not just have an imaginary friend, I had an imaginary *team*. We played football, talked, everything. I don't seem to have outgrown it.

I rang the doorbell and Officer Pete Schram, who I didn't know well but did run into now and again on various cases, answered. "Detective O'Malley? What brings you here on such a case? Did you find the car already?"

He guided me in but to say I was confused was an understatement. Before I showed my cards, I was more interested in why a street cop was here already. "Can I ask what case you are here for?"

He straightened his back and arched his head stretching his neck. The gesture clearly gave the impression he was over exaggerating his surprise at the question. "I am here for the stolen car. The daughter went out this morning, started it to warm it up, and when she came back out to head to cheerleading practice before school, the car was gone."

"The Malecha's car was reported stolen?" I asked. "What time?"

By this time three individuals came wandering toward the door to see who had arrived. It was a man, a woman, and a female teenager in a cheerleader's outfit. I know what you're thinking, the mother, the father, and the daughter. My thoughts too.

Officer Schram picked up his phone and checked the time of his call. "I got the call from 911 at 6:57." He then turned to those who arrived. "This is Peggy and Dan Malecha and their daughter Leah. Leah is the one who started the car, came in to grab some fruit to take with her, and when she came back outside, the car was gone. She said she was gone less than five minutes."

I nodded understanding and without speaking, I picked up my phone and hit speed dial number eight.

"Dispatch, Jasmine speaking."

"Hey Jas, this is Detective O'Malley. What was the time of the 911 calls for the accident this morning? The one on Keystone Place."

"Let me get that for you, Tommy," she replied, sounding pleased to hear my voice compared to an emergency call. "It looks like the first call came in at 7:08 and then there were at least eighteen calls in the minutes following."

"Interesting..." I replied. I thanked Jas and hung up.

"What do you know that I don't know?" asked Officer Schram.

I turned to address the group of four altogether. "Hello folks, I'm Detective Tomas O'Malley, but feel free to call me Tommy if you prefer. Can I ask that we all sit down as I have some news about your car and I need to gather some additional information?"

We meandered into the kitchen. The house was a nice two-story, very traditional. Items were clean and organized, granite countertops, stainless fridge, and so forth. Basically, a standard middle-class home. Dan and Peggy appeared slightly on edge, but not overly concerned. Leah did not appear worried about her car much at all. If anything, she was surprisingly calm. She did check her phone a few times. I thought before I went into the situation at the Schulman's house, I would start with some open-ended questions and the time check was as good as any.

After we all took seats, except Dan who had to fetch an additional chair from the dining room, I turned to Leah. "I have noticed you checked your phone several times even since I arrived. Is there something important going on?"

Without hesitation, she replied, "I'm just checking the time." She held up her phone and on the locked screen appeared the time. "I'm late for cheer practice and that usually does not go well. I'm not too worried because I will have a police report to back up my reason, but we are also working on our performance for the upcoming regionals."

I smiled and that seemed to put everyone a bit at ease. Still speaking directly to Leah, I said, "Great. Can I ask, have you gotten any texts or calls this morning about an accident?"

She twisted her lips slightly and shrugged. "To be honest, with this car thing, I have not even opened my phone. I heard it beep a few times, but my first concern is getting to school. Dad was going to drive me but the 911 operator said an officer was very near and would be right over so I waited."

The story was actually making sense. There were really two options here. Either she was telling the truth and the car was stolen, or this was an elaborate setup and the 911 call on the stolen car was the alibi. However, to do that, either the girl had to be the driver or one of the parents were and none of the three were acting like they had just committed their first murder and were holding a story together to cover it up. It was time to drop the bomb and see what the reaction was.

"Well, folks, I have some really bad news."

Dan interrupted. "What is it? Did some joy rider wreck the car?" He turned to his wife. "I told you. Some kid took the car and trashed it."

I let the comment sit. "You are correct, we have located the car. However, it appears the car was targeted for its use, and based on the limited information I have, I believe your car in particular was targeted."

The three looked at each other and then back to me. "What? What's happened?" Dan again interjected.

"I don't think I mentioned, I'm a detective in the homicide department. Your car, the car you reported stolen at 6:57 AM, was used in a homicide at 7:08 AM less than a mile away."

That was the statement. The statement where my job was to look for the *tells*— similar to an average poker player showing his cards by his reaction. The mother and daughter did not have anything to do with the murder of Mark Schulman, I was sure of it. The deflation in their bodies was evident, but it again was Dan who stood out just a bit. It could have still been his anger at a wrecked car, but he clearly was stressed about something.

Dan looked up directly at me. "What do you mean our car was targeted? Are you saying we know who did this or who was injured?"

That was the question that made me pause. The news was probably already all over social media at the school. If Leah had checked her phone, she would already know as well, but it was clear she did not. I pressed my lips together and then formed my answer. "As a reminder, I'm a homicide detective. I am not talking about an injury, but a death. And to answer your question, I am sure you know the victim. Your car was used to run down and kill Mark Schulman, a senior at Fenton Northwest, and former boyfriend of your daughter."

The reactions were as follows. Peggy, instantly deflated as I would expect. Mothers mourn for the pain of other mothers when their child dies. Dan, slight deflation but also something in him saw satisfaction. Not that he would ever want the boy dead, but he definitely believed that boy hurt his daughter. And then Leah, denial.

Leah looked at me shaking her head. "No, no, no, no. He can't be dead. He can't be dead. I love him. I wanted him back." Tears began to flow and she dropped her head on the table.

Peggy put her arm around her daughter and pulled her close. "Leah, it will be all right. It will be all right."

I mean, what else do you say to your daughter? I gave them a minute or so to let things settle, but I did want to ask some additional questions. However, Officer Schram tapped me on the shoulder and motioned me over. "Do you want me to stay? I was going to fill out a stolen car report and get the info, but if we have the car, then…"

I raised my hand. "Nope, you can go. Good seeing you again, Pete. It's been a while. I will take it from here."

"Good seeing you also, Tommy. Good luck on this one."

Pete made a brief nod to those at the table which was the most polite way he could bid himself farewell as his services were no longer needed. I slid back to the table ready to continue with some questions.

"I know this comes as a shock to all of you, but my primary goal here is to find who did this. Believe it or not, one of our first suspects was your daughter. However, I am at this time ruling her out based on the evidence I've seen so far. Therefore, I need the three of you to walk me through your entire relationship with Mark, everything that happened at the Christmas party and since then. I also want to know everyone who knows about it." Then, turning just to Leah, "Tell me everything about this morning. What you did. When you did it, and anything no matter how small, that happened."

The family nodded and over the next hour they walked me through the entire history. They dated, they were happy, he wanted to advance their relationship and she was not ready, and at a Christmas party, they believe he spiked her drink and took advantage of her. They met with the school, and a group of three teachers, the principal, and her counselor formed a team to investigate the incident. Through that investigation, they could find no corroborating evidence. Because she did not go to the police or the hospital originally and because she'd been allegedly drinking, albeit not knowingly, they convinced her that Mark would never be found guilty and this would only negatively affect her. What I did not expect was the feelings she still held for him. She was considering taking him back. In her words, he was the "catch" at the school and he liked her.

The description of the morning was not that useful all the way up until Leah's black cat appeared in the kitchen and jumped on her lap.

Right as the cat hit her legs, Leah said, "Oh yeah, something scared Inky."

My eyebrows raised. "What?"

"Yes, I almost forgot, but when I went out to start my car, something scared my cat in the bushes. She darted off like there was a dog nearby or something."

Bingo, I thought. "Can you show me where? Where the car was parked? Where you were, and where the cat ran from?"

"Sure," Leah replied.

We walked outside and she walked me through the whole layout. There were several drops of oil on the ground in relatively nearby areas. "I always park here and the car has an oil leak they said at my last oil change. You can see the spots. When I got out of the car here, Inky came to me briefly but then made a screech and darted to the garage from right under that bush."

The driveway was lined with bushes. Not only would they create a nice shadow from the light on the far corner of the garage at night, the side of the driveway went into a hill so if someone was hiding back there, they had the protection of the bushes as well as being below driveway level. "Was it light or dark out?"

"It's always dark when I leave for cheer practice. In fact, I think it may have been even darker than normal. Now that you say it, I think the garage light was burned out."

I walked over to the garage and with my height I was tall enough to reach the bulb. It was a simple light. An arm came straight out with a decorative glass casing around it but the bulb could easily be removed from the opening at the bottom of the case. It appeared to be a dusk-to-dawn light as it had a sensor on it. I turned to Dan who was outside with us. "Can you verify the switch is and has been on?"

He stepped quickly back into the house and in moments came back out. "Yes, it is on and I am sure it has been the whole time. Because it is next to our main entry switch, I put tape on this one to keep it turned up so it accidentally does not get turned off."

I nodded and put on some gloves. I then placed my finger over the light sensor. The bulb did not come on. With my other gloved hand, I turned the light bulb about a quarter turn and the light came on.

Dan's eyes widened. "What the hell does that mean?" he asked.

"It means someone intentionally stole your car. They dimmed the security light outside to lower the chance your daughter would see them. For her good fortune, she did not, or something terrible may have happened to her as well. Let me grab my flashlight as I want to check the bushes as well. I also am going to call my forensics team here. We need to search the area for evidence."

I grabbed my flashlight and was careful not to disturb the area. However, it was very clear by the dirt under the bushes that someone had been positioned there. I walked back up to the driveway where the three remained standing, Dan and Peggy in shock that this could happen to them and Leah still in and out of tears. "Hey folks, why don't you go back inside? I'm going to have to block off this area until we can collect any evidence left behind. Based on what I saw at the accident site, the individual who did this is not careful. We should be able to obtain footprints and maybe even DNA. However, I need to ensure nobody contaminates this area. It will take me a while to section it off. Secondly, I called my team in. We are going to need formal statements from each of you. You will have to repeat much of what you said to me so it will be tedious. Drink some water and do your best to relax. This will most likely take up your entire morning. My team will be here shortly."

They seemed to understand and right after calling it in, my phone rang. I looked at the caller ID and was pleased to see who it was.

"What do you know, Franky?" I answered.

"Hey Tommy, we probably need to compare notes. I heard your call for support at the owner's house. Do you think they are a viable suspect?"

I looked up to ensure the family was back in the house and out of earshot. "No, I really don't. Either they are collectively the best acting family who put together the perfect conspiracy, or they are not the killers. Everything they heard brought them to their knees. The daughter wanted the boy back even after the alleged rape. Something is off with the father, but I can't tell if it is anger or he knows something."

Franky acknowledged the comment and returned with information of his own. "Interesting, and listen to this. Based on the Schulman boy's text messages and some social media exchanges with her, he was trying to do the same. However, that's where his nice boy communication stops."

Although there was no mirror for me to see, I'm sure my eyes opened wider. "What do you mean?"

Franky didn't answer immediately, and it sounded like he was walking outside. "Sorry, but there are so many people around, I want to be sure this is for your ears only." He paused, coughed a little to clear his throat, and then continued. "The kid was a Grade-A asshole. He broke everyone down. Anything someone did that could be made fun of, he posted it everywhere. Somebody slips in gym and he catches it on video, it's all over school. One time at weight-lifting a small kid struggled with 80 pounds, he posted pictures of him dropping the bar and titled it 'biggest pussy in the school, can't lift 80 pounds.' There are literally hundreds of these."

"Jesus, and the school didn't do anything about it. Did anyone complain?"

Franky coughed again before continuing. "I have not talked to the school yet, but they have been informed of the accident and death. We wanted to give them time to get counseling in place."

"Makes sense," I replied. "Anything so serious it would cause someone to do this?"

"There is one that was especially bad." Again he paused, but this time I think Franky was looking for the right words. "There is a boy, Nate Kittleson. He has come out as being gay, and to say Mark was rude to him would be an understatement. There is video of him beating him up, calling him names, forcing him to drink things they created that looked like semen, and so forth. It's horrible. I do know the boy and his parents went to the school, but there are posts from Mark about how nothing could be proven. I think the school covered it up. Had they come to the police we could have subpoenaed his phone and found all of this stuff."

I guarantee I had a look on my face as if I had just vomited in my mouth and had to swallow it. "So we have a kid who was Mr. Popular Sports Guy but was so unconfident he had to exploit everyone else's faults to make him seem bigger and better. All of this was fine when he was dating the hot cheerleader, but when he was accused of rape, the message could have gotten out that he can't get sex on his own without forcing it. Therefore, he had to show how macho he was so he took it to the next level and completely destroyed the one homosexual boy who had the courage to come out in high school."

Franky replied, "That is an interesting overview, and absolutely possible."

I shook my head as I continued. "It pisses me off that his parents can't see this asshole for what he really was, but I suppose that goes with the territory. We need to do two things: We need to get to the school and meet with the principal and his discipline committee, and we need to meet with Nate Kittleson and his parents."

"There is one more thing," added Franky. "The note left on the car. It was definitely left by the perpetrator. It is simply two sets of numbers in the form of an equation. I will send you a picture of it to see if you can make heads or tails of it. We don't have any ideas yet but we are sending it to the lab for a full forensics workup."

"Okay, I have to wait for the team to arrive before I can leave. If you're done at the house, why don't we meet at the school and then head to the Kittleson's? The boy may even be at the school, and we can talk to him there."

"Sounds good, Tommy. I will text you that series of numbers and then text again when I'm leaving. I already called to have a cruiser brought out after your took my car so I can leave directly from here."

I clicked my phone off and almost immediately a text came through. I opened the screen and clicked the incoming message which had an attachment. Opening the attachment I saw a picture of a normal piece of typing paper with two long series of numbers printed across it: 41.3881832-87.1623177. I looked at it but it meant nothing to me. I did the equation quickly in my phone and came up with -45.7741345 which also meant nothing to me. *More time for that later*, I thought to myself.

•　•　•　•　•

Thirty minutes later I received the text from Franky that he was done at the house, was headed to the school, and that he would wait for me there. The forensics team had arrived at the Malecha's house and was doing a great job securing the area and Carter had sent two other detectives to take formal statements from the family. With everything under control, I replied to Franky that I too was on my way. The school was only ten to fifteen minutes from here and with it rolling on 10:45 AM, we should be able to arrive before lunch kicked in at the school. I was familiar with the school. I had considered it for my kids when they were growing up. The conversion from a boys' school to coed was to take place when they were in high school, and I sensed some issues around it. Between that feeling and the fact my ex-wife wanted no part of them attending school in downtown Chicago, I placed them out in Plainfield, the western suburbs where Stephanie had moved and eventually remarried. The schools there were better anyway—at least that's what her lawyer and future second husband told me at the time. As I did eventually learn and accept, the schools out there were great and provided a strong base for my kids.

I pulled into the school just before 11:00 AM, and just like Franky, instead of looking for parking or even taking the visitors' spots, I pulled right up to the curb. I was still driving Franky's car and he had taken a cruiser so as far as who looked more intimidating, I gave the vote to Franky. There were some kids scattered outside, as usual, which I never understood because class was in session. However, who am I to judge. I missed a class or two in my day as well.

We walked in and I liked what I saw. The kids in the area were all in uniforms and well behaved. A guard was stationed at the front entryway and there was a mess of security cameras I could see behind his desk. To be honest, I think the TVs were more for show. The school had more than 800 students and there were only six TV feeds, but it still sent the message, Big Brother is watching. Franky and I showed our badges and the guard got up and escorted us to the main office. My stereotype of a high school security guard would be one of two things: Overweight thirty-year-old who tried to make it as a cop and couldn't, tried to make it as a TSA agent at the airport and couldn't, so ended up in a high school. The alternative, a sixty-five-year-old retired cop who was good with kids and wanted to stay active. This guy was neither. He was approximately twenty-seven years old, in perfect shape, and looked to be straight out of the military. There was no way this guy could not have made it through the police academy as he looked like he could bench more than 350 pounds without working up a sweat. *Brick shithouse* comes to mind.

He shook both our hands and introduced us to the receptionist. He handled the discussion by explaining that we needed to see the principal immediately without leaving anything open to interpretation. If the principal was busy, she was to make him not busy, and that was simply how it was to be. He turned back to us, shook our hands again, and said, "Detectives." And he left.

The receptionist behind the desk looked up at me and smiled. "I will get Principal Bales for you right away. He was speaking to a group of students about the tragedy that occurred this morning but I think he is back in his office now."

"That would be great," Franky replied, his tone much softer than it needed to be. I glanced at him and then followed his eyes as he watched her walk back through the office to a wall of closed offices in the back.

"Are you kidding me? You're fishing now..." I whispered.

Frank Sullivan was a widower. His wife had passed away years earlier, and to the best of my knowledge, he had not dated since. He had a huge dog, a Newfoundland named Vader. That dog was his sole companion. However, he always felt he was a ladies' man and he could flirt like none I had ever seen. He didn't call it flirting, but fishing. I believe he loved it when they flirted back, but history had shown when that happened, it was enough for him. He could throw them back with no harm done. I think he just wanted to know someone could like him again, not that they really needed to.

Franky smiled but didn't take his eyes off her walk. "No, partner, I am not fishing, just enjoying the pond. Haven't you ever done that?"

"If you're just enjoying the pond, why the hell did you use the Frank Sinatra voice just now?"

He turned now to face me and looked at me like Obi-Wan Kenobi first looked at Luke Skywalker, as if a master was there training some raw and innocent child. "You never know how you might be able to change the motion of the water with a little encouragement."

"I don't even know what that means, and I don't want to."

He held his smile but said no more as the receptionist was returning with a short, gray-haired man in her wake. Frank turned his smile toward the woman who clearly smiled back in return, and I was pretty sure she was just being polite, but my fear was I would be reliving this story of their exchanged glance of love later at Flap Jaws.

The gray-haired man reached out his hand. "Detectives, I am sure you know we have had a busy, not to mention extremely tough, morning. I am Principal Robert Bales, but you can call me Bob. Why don't you come back to my office?"

We shook hands and introduced ourselves as well and then proceeded back to his office, which was clean and organized. He was in a suit and looked the part as well. His walls were covered in degrees and it appeared, without looking too closely, he had several awards that were either his or accomplishments of the school. There were also several football trophies that captured my eyes as much for their size as how they were prominently displayed.

"State football trophies," Principal Bales said, noticing my stare. "The smaller ones you get from just making it to the championship game and the larger ones are when you win. We have seven in all which is incredible for a school of this size."

"Is football important to you then?" I asked, jumping right to the point and doing a little fishing of my own.

Bales sat down behind his desk and motioned for us to sit as well in the two chairs on the opposite side. "I know what you're implying. I spoke with Mark's parents."

I nodded, supporting that he felt he was all-knowing. "Why don't you just tell me what I am implying?"

"Mark was killed. The car that killed him was owned by a girl who reported she had been attacked by him."

"Raped," I interrupted. "A Class 1 felony."

"You're implying that the school did not act appropriately once it was informed about the alleged attack. You're implying that I worked to keep it quiet to protect a football player."

Bingo, I thought. *Maybe he should be a detective.* I can't believe he went straight to the point. I had never seen anyone implicate themselves so quickly. I was starting to boil and it had only been about twenty seconds since I met this jackass. "Listen, Principal Bales, since you seem like you want to cut to the chase, I am not implying anything. This school has no business investigating rape allegations. We have an entire police department whose job it is to do that very thing. These are kids, and one of them in the early stages of this investigation seems to be a pretty good one; the other seems to not be so nice. But when that one kid who is not so nice is the star football player and the school principal wants to have more trophies around his fucking office, then I guess the fact he raped a girl can be pushed under the carpet."

Franky lifted his arm and placed it on my shoulder telling me without speaking to calm down, but I didn't.

"Now you just wait a minute, Detective. You don't even know the facts." Bales' voice cracked a bit and I could see he was moving into heavy defense mode. "The facts are, this girl you say is so good was drinking. Nobody saw her or him any time after the dance. She reported it two weeks later. There was no rape kit. We took this very seriously. I put together a team and we interviewed everyone. Not one person could corroborate her story. Not one. Even her friends on the cheer team who would defend her to the end could not say they knew about anything that happened. In fact, to the contrary, they spoke highly of Mark and said he couldn't do it. How would that have gone for her in court?"

"Last time I checked, you are not a judge or a lawyer and neither am I. It is not our place to answer that question, Principal." I paused but I wanted to keep control of the conversation. I wanted to keep him off guard so I fired this one off the bow. "Tell me about Nate Kittleson."

It was clear the moment I said that name, he did not expect or want to go there. "What about Nathan?"

"I thought we were cutting to the chase, Principal Bales. Are you going to tell me you don't know anything special about Nate Kittleson and his interactions with

Mark Schulman?"

"No, I asked you, what do *you* want to know about him?"

I smiled. "Oh, I suppose my original question was not cut-to-the-chase enough for you." I tilted my head in closer. "Why don't you tell me how you handled the bullying accusations put forth by Nathan Kittleson? Why don't you tell me about them now?"

Bales sat back in his chair as if he was about to light up a smoke and tell some fantasy story about how he used to slay dragons. The look was odd to say the least. He turned his lips into a smile and then tilted his chair back. "Nate is a troubled kid. He's a kid that's constantly getting in trouble." *In the dictionary, under the word 'redundant,' it says 'see the word redundant,'* I thought. Bales continued as fortunately he couldn't hear my thoughts. "He tries to buck the system around every corner, and in short, causes problems." He paused, let that sink in, and then continued. "Regarding his concerns with Mark Schulman, again, I had a team put together, we investigated the accusations, and found no evidence of any incidents that warranted further action."

I began to reply but Franky placed his hand back on my shoulder and held me back. "Principal Bales," Franky began, "can I ask you to look at this?"

He held out his phone and began to play a video. He stopped it immediately. "Sorry, let me put the sound up as I think it tells even a better story than the video."

He made an adjustment on his phone and then hit play again. This time the sound came through with the video. I couldn't see the video from this angle, but I could hear the sound perfectly.

In a shouting voice I assume was coming from Mark Schulman, I heard the following:

"Nate Kittleson you are a fucking gay prick. Stop talking to our girlfriends! Stop looking at me and the rest of my boys with those homo gazes, and stop checking us out in the locker room. The next time I see your faggot ass after school, I will beat the living shit out of you."

During the entire ordeal, without seeing the video, I could tell Nate was either on the ground being kicked or being held up by others and being punched. There were others in the video because I heard their laughs and jeers in the background.

Principal Bales' face noticeably dropped. His voice was also saddened. "This is the first I have seen this video. Had we seen it, of course we would have taken different action. He would have been suspended or at least missed a few games."

Oops, that did it. I stood up and was actually yelling. *"Miss a few games!"* I exclaimed. "What in the hell are you talking about? This guy threw out numerous discriminatory slurs, beat the crap out of the kid, all for what? To make him feel more manly? And you would consider having him miss a few games. Further, had you handled this the proper way, this and the other videos on his phone would have been found by the police investigation. I wonder what you missed in Leah Malecha's investigation. Maybe this jackass videotaped his rape. Did you ever think of that?"

Bales stood now and appeared equally mad. "We have over eight hundred kids here, Detective. We followed policy and showed no favoritism in either case. Our team investigation was thorough. We cannot control if students lie. This video will open a new investigation and we can leave it at that."

"*A new investigation?*" I exclaimed, even louder than before. "The kid is dead. Regardless of his actions, this could have been avoided. You might as well have driven the car yourself."

"Hey," interrupted Franky, "let's all cool down. The goal here has not changed. We are going down the wrong path. Yes, it is important to know the past, but our true goal is simple, we do want to find the real driver of that car. Despite anything else, that person committed murder."

Bales still stood and turned now to address Franky. "Then I guess you and your partner might want to talk to Nate Kittleson. He seems to have quite a bit of motive, and he is disturbed enough to do it."

"I am sure we will talk to him," Franky continued. "But we have been on this investigation only a few hours and came up with two people with serious motive. This leads us to believe there may be others. I would suggest based on the discussion we just had that you let us know about anyone else who had an issue with Mr. Schulman. The best thing you can do for yourself and the school is to help us unconditionally."

Principal Bales' voice changed and became slightly contrite. "I would love to, gentlemen, but all I can share with you now is Mark Schulman's file. When I talked to Mike and Runae this morning, they authorized its release to authorities. For any others whose names you come up with, I will need parental permission before I release it."

"Of course you will," I added snidely.

"Unless you have a court order to the contrary," he added.

I shook my head and got up as if I was going to leave then turned back. "One more thing, Principal Bales, I need a list of everyone who was on each of the committees that did the investigation into Leah Malecha's allegations as well as Nate Kittleson's."

"No problem, Detective. In Mark's file you will see all their names. They are still here and available if you need to speak to them, except Dawn Wells, the counselor. She left a message a few days ago requesting personal time, saying she had a family emergency and wouldn't be back for a week. We have her cell phone, however. It's too bad. I need her here today for obvious reasons."

I looked back at him with a touch of concern. Another little voice moment. "Has she done that in the past? Simply left a message and then been out for a family emergency?"

He didn't hesitate. "Not that I'm aware of, but I guess you can say that about everybody until the first time they have a family emergency."

I am not a big fan of things out of the ordinary happening for the first time right around the time of a murder. Therefore, I thought this was worth pushing further. "Can I get her number now? I think it's pertinent we talk to her."

Bales rolled his eyes a bit giving the impression that he thought this was a wasted effort. He reached out his hand and pressed an intercom button on his phone. "Marci, will you please provide these two detectives with Dawn Wells' cell and home phone numbers, as well as her address. They would like to check on her well-being and speak with her if possible."

"No problem, Robert," a female voice said through the phone. "Have them stop by my desk on their way out."

Bales looked up at me. "My secretary," he paused and added, "Oops, I mean *Administrative Assistant* sits in the cube to the far left as you leave. She will have the information for you. Now, if there's nothing else." He stood as if he was going to show us to the door but did not move from behind his desk.

I leaned in and placed both my hands on his desk so my face was much closer to his than I think he would have preferred. "Principal Bales, you strike me as someone who not only does not have the best interests of your students in mind, you would even allow harm or bring harm to them to protect your school or reputation. I bet if I stopped to ask your secretary, oops, I mean Administrative Assistant, she would tell me you made sexual jokes toward her, and made derogatory comments about students who are in the chess club or gay or anything else that doesn't get you a trophy you can display in your office. Maybe you even look the other way when the 'cool' kids hurt the not-so-cool kids. Do you think she would tell me those things?"

"Detective O'Malley," he began in a softer voice that Franky may not have been able to hear, "get the hell out of my office."

I smiled, turned to Franky and said, "I guess that's our cue to go. Thank you for your time, Principal Bales."

We swung by Marci's desk on the way out and she had a small notepaper with all the requested information on it. I looked back to Bales' office and he was standing in the doorway watching us. "Marci, I also need the names and numbers for all the teachers or administration individuals who were on the two committees reviewing Leah Malecha's allegations as well as Nate Kittleson's complaints on Mark Schulman."

The minute I said Mark's name, her pleasant demeanor vanished. Marci was young, probably 28-30 years old. She was also very cute. I would put her in the category of probably not the homecoming queen in her high school, but the runner-up—the type of girl you would want to marry. She looked up with what Webster's dictionary would use as the photo definition for puppy-dog eyes. I actually thought she may start crying right then. "It's so awful what happened to Mark. I can't believe how this is going to impact the school. I hope you find who did it."

"We will do our best, ma'am," Franky added in his Frank Sinatra voice. "Now, the contact info please."

Marci's sadness seemed to vanish when she was put on a task. "No problem. The committees that investigate complaints like that are made up of the same people each year. Then they rotate to new people. These incidents occurred this school year so the individuals are the same. There was Principal Bales, of course..."

"Of course," I supported, trying to sound positive about the individual who in one short conversation I had grown to hate.

"Dawn Wells, the counselor, Eric Graham, the physical education teacher and soccer coach, Herb Whychoff, the senior English teacher, and Bill Ronin, chemistry." She paused and let out a sigh. "It will take me a minute to pull all the information up. Would you like a cup of coffee while you wait?"

"No, thank you," I replied for both of us, not concerned if Franky actually did want some. "It is just so nice having someone so helpful to work with us."

She seemed to like that and smiled in return just as her phone made a long solid tone. She pushed a button, "Yes, Robert?"

"Will you pick up, please?" Principal Bales asked through the intercom.

She picked up the receiver making the speakerphone turn off. "Yes. Yes. Okay. Sure, I will do that."

She put the receiver down and looked back to us, that recent smile now faded. "I'm sorry, but Robert was asking if you were requesting more contact information. He believes, upon second thought, he should talk to the individuals involved first to let them know what's going on. It has been a crazy day and he doesn't want to make a decision that could make things worse because he's not following the required protocols."

I reached out and took her hand in a soft shake. "Of course, we wouldn't want to put anyone in a negative situation just because we're trying to solve the murder of a teenager." I swung my head back to Principal Bales but didn't show any emotion. The last time I checked, we were detectives. It would take less than five minutes to get every address, phone number, alias, or anything else I wanted to know about the names she just provided. My job here was done for now, but something told me I would be speaking in detail with Principal Robert Bales again.

4 WE MET OUTSIDE the school and although we didn't say it, I think we both had an uneasy feeling about the missing counselor. I dialed a quick call into dispatch and asked to have someone start the process of locating Ms. Dawn Wells.

"How do I know that name?" I asked Franky.

"Easy," he replied smiling. "Ginger or Mary Ann?"

What do you mean? From *Gilligan's Island*?" *Gilligan's Island* was an old TV show I watched religiously when I was a kid. I don't believe there were more than 35-40 episodes but boy, did I love the show. A group of castaways end up stranded on an island and in every episode barely miss getting rescued. That being said, I have no idea what *Gilligan's Island* had to do with Dawn Wells. However, every guy my age knows the answer to the question, Ginger or Mary Ann. Although I think the show wanted Ginger to be the one most desired, all my friends were all about Mary Ann, but all my friends at that time were from Kansas, like me.

"Sure," Frank continued. "Ginger was played by an actress named Tina Louise, but Mary Ann was played by Dawn Wells. I think she's still out in California."

I am not sure why I needed to know where she lived, but I guess it was Frank's way of showing how much he knows about critically important information. "Wow, Mary Ann..." I said slowly as if remembering an old girlfriend. "She was something." With that, we let the matter drop but I made a mental note to add meeting Dawn Wells to my bucket list—not my missing counselor but the actress now living in California.

I opened my car door...actually, the car I was driving was Franky's car... but I stopped and leaned on the roof of the car looking toward my partner. "What is our next move? We still need to go to the Kittleson's, but I want to talk to the boy and since school is in session, maybe we should pull him from class."

Franky shrugged a bit. "Carter wanted to see us after we were done on the scene. We are much later than I think he would have ever intended. Therefore, we should head to the station, have our meeting with Carter, then see what evidence they've turned up from the accident scene. We need to determine what the numbers on the letter left behind mean, we need to schedule meetings with this team of teachers that determines the law for the school, and we need to talk to Nate Kittleson and find out where he was this morning."

"Very well," I replied. "Let's both head to the station. You can dump off that car and we can take this one to pick up my car later."

"Sounds like a plan, Tommy. See you at Carter's office."

I still didn't know what Carter needed to see me about. I hadn't done anything too terribly wrong in some time. In fact, ever since the Polino and Moretti case closed months ago, I had kept things pretty clean. Just thinking about the case took me back to my morning and the "need to talk" comment I got from Tammi. "Sucks!" I said out loud, then pushed the gas.

●　　　●　　　●　　　●　　　●

I walked into the department and several other detectives were noticeably not talking to me. I didn't know what it meant, but I also didn't pay it much mind. I wanted to get through the meeting with Carter and then get back to solving this case, starting with the sheet of numbers left on the car. That had to hold some answers. Franky was not at his desk but his paperwork from the morning was there so I knew he had beat me in. I assumed he was already in with Carter. I dumped my stuff on my desk and headed that way. Again, a detective actually walked around a desk to avoid me passing directly by him. *What the hell was going on?*

Sergeant Carter's office was glassed in but the shades were drawn. I probably had been in his office a hundred times. He only closed the shades when he was going to tear someone apart. I'm not sure I had seen them open from the inside before. Today would be no different, but I still didn't know what I had done. When I opened the door, however, all things came front and center.

"Officer Halterman," I stated when our eyes met. "I should have guessed." Now I knew based on her text message that she was actually a detective, but because I did not know what detective she was or from where, I felt that sticking with "officer" seemed appropriate.

"Goddamn it, O'Malley, get your pompous ass in here and sit down." Carter was not yelling, but he was definitely speaking with authority. "I already heard about all your crap out at the scene. In fact, it's that type of bullshit that brings us in here right now."

I raised my hand. "Now wait just a minute, Sergeant. I don't know what the hell she told you, but the scene was in shambles when we arrived. To her credit, she cleaned it up quickly, but all I did is light a fire under the cleanup process. Whatever she told you is crap."

She had a look like she was about to speak, but then she didn't. I hadn't even noticed Franky to my left also standing with a woman. A woman I also did not know but in an officer's uniform. I started to continue with my comments about her performance when Franky interrupted. "Hey Tommy, you might want to listen to the sergeant here for a bit. He has some news about us."

I turned to my partner and saw the message clearly in his eyes. *Shut the hell up. No, wait, shut the hell up now, jackass.*

Sergeant Carter smiled. "So that's what it takes. You listen to Franky but you don't listen to me?"

I did not smile though my first instinct was to do just that. Instead, I backed down. I saw the look in Franky's eyes. This situation was not good. "I meant no disrespect, Carter. I was just a little blindsided at the scene and then back here, I just—"

"Shut up, Tommy!" he interrupted. "I already told Franky, and now I'm telling you. The department was approved for some new detectives. We also are reevaluating our current policies. No detective is to work alone. You and Franky have somehow slid under the radar with that rule for several years. Today that ends. Detective Halterman here just transferred in from Joliet vice, and Detective Huston is from Springfield."

I nodded to both of them. However, I never took my eyes from Carter. "Do not finish your statement. The next words you say are simply that these two new detectives are going to be partners and you need me and Franky to show them the ropes."

Now Carter smiled. "Great idea, O'Malley, but not quite spot on. A better way for me to say it is, meet your new partner, Detective Patricia Halterman. Huston is with Sullivan."

I tried to control my speech, but it was not possible. "Goddamn it, Carter, was this your idea? This is crazy. Franky and I are our own partners. We don't need anyone else and nobody else wants us. Look at these two." I motioned to both of them. "They don't want to work with us."

"Shut it, O'Malley. This is not open for discussion." Carter was leaning over his desk now and his face was turning a deep red. He looked like an apple.

Halterman then broke in. "Listen, Detective, you may not want to work with me and you sure as hell are making me feel like I shouldn't want to work with you, but I have worked my entire career for this, and I am not going to let a deadbeat male chauvinist pig keep me from it."

"What did you call me?" I snapped at her.

"She took a step closer. "I'm sure you heard me, but I'm not sure you know what the words mean. Let me rephrase. I am here to work. I will work with you or anyone else in this department and I will kick ass every day. You may not want to work with me, but..."

I waved my hand and stormed out of the office slamming the door behind me.

"Give him some time," stated Franky in a much softer tone but it didn't calm anyone down. "He has not had an official partner since Dixon."

Carter instantly faded back a little at the mention of his name. Detective Halterman noticed the immediate change and asked, "What happened to Dixon?"

Carter and Franky looked at each other, but it was Franky who answered. "Tommy and I had been partners for years. We worked well together but we can both rub each other the wrong way at times, just like anyone I guess. Well, we were at one of those lower periods and had the opportunity to work with a young up-and-coming detective. The guy was a hotshot. Cleared many cases, including a serial killer, as an officer. He chose Tommy and to be honest, I think Tommy chose him. Two months into the job, Dixon takes one in the neck. It was a routine follow-up on a murder. They knocked on the door and shots started coming. Dixon died instantly. Nobody would have handled it any differently, but Tommy had been joking with the kid about how the rookies do all the carrying of equipment, driving the cars, knocking on doors. He was just playing with him, but Tommy felt if he hadn't been joking, the kid would be alive."

The room was deafly silent until Carter added. "A few things you need to know. Tommy O'Malley is one of the best damn detectives I have ever known, and that moment changed him. Not just because his partner died in his arms, but because the guy who shot him got away. He vanished."

"Seriously?" asked Karen Huston. "You guys never caught him?"

"Carter is right," added Franky. "The guy just vanished. He had the entire Chicago Police Department after him, and we turned up nothing."

"Tommy still has the guy's picture in his locker. Jessie Molden." Carter let the story die there and again everyone fell into silence.

After several moments, Carter turned to mostly address Franky. "Sullivan, I wanted to go through this with both of you, but at this stage I will give the three of you the overview and between all of us, we can bring Tommy up to speed. A kid's death is a press killer. I want two teams on this one and it's going to be both of you. Tommy and Halterman will take the lead, and you two ride shotgun. However, if he can't figure this out, I will pull the two of you"—he motioned to Detective Halterman—"and find a team that can handle it. You got it?"

Halterman shook her head but Franky was who responded. "Tommy will be fine, Sergeant." Then turning his speech more to Patricia Halterman, he added, "He's all show. He wants to appear as a hardass so he can control a situation. This situation is just a bit out of his control right now."

"We'll be fine," Halterman added. "I've been around much worse."

"Good," Carter said. "Then the three of you go gather his ass up and run through the case together. I want a preliminary report on my desk by 5:00 PM tonight."

Franky rolled his eyes because he knew there would be no report at 5:00 PM. That was for the newbie's benefit. Carter needed to posture just like Tommy did; he just did it better. Franky smiled. "Will do, Sergeant. Tommy and I will get on that report right away."

He motioned to the other two detectives to follow and then opened the door, letting them lead the way out. He turned back to Sergeant Carter. "A report at 5:00 PM?" he asked softly.

"Nice touch, wasn't it?"

•   •   •   •   •

Franky led the two detectives through the different desks that really had no organized layout. Detectives pushed their desks wherever they needed to at the time, so navigating through them was something you should never do in the dark. That being said, I was amazed when I watched them from across the room. The detectives that had run for cover as I walked by, which I now knew was because everyone but me was aware that I was getting a new partner, now ran up and greeted the two new detectives as if they had been long-time friends. They did this not because they were new detectives, but because they were new *female* detectives. And I didn't need to be known as the best detective in Chicago to figure that one out.

As they all exchanged a few polite greetings, they made a path to my desk to relay the direction from Carter. "A report by five o'clock, huh?" I muttered.

"That's what he said," replied Karen Huston, Franky's new partner, with confidence.

"Well then, we will have to get right on that" I replied with Franky giving me a slightly turned-up smile as our eyes met.

We headed to an open interrogation room. We labeled our rooms by local sports teams. I'm not sure why and I don't think it was a positive for criminals, the city, or any other entity, we just liked it. We had the Bulls, the Blackhawks, the Fire, the Cubs, the Bears, and the Royals. The room used to be the White Sox, but having a father from White City, Kansas, who drilled the Chiefs and Royals into me for my entire lifetime, there was no way I could let the White Sox room stay. Therefore, after about a year of replacing the gold White Sox sign with a handmade Royals sign, the department actually made a permanent Royals sign and the name stuck. It was often the only room I would use, and coincidently, the last room everyone else would use. We headed directly there.

"Why is it called the Royals room?" Huston asked as we entered.

I just smiled.

5 TWO HOURS LATER we emerged from the Royals room and to her credit, Detective Halterman was a skilled dictation specialist and in very short order took everything Franky and I shared, combined with the information she had gotten, and packaged it into a formal report. As I looked through the documents, I was dumbfounded at how thorough it was. Another detective could pick up this report and take off without missing a step. Carter may actually stop breathing for just a brief second when she sets it on his desk.

We had discussed the next steps. The two newbies would deliver the report to Carter while Franky and I headed to the lab. During our meeting, I had received a text from Doc G saying she had sent the report over and I had also gotten a text from the lab saying they had an idea about the numbers on the mysterious note. Adding these two bits of info to the mix should give us an excellent direction to take.

•   •   •   •   •

Before heading to the lab, I had to make a quick stop at the vending machine to make sure I came bearing gifts. At the lab, I knew Doc G's report would have a great deal of information, but if my hunch was correct on those series of numbers, they could lead us directly to some answers, so that was going to be our first stop. We walked through the lab, which was set up like a high school chemistry lab. This part is where most of the forensics takes place. There's a separate room for blood spatter analysis and DNA testing, but I wanted to go to the lab guy's offices. It was there that I assumed the answers to the mysterious envelope would be.

When we walked into the office area, immediately I saw a face I recognized.

"Swanny, how the hell are you doing?" I asked him. His name was Craig Swanson, but everyone called him Swanny.

The large man, in what had to be a 5XL lab coat, turned his head toward me when I entered and smiled broadly. "O'Malley, you still work here? I thought they fired you for one of your forty or fifty violations over the last thirty years."

I smiled in return and as I approached, I reached my hand out to greet my old friend. "What? Please don't tell me you run this lab now?"

For a very brief second, he appeared stung as if the news of his promotion had not made it up to me. But as I had seen him several times in the last few weeks and congratulated him every time, the dots connected, and he realized I was just toying with him. As we separated hands, I took my other hand and slid it around as if to give him something secretively. He looked down at what I placed in his hand, and instantly a big smile crossed his face.

"A Clark bar? You must really need some information."

Franky shook his head. "Seriously, a candy bar, O'Malley?"

"Hey Franky," replied Swanny, meaning it as a greeting as well as an interruption. "Don't kid yourself. Tommy knows how to get information from a guy. That's why he has moved up the ladder so quickly." His smile began to break through but he held it just a bit longer. "What has it been, Tommy, twenty-two years as a homicide detective?"

"Something like that?" I replied, careful to not let my smile show through too clearly.

Swanny opened his Clark Bar and took a bite. Through chocolate-filled teeth, he asked, "What do you need that is Clark Bar worthy, Tommy?"

Instantly my face hardened. "The hit-and-run this morning – The teenager pinned in the car. There was an envelope left on the hood with some numbers. Who took that one?"

He walked over to a bench about ten feet away along a wall. It had several fairly cool-looking gadgets on it, but in the center of them in a plastic bag was the seemingly harmless piece of notebook paper with numbers on it. He picked up the plastic bag and held it in front of us like a trophy.

"I'm actually glad you came down because I was about to give you a holler. I did every test imaginable on this paper. It was completely clean. So much that I don't think it was ever touched directly by human hands. Additionally, it could not have been a more common paper. By weight, color, fiber count, everything. I can't even estimate the amount of paper just in Chicago alone that matches this."

"So you have nothing," said Franky during the pause.

He smiled. "I got nothing from the paper. However, the writing was another story."

Now I was intrigued. "What did you find out? What did the numbers tell you?"

"They were written with a left hand." He pointed to several numbers and the angles used. "You see here and here. Clearly left-handed."

Franky and I saw it as well, but something else struck me about the writing. "Whoever wrote this is a horrible writer."

"Exactly," added Swanny still smiling. "The person who wrote this with their left hand is most likely…"

"Right-handed," I finished for him. "He was trying to fool us."

"I do believe that is the situation," Swanny added. "I don't know what it means, but it is unique to say the least."

"What else?" I asked. "What do the numbers mean?"

Swanny shrugged showing his frustration. "Up until about thirty minutes ago, I feared that I'd have to tell you I had no idea. We tried everything from series code, simple math equations, phone numbers, portions of addresses, and so forth. We came up with squat. I had the whole team on it for a while." He paused a moment I believe to add to the drama, because I could tell from his demeanor that he had something. He was too pleased with his story for it to have a bad ending. As a side note, I of course was pleased to hear they also tried the math equation just like I did. I could easily be a lab guy or a detective. I basically knew every job.

"Are you okay, Tommy?" Swanny asked.

"Yes. Why?"

"I don't know, you just seemed happy all of a sudden."

I waved my hand. Inside I was slightly embarrassed. Outside, I truly did not care. "I was just thinking about how frustrating it must have been trying to figure this out. But, on the other hand, I can tell you found something. What do the numbers mean?"

"Well," he began slowly holding up the numbers so Franky and I could see them. "My team came up with latitude and longitude as a direction instead of a math equation. The longitude is simply a negative number."

"Holy shit!" stated Franky. "Where did it take you?"

He shrugged again. "Unfortunately, nowhere at first, but one of my guys was an Eagle Scout as a kid. He knew right when he looked at them that they had too many numbers compared to how they are typically reported or traced. We took a look at the numbers." He laid the sheet down in front of us so we could clearly see them again. He read off, "41.3881832-87.1623177. We started trying to remove a number from each one, then looked for a pattern."

Franky and I stared at the numbers for what seemed like too long. I think Swanny sensed it and answered our unasked question. "The first number after the decimal point is the equivalent to the second number subtracted from the first. In this case"—he pointed to the first number—"the three is equal to the four minus one. Maybe it's a coincidence, maybe it was planned. Regardless, when we removed the first number after the decimal, the latitude and longitude takes you directly to downtown Chicago, specifically an alley behind Rush Street."

"Are you fucking serious?" I asked rhetorically. "You have an address for us?"

"I do," he said proudly. "I don't know what's there. I Google-mapped it and it looks like a simple dead end, but here's the print out."

I snagged the paper from his hand and turned to Franky. "Let's grab the lab file and scan it on the way. I'll drive."

"Whoa Tommy, aren't you forgetting something?"

I looked puzzled at him briefly then shook my head and smiled. "Sorry, you are correct." I turned to Swanny. "Thank you, buddy. There's another Clark bar in your future."

He acknowledged the thank you but it was Franky who again replied, "No, not a thank you and candy bar. We have partners now. We can't just go running off with the main forensics file and an address and leave them behind."

"Partners?" inquired Swanny. "You're kidding me. Who the hell would work with either of you?"

"Exactly," I stated. Then turning to head out, I asked, "Can we get the file on the other evidence collected and Doc G's report?"

Swanny got up and walked with us. "The only thing we have so far is a full rundown of the victim's phone. In a word, he was a jackass."

I stopped. "First off, I believe jack ass is two words. Secondly, what do you mean?"

Swanny continued by me and headed to a lab bench near the entrance to the room. There was a stack of files in a vertical divider. He scanned through the tabs and pulled two out. "I made duplicates of everything we had so far. Here's the phone breakdown and here's the report from the coroner." He reached them out to Franky who was closest. "Regarding why he is a jackass, which is definitely one word by the way, he literally destroyed everyone on social media, but one kid was especially vulnerable to his attacks." He peeked in the file and repeated the name, "Nate Kittleson. I'm surprised the kid still lives in town."

Franky and I looked at each other. We needed to start reaching out to some teachers, we needed to follow up with the Kittleson family, but the address we just received was at the top of my list. "You and your partner head to the Kittleson's, and my partner and I will take the address from the note?"

"You mean Detective Huston and Detective Halterman?"

I don't know why I didn't want to say their names. Saying "partner" was probably worse, but it just made it real to say their names. "Yeah, you and Huston and me and Halterman. Good enough?"

"Let's go gather them up and hit it." Franky turned back to Swanny. "Thank you, Swanny. Great work."

"As always," I added with a handshake.

•   •   •   •   •

As we entered the hallway, we saw our two new partners headed directly toward us. It was like watching a teacher coming at you in high school when you knew you had been busted doing something wrong and you were just waiting for them to assign your punishment. That was not at all the situation. We hadn't done anything wrong, but I still didn't want to see our two partners, just like kids didn't want to see teachers.

"Hello, partner," said Franky with a surprisingly cheery voice.

"Carter was pleased with the report," replied Halterman. "In fact, he almost seemed surprised we had it."

Franky nodded in return. "Yeah, that's how Carter is sometimes. He always seems like he holds no expectations even though he does."

"What did you guys find out down here?" asked Huston.

"We will fill you both in on our way," I answered. "You and Franky are headed to interview the Kittleson family. Our victim bullied their son to an extreme degree on the Internet and the school did not act on it. Halterman and I are headed to the location on the note. Those numbers are coordinates that lead to an address in downtown Chicago."

They seemed pleased with the direction and strangely enough, in that moment, it was okay to have a partner. My only issue was it should have been Franky. We headed to the lot and piled into Franky's car.

"What, we're splitting up by driving together?" asked Detective Halterman.

"No," I replied. "I left my car at our breakfast place and we rode together. We need to swing by Mr. J's and pick it up."

"Mr. J's?" Halterman replied, a questioning nature carried in her statement.

"You wouldn't know it, Halterman," I replied, almost with a bitterness in my tone.

"Oh, I know it," she said snidely. "There's nothing better than a Dagwood after a long day. I'm just surprised you would go there."

My jaw dropped. Hopefully it didn't drop as far as Franky's did, but I'm sure she saw it even with me in the front passenger seat. Franky quickly fired back in her direction. "Hell, Halterman, if I was going to give you a way into Tommy's world, you just beat anything I could come up with."

"Maybe Tommy just came into my world." She paused and let her comment sit in just a bit. "What do you think?"

I didn't answer.

• • • • •

We reached Mr. J's and split up. To say Detective Halterman was not impressed with my car was an understatement, but to her credit, she kept her feelings mostly to herself, other than the sour expression she simply could not hide upon first sight. I sensed she believed I should be driving a sedan or even a black SUV, but a '74 shit-brown Camaro was not on her short list of options. First off, it was a two-door. How could I ever bring a suspect back in this car? Secondly, and most importantly, there was no interior room for anything. To her credit, she said not one word about it.

"Nice car, huh," I said proudly.

She glanced at me to see if I was kidding and saw no smile in my expression. "Why yes, very nice."

We drove for a few blocks without another word. I think she was scared to say anything.

She glanced back to her GPS and it showed we were only one minute away. "What do you think we will find?" she asked.

"No idea," I replied. "But whatever it is, the driver of that car wanted us to find it. My gut tells me it's simply some evidence implicating the victim in some bullying crimes. Basically, I think the driver of the car wants us to justify his actions."

"That was my thought too," she added. "I think they are trying to build a case such that if we find out who they are, we will not arrest them."

"*When* we find out who they are," I interjected, "and they are wrong about that one. I don't care what kind of asshole that kid was, he did not deserve to be split in half at age eighteen." I paused then turned to her. "Do you have an issue with my language?"

She smiled. "No, I grew up with a plumber for a father and two brothers. There's nothing I have not heard before."

"Fucking-A," I replied joining the smile.

Her GPS dinged and the British female voice said, "You have arrived."

We were sitting on a side road between downtown buildings. Coming off in both directions were two dead-end alleys. Neither had any of their own lighting but with daylight still left, although protected by the buildings, both alleys were at least partially lit all the way to the end. I had a déjà vu experience remembering finding my good friend Tom Clark's body in an alley just like these several months ago.

"You okay?" Halterman asked.

"Yeah," I replied, my voice cracking ever so slightly. "Let's get to it. Which one do we want to inspect first?"

She pointed left. "That one looks pretty empty. Let's go this way. Much more debris down at the end."

I grabbed my flashlight and began walking. To my side, my partner did the same. I have to say I was a little nervous. No matter how long you are a cop, when you enter an area that may not be safe, you can feel it in your body. It does not slow your steps or change your actions, but it does make you feel just a bit weak in your knees. I reached down and unsnapped the buckle on my gun. Although I did not speak or suggest she do the same, through my peripheral vision, I could see she followed suit. Our flashlights scanned every corner on our walk to the end. There was trash, signs of urination, and even a cardboard bed or two left unattended, but to that point, there was nothing unexpected. At the end of the alley was some wood stacked up on what appeared to be a trash bin. We approached the area, scanned our flashlights around, and then stopped and looked at each other.

"Well, there's nothing here unless it's in this mess," she stated, pointing at the pile of trash.

I shook my head and looked a bit closer at the debris. "Let's dig through this." I pulled two pairs of gloves out of my pocket and handed her one. "Put on some gloves and let's go through it. Check out anything with writing, papers, etc., and set them aside just in case we find anything. Once we clear the debris, we will need to go through the trash barrel."

She took the gloves and began filtering through the mess. As she pulled a large board off the stack, she turned and said, "Do you think this is odd?"

"What?"

"The main part of the alley is empty. The other side appears to be completely empty, but here, there is this large pile of crap. Several of these boards are fairly nice, almost unused and definitely not weathered." She paused, then added, "It just seems, I don't know..."

"Out of place," I finished for her.

"Yes, out of place," she repeated.

"I was thinking the same thing. And the barrel is not a trash barrel, it's like a 55-gallon storage barrel. There's no way this would be left here for more than a day or so. It would be highly desirable for the homeless."

I pushed a large pile over exposing the barrel. "Let's check out the barrel first. We can go through the rest when we see what's in it." It was sealed and the top had a locking mechanism to hold the lid in place but it was not physically locked. I pushed on the top and met with tremendous resistance. "What's in it is heavy, very heavy." Then I froze when I saw what was on top. "Halterman, look at this."

She came closer and saw what I was referring to. "That's an Illinois driver's license taped on top."

"Yep, and do you see whose it is?"

"Holy shit!" she replied. "Dawn Wells, the counselor."

6 BY THE NUMBER of emergency vehicles in the area, you would have thought we had just found the burial place for all of the victims of TV serial killer Dexter, especially considering that we hadn't even determined if there was a body in the drum yet. It was about 4:00 PM when I called Franky to let him know what we had found but agreed with him that they should continue to the Kittleson's. Although we had a few suspects, none of them were truly viable yet. I was very pleased when Doc G showed up.

"Hello, Tommy, what do you have for me this time?" she asked, reaching her hand out to me but looking toward Detective Halterman.

"We followed a lead to this alley and found a sealed drum with the driver's license taped to the top. The license is from a woman we were searching for on this case. My fear is..." I stopped when I saw her eyes had not left my partner. "And this is my new partner, Detective Patricia Halterman."

They shook hands. "Please, call me Patti."

"And I am Doctor Elise Gerstenberger. And you can call me whatever you are most comfortable with. I believe I saw you at the accident scene this morning. I had no idea you two were partners."

"Yes, I was there and saw you also. I was in my officer uniform and I don't think Detective O'Malley even knew we were going to be partners so I didn't push any introductions earlier."

Elise smiled toward me as she knew very well had I known about this new partnership, I would have been very boisterous about it earlier that day. "You were saying, Tommy? Your fear is?"

I returned her smile knowing we were thinking exactly the same thing. Then, as I started to speak, the smile quickly faded to one of disgust. "My fear is, the missing school counselor is in this drum, but I can tell you just by pushing on it, it is more than just a body in there."

"I see," she replied eyeing the drum. "It's fifty-five gallons and could easily hold a body, but there are obviously a ton of other possibilities."

Just as she spoke, another individual who I recognized from various crime scenes, but wasn't sure I'd ever met, walked up to us. "Hello, Doctor Gerstenberger. We have tested and photographed the area and the drum. There was no trace of blood or fingerprints on the drum and to be honest, the entire alley was surprisingly clean of any evidence. I think our best bet is to open it here and control what might be inside."

"Thanks, Dick," she replied. "Tommy, Patti, you want to assist?"

The last thing I would sign up for was opening a sealed drum that could have a human body inside, but Patti jumped right up and was willing to help, so that meant, you guessed it, "Sure, Doc, I will be glad to assist."

She noticed the slight hesitation. "This is not some macho thing, is it? Your new female partner is ready to go but you don't want to help?"

I didn't mean it, but they both heard the defensiveness in my quick response. "No way." Even I thought I sounded like a douche.

Nothing more was said on the subject and to be honest, I was glad. There was a group around the drum, but Doc G asked for just two from her team and then Patti and I. She seemed concerned with onlookers, even the professional emergency response individuals were asked to move back behind the police line. She turned to Patti. "I know Tommy has seen things no human should ever see. I cannot speak for you. However, my team and I have witnessed things that will melt the strongest stomach. When you have a sealed container, decomposition changes. Bodies don't look the same, they don't smell the same, and neither are improved. I am telling you this because if you are going to be sick, do not contaminate my scene. Understood?"

"I understand," Patti replied without hesitation.

Doc G glanced to me and I nodded acceptance as well.

We approached the drum. I went to the far side. "It's a simple ring clamp. When I pull the clamp, it will release and the ring will come off. I will pull the ring clear and as long as there's no pressure, the lid should remain in place and then lift straight off. If pressure has built up at all, it could pop off on its own and some of the contents with it."

I reached out and placed one gloved hand on top of the drum and the other on the ring clamp latch. I slowly pulled the clamp and after opening it about one inch, the latch released and the ring popped open. The lid didn't move so there was no pressure from inside. I glanced to the others who were all watching intently. Doc G was standing next to Patti and her two colleagues were behind the two. She nodded and I removed the ring from the drum. The lid seemed to have a seal which kept it in place and any air from escaping. I reached slowly forward and gripped each side of the cover. I glanced back toward Doc G and then Patti and both seemed ready. I wasn't sure how tight the seal would be so my muscles tightened just a bit as I arched to pull the cover off. The seal broke.

The first thing that hit me was the smell. It was immediate and intense. I hadn't had a chance to talk to my new partner about her history or experiences. I can tell you every time, no matter how often, you smell aging human flesh you cannot get that smell away from you. When I lifted the lid, it was angled away from me so I couldn't see directly into the barrel. Doc G and Patti could. Doc G's eyes widened slightly, a reaction I'm not sure I had seen in her or any medical examiner before. Detective Halterman's belly surged inward causing her to double over to about forty-five degrees. She dry-heaved and then walked away quickly. I don't know if she ended up throwing up or if she just needed some fresh air, but either way, she left. Exiting beside her was one of Doc G's team members, leaving just the three of us behind—Elise, her colleague, and me.

I pulled the lid the rest of the way off and the smell was almost enough to bring me to my knees, but when my eyes fell to the inside of the drum, my only answer was to look away or my knees would have been the best option. Inside the drum was a liquid, brown in color but in its initial form it may have been clear, white, blue, or who knows. There were the remains of something. There was hair, some bone, and other miscellaneous material. I'm not sure how much time went by as I just stared.

"Caustic," stated Doc G. "It eats human flesh." There will be very little left for us to work with. We'll be able to get enough DNA to make a positive identification, but beyond that, even cause of death will be a stretch."

"What the hell is caustic?" I asked.

"Have you heard of lye?" she replied. "How about the Sausage King of Chicago, Adolph Leutgert?"

I knew the story, but had not ever heard it called caustic. Adolph Leutgert was found guilty of murdering his wife and dissolving her body in a tank of lye at his sausage factory. "Yes, I have heard the story of Leutgert. Early 1900's I think. What does that have to do with this?"

"Nothing other than this individual is dissolved in the same material. A material you can't just go buy at any Wal-Mart."

Now I understood. In two short sentences she had said so much. There would be nothing her team would get from the body, so our best lead was the caustic. "How many places use caustic in their processing?"

"I am no expert, but after you check for a chemical plant manufacturing caustic, I would look for specialty food plants. They often use it for cleaning and sanitation or even in their processing."

"Sorry," Patti said as she had slowly made her way back over. Freeing the smell from the drum was an initial blow to everyone in the area. Now the scent, though still potent, was much more tolerable. "The odor was more intense than I have ever smelled before. It was just too much."

"I understand," I replied. "I hope you're not around this stuff so long that it never becomes too easy to take."

Doc G interrupted. "We are not prepared to handle this right now. My team will need several hours to clean this up. We will also need a Hazmat team. The chemical needs to be controlled to help preserve whatever, if anything, we can get from the body that's in there...whatever is left of the body, to be more accurate. This will take some time. You might as well follow your other leads now and I will call when we have anything."

"How long will it take you to do a DNA match to Dawn Wells?" I asked.

"We will need some DNA to match it against, but once we control the caustic, the DNA test is the easy thing. Only a couple hours additional."

Patti responded. "We will get you a DNA sample to match it against by the time you do the test."

I was surprised at her defined direction but also knew she was correct in that we could head to the Wells house and get a toothbrush, hairbrush, whatever we needed. I was not aware of her family situation, but we would have to deliver notification as well. Based on what was left in the barrel, a positive identification may not be possible without the DNA match. There was a web of hair above the surface, some bone and material, but almost all the biological material was dissolved into the caustic. The smell was beyond disgusting and was different than typical rotting flesh. I was not able to define it. It was like nothing I had ever smelled before.

I could see in Elise's eyes it was time for us to go. She was concerned about what she'd be able to do with the body and caustic mix, and she didn't want a couple of detectives hanging over her shoulder. I don't think Patti recognized the look, but she would in time. I did not speak but motioned with my head for her to follow. She did and we slowly made our way out of the alley back toward the crime scene tape and wall of emergency and press vehicles in the street. I placed a quick call to dispatch to get Dawn Wells' address and family history. She was married but with no children. I asked to have her husband's name and number texted to me and within seconds, my phone beeped with an incoming text.

As we reached the end of the alley, the press immediately made its way over to us. Through a barrage of questions and unwanted camera shots, I raised my hand and made one simple statement. "The City of Chicago has no comment at this time."

One reporter interjected, "May we assume that there is a murder victim in this alley, Detective O'Malley?"

I liked how everyone knew my name but I didn't know any of them. I guess that's why I'm one of the most famous detectives in all of Chicago. "Last time I checked, Mr.?

"Simpson. James Simpson with the *Chicago Sun Times*."

"Last time I checked, Mr. Simpson, *no comment* meant"—I paused, placed my fingers on my chin as if deep in thought, and then continued—"*no comment*."

We brushed by the group to a smattering of soft laughs in the background, one of which came from my partner.

When we reached the car, Halterman said, "I thought you were going to give him something, then when you grabbed your chin, I had to just laugh, especially when I saw his face."

"I learned a long time ago the easiest answer is to simply say 'no comment,' as it takes the pressure off you to not mess anything up. If you say nothing, you cannot get in trouble."

"Thanks for the tip," she replied with complete seriousness in her tone. It was very respective in that she meant that the simple handling of the press situation was legitimate learning for her. She was taking this seriously. She continued once in the front seat. "Are we headed to Dawn Wells' residence?"

"No," I replied. "We are headed to her husband's place of employment, the United Center."

"What does he do there?"

I shrugged as I started the car. "I'm not sure, but his title is Contract Manager so I assume he's either tied to procurement or customer service. We will find out when we get there."

"Why are we starting there? Why don't we have him meet us at his house so we can get the DNA sample?" It was clear she thought going to the house was a better idea since it would kill two birds with one stone.

I turned to her. "Because I want to understand why, after she was missing for forty-eight hours, there's no missing person's report, and I don't want him to have time to think about his answers. I want to see his reaction immediately after telling him we believe his wife of six years was dissolved in a vat of chemicals."

She nodded understanding. "We are only ten minutes from the United Center. It is late in the day. Are you sure he's still there?"

According to my text from dispatch, he scanned his badge in at 7:30 AM and hasn't scanned out yet. We will see when we arrive."

• • • • •

Franky and Karen arrived at the Kittleson's house around 4:30 PM. They lived in a middle-income house tied to the outskirts of the same neighborhood where the accident took place. Although there was probably only a mile between the two, Mike and Runae Schulman's house was probably $200K more expensive than the Kittleson's. Franky's initial thought was that was simply another way Mark

Schulman was better than everyone else—his parents were rich.

Karen broke the silence as they pulled in the driveway. "The plate of that Taurus matches one of the cars registered to Becky Kittleson, and judging by the look of it, it's the kid's car."

"Yeah," Franky replied. "It has that typical teenager look."

"Maybe the mom's car is in the garage," she added. "The parents are divorced. The father lives in Lakeville, Minnesota. According to this"—she was flipping through pages as she spoke—"he has remarried."

"So a single mother raising a homosexual boy in downtown Chicago most likely scraping by to pay for private school finds out her boy is being bullied and the school is doing nothing about it. She is clearly down on her luck because her ex-husband has remarried and moved away. She gets to her breaking point and drives over in the morning to confront the boy bullying her son, and timing is what it is, she sees him come out and she cracks and drives right into him." Franky paused and looked at his new partner. "Well, what do you think?"

"Great theory, but what about the car switch. When and how did she steal the car and use it?"

"Damn," Franky replied. "And I was on such a roll. Let's go, but if the mom is not here, we can't question the boy."

"Understood," she replied as she reached out to ring the doorbell.

After a brief moment, some rustling was heard and the sound of someone walking toward the door shortly thereafter. The lock popped and handle turned revealing a good-looking, clean-cut teenage boy. He was wearing a polo shirt neatly tucked in, belt, jeans, and socks. His shoes were stacked neatly to the side by the front door. "Can I help you?" he asked.

"Hello," Franky began. "I'm Detective Sullivan and this is Detective Huston. Are you Nate Kittleson?"

Hesitantly he replied, "Yes?"

"Is your mother home? We would like to talk to you about an accident that took place this morning and your relationship with the victim."

His body seemed to tense a bit. It was not what Franky would call a guilty tense, just an uncomfortable tense. "My mother just texted me. She's five minutes away. I'm not supposed to let anyone in the house when she's gone." He paused, smiled a bit, and tried to appear slightly macho, which he could not pull off. "You know, mothers worry and all."

Not missing a beat, Franky replied, "I think that's a good rule to follow. We will wait outside until she arrives, but next time, why don't you ask who it is before you open the door."

As if on cue, an older model Ford Escape pulled in just as Franky and Karen were turning from the door. "There she is," Nate said from behind.

In the front window a woman sat with a death stare on the two detectives. The automatic garage door opened and she pulled the Escape inside. She had picked up groceries but left them and her work bag in the car and proceeded directly to the front door. "Can I help you?" she said with a harsh tone.

"Yes," Franky again took the lead in the reply. "I am Detective Sullivan and this is Detective Huston. We stopped by to have a few words with you and your son on his relationship with a boy who was the victim of a car accident this morning. If possible, we would like to go inside and see if there's anything he can help us with."

Her voice was questioning. "I know who you're talking about. First that boy wrecks my son's life and you guys don't do anything about it. Now he gets in a car accident and you want to talk."

"Ma'am, I don't know anything about the history here. We are with the homicide department. The boy was murdered and unfortunately, we need to talk to anyone who knew him, whether they were friends or enemies, we need to determine how he ended up as he did."

The word homicide seemed to hang in the air. Becky Kittleson's voice was softer. "You mean, it was not just a car accident? It was..."

Franky stared at her. It was clear just in that reaction that Becky Kittleson had nothing to do with the murder. A first-year traffic cop could have seen it. This was a mother reacting to another mother's pain of losing her child. Franky finished her comment. "Yes, it appears this was a hit-and-run targeting the young man."

She didn't speak again but motioned Franky and Karen inside putting her arm around her son as she passed to take the lead. Becky Kittleson led the small group to the kitchen table motioning for all to sit. "Can I get either of you anything?"

"I'll take a soda," Nate answered.

"I was actually talking to the two detectives. You know where the soda is." She turned back toward Franky.

"I'm fine," Franky answered.

"Me as well," added Karen.

Hearing that, Becky took a seat in the chair next to where her son was going to sit. When he returned, she fixed his polo shirt collar that had become partially turned up then pushed her lips slightly together before responding. "I am almost scared to ask, but what happened and why do you need to speak to my son?"

Karen turned her eyes to Franky and gave him a small nod. With that, he answered, "Early this morning in his driveway, Mark Schulman was run down by a stolen car before he could get in his vehicle. The driver fled on foot to what we assume was the perpetrator's car. The young man was killed on impact."

Franky let them absorb that information and watched their reaction. It appeared that Nate already knew the story. He had been at school the entire day and Franky was sure word had spread. However, it also appeared that Nate hadn't told the specifics to his mom. Franky wondered why. Becky hadn't removed her hand from her son, and although it was clear she felt pain for Mark Schulman's parents, there was something working against it. "That is truly horrible for the family," she said softly. "But again, what does that have to do with my son?"

Franky expected the question. "Well, Nate, I was wondering if you could tell me about your relationship with Mark?"

Nate was about to answer but his mother cut him off. "What does that have to do with anything? Nate was no different than any other kid at school. Mark Schulman was awful to him. He taunted him, hazed him, beat him up, and bullied him at every opportunity, but because he was a football player, the school did nothing."

"Mother, I can answer the detective. I'm okay with it."

She was going to say more but softened when she heard his tone.

"Am I a suspect, Detective Sullivan?"

"An interesting question, Nate," Franky answered. "Should you be?"

He put his lips together. "I guess so." He paused. "I mean, if you go by the social media world you're going to see a whole bunch of horrible stuff. The guy was a real asshole."

"Nate, your language..." interrupted his mother.

"Mom, let me talk." He shot a glare back toward his mother as he spoke, and then pulled out his phone, clicked a few apps open, and handed it over to Detective Huston who was sitting closest to him. "I saved everything. They are all stored in that file. Even the Snapchats he sent that erase immediately, I took a screenshot and saved them as well. The guy tore me apart for not being in sports, for being a straight-A student, but most of all, he bullied me for being gay."

"What type of things did he do to you?" Franky asked.

"A little of everything," he replied. "The social media was the worst. I kept trying to block him but he would get to me through other accounts. I think it became a challenge to him to find his way back into my account. Then he would push me in the halls, knock my books on the floor, urinate in my locker, and a few things I don't want to say."

"And you told the authorities at school?" Huston asked.

This time Becky broke in again. "We not only told them in writing, we met with the advisory board in person and showed them all the evidence. You know what they did..."

There was a pause that went long enough that Franky had to reply, "What? What did they do?"

"Not a goddamn thing," Nate answered. "If anything, they made it worse. They gave Mark absolute, untouchable power. The bullying didn't stop, but now he added the fact that I tried to get him in trouble, and the school agreed with him. His most common taunt was, 'There's no place for faggots at Fenton.' " He paused and forced out a fake smile. "Catchy, isn't it?"

"No, Nate, it is not catchy at all," Franky replied.

Karen now asked a question in a softer tone to match Franky's. "So, you just implied that with all these things going on *you* should be considered a suspect. You definitely had motive. Can you tell me where you were this morning?"

Franky would not have gone right to the punch, but since Huston did, the punch was laid out there. Let's see if it landed, he thought. The boy looked right to her almost in disbelief. The reaction was good, but something about it still left a little to be desired. It was as if there was some guilt there and he was trying to force surprise.

"What do you mean? I couldn't kill anyone, even an asshole like that."

"What business do you have asking my son that question? He is here to help you understand the kid. Now I can tell you for sure, no parent deserves to outlive their child, but if you think either one of us will shed a tear over him, you're wrong. But that does not make my son a murderer."

"We were actually friends when we were kids. We were in school together for at least nine or ten years. It was only in high school when things changed, but I guess that's when *I* changed," Nate added softly.

Franky broke in. "Tell us about your morning. When did you get up? Where did you go? All that stuff."

Nate looked at his mom and she gave him a slight nod to go ahead. "I don't know. It was normal. My alarm rang, I got up, and I went to school."

"What time did your alarm ring?" Franky asked.

"Five-thirty or so. But I snoozed at least once."

"Five-thirty? That's awfully early, isn't it? What time does school start?"

Nate shuffled a bit in his chair. "It takes me a while to wake up so I give myself extra time. I also like to watch the sun come up and reflect off the lake so I drive downtown."

"You drive into the city?" Franky was taking notes as he asked questions.

"Not every morning, but I did this morning." He looked up almost appearing eager. "There, you see, I couldn't have done it. I was on Lakeshore this morning before school."

Karen now interjected. "Did you stop anywhere? Even for gas or a donut or something? Was anyone with you? Did you see anyone who can place you there?"

He appeared deflated. "No, not that I know of."

Becky Kittleson now stood up, taking both detectives a bit by surprise. "No more questions. I don't know where this is going but I definitely don't like what you're implying." She stood behind her son and placed both hands on his shoulders. "No more questions at least until I speak with Nate's father."

Franky took the opportunity on that lead-in. "Speaking of his father, where is he?"

"Jack and I divorced five years ago. He moved to Minneapolis shortly thereafter."

"Is he involved in Nate's life?"

Nate answered this one. "Yes, we talk every day and he drives down almost every weekend. In the summer, I go there for a few weeks at a time." His voice trailed off. "He probably spends more time with me now than when we lived together because the time is not interrupted."

Becky continued. "Jack traveled for work. It was hard."

It was clear to both Franky and Karen that Becky Kittleson was a peacemaker who still had feelings for her ex-husband. Perhaps not feelings of love as in a marriage, but love as in a father to her only child. "We're going to want to talk to him as well, and we would prefer it be in person. When you talk to him, can you ask how quickly he can make it down here?" Franky stood which gave Karen the signal they were done. She seemed a bit surprised but didn't say so in front of Becky and Nate. That comment would wait until they were back in the car.

Before turning to walk away, Franky asked one more question to see if it would be answered. "Say, Nate, I don't normally go downtown that early. I assume traffic is not bad so you could even jump on the Interstate without a problem. Is that what you do?"

Becky instantly frowned but when Nate looked to her, she nodded again. "I could take the Interstate but there's no point. It would take me longer to get there, get on, and then get off. I take Fullerton to Grand and take Grand all the way into the city."

"Oh, right, right, right. That makes more sense." He paused, smiled, and then added, "How was the sunrise today?"

"A clear, crisp day like today electrifies the water. It was excellent."

"Enough questions, Detective. Take it up with Jack when he gets here." Becky's eyes clearly stated the interview was over even more than the words.

Franky nodded. "We will show ourselves out. Thank you both for your time."

They got to their car and Karen could barely wait until the car was started before she asked the question. "Why did you let them off the hook like that? We could have pushed harder."

"Do you think either one of them did it?" Franky asked.

She turned forward. "The mother is clean. She didn't know anything about it and was not faking. However, my gut tells me the boy didn't do it, but he was lying about something. Something about his morning drive to watch the sunrise doesn't fit. Maybe he was lying about the murder, but maybe it was something completely unrelated. I couldn't tell."

"My thoughts exactly, but as far as why we're not still there questioning him, we have enough to verify his story. There are at least a dozen traffic cams on Fullerton and Grand. If he was there this morning, we will be able to confirm it."

"And if we can't confirm it, then we will have a different set of questions for him next time. That's why you asked for his route downtown."

Franky smiled. "Yep. It will be much more powerful with evidence behind our questions. I agree though, he was lying about his time this morning, I just don't know if it was because he was at the Schulman's house, or if he was hiding something else."

7 "WE ARE HERE to see Donovan Wells," I said to the guard. And yes, Don Wells was married to Dawn Wells. It must be tough when someone calls and asks for Don, I thought to myself.

The United Center was an awesome arena. When you think of it, you don't think about procurement or offices. You think about Michael Jordan and the Chicago Bulls. Basketball is my favorite sport to watch. Chicago had all the sports franchises so at any time you could see the Bulls, Bears, White Sox, Cubs, or Blackhawks. They also had soccer which we all know is not a real sport. That being said, I was a college basketball fan and partial to the University of Kansas Jayhawks. March Madness had just started and as always, the number one seed Jayhawks were rolling through the first two rounds.

"Donovan Wells?" the guard replied questionably. "You mean Donnie?"

I pushed my lips together showing slight frustration. There are three levels of individuals in the world: those who are cops, those who have no desire to be cops, and those that tried and failed. Some key examples of those in the last category are TSA employees at airports, and front-desk security guards in downtown buildings. "If his birth name is Donovan, then yes, I mean Donnie."

"Donovan. I can't wait to start calling him Donovan," the guard replied smiling.

"What is this, the fourth grade?" I said to myself.

He picked up the phone, dialed four digits, and waited for an answer. "You know, I don't even know your names."

Great security. "I'm Tony Kucoĉ and this is Dorothy Hamill. We just need to ask him a few questions." Pulled out a couple Chicago athletes without thinking twice.

The security guard didn't blink an eye. He never asked for badges or any identification. "Hello, Donovan." He laughed out loud more so we could hear than because he was actually laughing. "I have a couple people at the front desk here to meet you." Something was said back to him. "'Oh, I didn't ask." He turned back to us. "Do you folks have an appointment?"

I pulled out my badge. "This is a police matter and we need to speak with

Donovan." I smiled back at him. "Immediately."

His voice was more hesitant on the phone. It was clear he didn't expect us to be police officers though we screamed it by our appearance. His voice was softer. "Donnie, these are police officers. They say it's urgent."

There were a few other short exchanges before he hung up the phone. "Everything okay?" I asked.

"Yep," he said, his voice still softer than before. "Donnie will be right down."

Back to Donnie, I thought. The joking mood must have gone away. "Great. We will just wait over there." I motioned that we'd sit in the chairs by the large windows looking out toward the city.

"Dorothy Hamill?" Patti questioned.

"Well, that was really just to prove a point that certain people have no business being in the positions they are. What if we were criminals, arsonists, or who knows what else? That yay-who is not going to stop anyone who actually had a plan to get in. We weren't even trying that hard."

Just as I finished, a man of about thirty years old walked up and spoke briefly to the guard. His eyes panned across to us. "Mr. Kucoĉ and Ms. Hamill?" he said softly.

"No, the guard must have gotten the names wrong. I'm Detective O'Malley and this is Detective Halterman. I think we need a private room if that's all right."

Mr. Wells' eyebrows lifted just a bit and I could tell he was nervous. It might just be normal nerves about unexpected visitors in the form of two homicide detectives, but perhaps it was more. The next five or so minutes should give me my answers. He hesitated, then continued. "Can I ask for your identification?" We both produced our badges with IDs and allowed him to look through them. Most people do a quick scan and if they even read the names, they accomplished something. He studied them. "Homicide? Can I ask what this is about?"

"You may ask, Mr. Wells, but as I said, I would prefer to speak in private."

He seemed to accept that answer. "Since it's almost six in the evening, none of our conference rooms will be taken. There is actually one on this floor level just around the bend. Why don't we go there?"

"Sounds good," I replied.

We followed him around what I would call the "end zone" corner of the United Center. It's the end where one of the goals would be for basketball or hockey. He approached a door, tested if it was locked. It was. He removed a set of keys, found the right one, and opened the door. "Why don't you come inside and grab a seat." To our surprise, this was not a conference room, but a luxury suite. It had a bar for food, a tap location for beer, and a long high-top bench in back and stadium chairs by the window overlooking the basketball court.

"Wow," I began. "What a way to watch a game."

Suddenly, Mr. Wells' tone changed significantly. "Listen, Detective, I'm sure you're not here to talk about seats and a basketball game. I have already said it's late, so let's get through this. What do you need to know?"

I did not like his tone, so I immediately changed mine to match. "We have been looking for your wife. Are you aware she is missing?"

His face did not change. "I have no comment on that."

What the hell does that mean? I thought.

"What the hell does that mean?" Detective Halterman broke in.

"It means just that," he replied. "My wife and I are having some difficulties. I haven't seen her for several days. We had a fight about her boss, that jackass Bales, and she stormed out. That was two days ago and I haven't seen her since."

Well, at least he answered the question as to why he didn't file a police report. Instantly my mind went to motive, at least for the death of his wife, but what about the Schulman boy. I raised my hand motioning for him to calm down a bit. "Okay, we have some information on your wife to speak to you about, but I have one other question first. Did you know or ever hear the name Mark Schulman?"

"I do know that name, but only from the news today. That's the boy who was in the accident this morning. It's been on the news all day and is big talk around the office. He was struck by the car right in his driveway, correct?"

I was pleased to hear many of the details were not released yet if that was as thorough as his information was. "Yes, so before today, you had never heard your wife mention him before?"

"No, should I have?" Donovan was much calmer now and in tune with the conversation.

"No, just a question," I replied.

"How does this involve Dawn?" he interrupted.

"Well, sir, we have some bad news. We believe we may have found your wife's body. It appears she was murdered, and it appears the accident involving Mark Schulman and this situation with your wife is related."

His face dropped. I have given too many notifications to count. Sometimes I have given them to the person who later turned out to be the cause of the death. You learn reactions. You learn involuntary body functions. Donovan Wells had none of them. He sat quietly without speaking. He did not appear nervous. His heart didn't start racing. He basically went someplace else. This was a reaction I had seen, but not very often. Most times there was denial. Sometimes when the person was guilty, there was way overdone denial. Donovan Wells did nothing.

"Mr. Wells?" Detective Halterman asked. "Are you all right?"

His head turned up and there was a wetness forming in his eyes. "What do you say when you are told something like this? Two days ago my wife stormed out of the house saying she never wanted to see me again, and she never did."

I don't know why, but my mind went to Tammi. *We need to talk.* I wonder if before she stormed out, Dawn Wells told her husband they needed to talk.

"Why do you think it's my wife?" he said after a brief pause. "And why aren't you sure it's her?"

Patti looked to me and without speaking said, *this one is all yours.* "Well, sir, a clue left at the scene of the Schulman case led us to a remote area of downtown Chicago. When we arrived, we found a barrel with your wife's driver's license taped to the top of it. In it were the remains of a body, but it was too badly decomposed to be identified at this time. We will need to do a DNA match."

He let out a sigh of relief. "Then it couldn't be her. I saw her two days ago. To be that decomposed would take much longer, wouldn't it?"

"The decomposition was accelerated with some corrosive chemicals." I didn't have to say any more.

"I called her several times. I left voicemails saying I was sorry and I wanted to work things out. I wonder if she ever heard them." His voice trailed off.

Although I could not be 100% sure, I felt fairly confident Donnie Wells did not murder his wife. He loved her.

We talked for a short while longer, and then escorted him back to his office, collected his things, and headed to his condo, a high-rise just off Navy Pier downtown. We offered to drive him but he was not able to leave his car at the United Center so he rode with me, and Detective Halterman drove his car. We arrived at 420 East Ohio, greeted Charles in the lobby, another failed policeman, and proceeded to floor number twelve. The condo was immaculate. It was two buildings down from Lakeshore Drive and probably had a wonderful view of the water until the new high-rise immediately next to it was built last year. Now their view was a tiny sliver of Lake Michigan between the buildings and the edge of the Ferris wheel at Navy Pier.

After recovering her toothbrush and hairbrush, I turned back to Donovan who was simply staring out the window, not even in the direction of the lake. "Is there anyone you can call to come over?"

He turned his head to me but left his body facing away. "No sir, we didn't have a lot of friends and both our parents are dead. Dawn has a sister in Kalamazoo. I should probably call her."

I nodded. "Listen, if there's anyone who can come over, I would highly recommend it. However, hold off on the sister right now. There is no reason to do that until we have the DNA test results. The coroner is still doing her work on the remains, and it will be morning before they even run the DNA matching test."

He nodded but didn't reply.

We began to move toward the door. "Please take care of yourself, Mr. Wells. Also, I know sometimes people want to get away from things. Please stay in town until we get this all sorted out." We continued to the door. "We'll show ourselves out."

.   .   .   .   .

We got in the car and I checked my watch. 7:30 PM. Where had the day gone?

"Need to be somewhere?" Patti asked.

"Yeah, the woman I'm seeing requested some of my time tonight. I am already later than she would have hoped. Probably not going to help."

"I'm sure it will be fine," she replied. "The fact that she wanted some of your time is a good thing. Most guys would scream for that."

I shook my head in return. "Well, it's not that kind of time. It's the kind of time that starts with 'we need to talk' in the morning and ends with, 'I am moving out' in the evening."

She was silent for a minute. "I'm sorry, Tommy. If it does go the way you're anticipating, I am very sorry."

"Thanks for saying that, Detective, and you know, I think that is the first time you called me Tommy."

"Yeah," she said smiling just a bit. "Can I ask you, was I such a bad partner for a first day?"

I pulled over and stopped the car about a block short of the police department. "Listen, Patti, it's nothing personal. Were you that bad of a partner? No, you weren't, but it was never about that. It's about David."

"David?" she asked.

"My old partner," I replied.

"David Dixon?"

My eyes swung to her. "How the hell do you know him?"

"Franky and Carter mentioned Dixon as your old partner's name, but not David, and they did not give any specifics."

I nodded understanding. "He was young, like you. I thought I could teach him things. I thought I could mentor him to become everything I wasn't. He was clean-cut, good, and incredible on the range with a gun. We had a follow-up to a murder. Not much different than what we did today. There was a murder and we needed to talk to those involved. I was riding the kid hard. I made him drive, I made him pump gas, wash the windows, fill out all the reports. Basically, anything I did not want to do and I even made up some things we didn't have to do—all those things went to him. We approached the house and were talking about baseball or something, I don't remember. I made some comment that rookies have to always knock on the doors. We were still exchanging verbal jabs when the first shot broke through the door. I pulled my gun but it had his brain matter all over it. His body was limp and he was dead before he hit the ground. I fired three times into the house and then fell to my knees to help him. I was not even worried about securing the scene or my own well-being. I just didn't want him to die. More than anything, I didn't want David Dixon to die."

"I'm sorry, Tommy. I didn't mean for you to…"

I cut her off with my raised hand. "So, Detective Halterman, when I am asked if I want a partner, my answer is always no. Because I never want to fuck up again like I did that day."

"You did not fuck up, Tommy."

"Tell that to Rhonda Dixon, David's mom. Or the future Kelly Dixon, David's fiancée."

She placed her hand on my shoulder. "It was a disturbed murderer. Nothing you could have done would have changed that."

"But he got away, Patti. He got away."

I put the car back in gear and continued the last block to the station. Nothing more was said. Patti said she would take care of the DNA sample and follow-up on where things were at. She would also update the report she had started. I knew I needed to put a call into Franky but now was not the time. I needed to get home.

Just after dropping Patti at the door, I saw Franky emerge from the building in her wake. My chance to get away was delayed if not cancelled altogether.

"Tommy, hold up," Franky yelled.

I stopped and rolled down my window. "What do you need, Franky. I'm late."

"I know, I know," he said breathing heavily. "I wanted to tell you two things."

He paused, and I don't know why but he seemed to be waiting for me to acknowledge he was making this great effort. "Okay, Franky, what are they, these two things?"

"First, don't take any shit from her. You are a good man and if she doesn't see it, then screw her."

I smiled. "And the second thing?"

"When she is done dumping your sorry ass, swing by Flap Jaws and I will buy you a drink."

I flipped him off and tried to drive over his feet as I left, although I was smiling. Franky always knows the right thing to say.

8 "TAMMI, I'M HOME."

I don't know when I realized she was gone. I think I walked around the place calling her name in every room. Then, I actually said out loud to myself, *she must be at the store.* I walked over to the kitchen table, and there it was—the note. It was folded up twice into a fan and looked like a business letter, although it was handwritten. I felt something in my heart. It ached. It was strange, a sensation I had not felt for some time, but it was there. It was fear. I was scared to even reach out and grab it. I looked at it in silence for some time. Then, the next thing I knew, it was in my hands. I read it out loud.

Dear Tommy,

I am sorry I have to write this down, but I needed you to realize this was important. I needed you home tonight. I know your job does not have hours, but our relationship does and sometimes, it just needs to come first. This is not a good-bye letter. I have an opportunity I need to talk to you about. I have been putting it off and that is on me. However, every time I build up the courage to talk, you are not home. You are a wonderful man..."

"You don't have to read that now. I didn't get on the plane," said a gentle voice through tears.

I swung my head around to see her beautiful face in the doorway. I hadn't even shut the door so she made no sound upon entering. She was crying. I walked to her. "What is this?" I asked, my voice cracking as well.

"How far did you read?"

I glanced down at the paper I still held in my hand. It looked to be about four paragraphs and I hadn't even made it through one. "Not even through the first few sentences. I read *'you are a wonderful man'* and then stopped when you spoke." I took her hand. "What is going on, Tam? Are you leaving me?"

"No," she said immediately. Then her voice softened. "Not really," she added.

"You can't partially leave someone, Tammi. Either you are here or you are not." I released her hand and turned away. "You know, when I walked in the bedroom looking for you, I saw your clothes were gone. Did I do something wrong?"

She took two steps toward me and took both my hands, crumbling the note I still held in one of them. "No, Tommy. Other than your job, which I hate, you are the man of my dreams. I have an opportunity. That is all. One I can't pass up right now."

"An opportunity? You mean like a new job? You have to move out because you have a new job?"

"Yes, Tommy, a new job." She paused then added softer as if it would not impact as much in a quieter tone, "In San Francisco."

I released both her hands. "You are moving to San Francisco? Have you already accepted the job?"

"I have."

"Without even talking to me! What kind of crap is that? I would never do that to you. We had been talking about our lives together. How does that work in San Francisco?"

"We can make it work, Tommy. If we love each other."

"Love each other? You have never even said the words. I say them to you and you just give me a kiss or change the subject. What the hell, Tammi? Now you love me, when you write me some Dear John letter and are already packed. Hell, you just said you didn't get on the plane. You were going to leave without even saying good-bye."

"You're mad. There's no talking to you when you're mad."

"You're damn right I'm mad. This is bullshit and you know it. No job makes you accept it and start right away. You always have a few weeks to transition. And you are talking about moving halfway across the United States. They would give you more time."

"They did, Tommy." She paused and let that sink in. "I notified the Chop House three weeks ago. I just couldn't tell you."

I paced a bit taking some deep breaths as I walked. Trying to calm down, I changed the subject to something other than my feelings. "What is the job?"

"Ozumo. It's the premiere Japanese restaurant on the West Coast. They are making me a managing partner. I can't turn it down, Tommy. It's the fulfillment of my dream."

That's when I saw it. The difference when she talked about me and when she talked about Ozumo. She could not live without Ozumo, but she could live without me. "Can you still make your flight?"

"What? No. I mean, yes I can make my flight, but I came back to be with you."

"Tammi, that is the difference. I don't want to be with you for tonight. I don't want you to love me the day you're leaving. Part of me knew this day would come. Your future is bigger than mine. We both know that. Go get on your plane. I'm supposed to meet Franky anyway." I turned and held her hands. "Tammi, I love you. I have known that for some time, but this is your chance to follow your dreams. If we are meant to be, we will find out what happens next. I'm a Midwest guy. I'm a Chicago guy. San Francisco is not for me. I hate the 49ers."

She smiled as that was not the last phrase she thought I was going to say. "What are you saying, Tommy?"

I am saying what you are saying. "Go get on that plane. That is the life you are choosing now. If our paths cross in the future, then we will see what happens."

Tears streamed down her face. "Tommy, this is not..."

I stopped her. "Tammi, please go."

She fell into my arms and although I loved the feeling, I did not return the embrace. I reached my arms inside and pushed her shoulders. "Tammi, please. You made the decision. You need to go." I took the letter now partially crumbled in my hand, walked over to the trash and threw it there unread. "I will miss you, Tammi." Then I walked back into the bedroom.

I heard the front door shut a few minutes later. I sat on the end of my bed in complete silence. I believe I could even hear the hum of the refrigerator from the other room, or maybe the furnace kicking on and blowing some heat. I felt a tear forming in my eye. I'm not sure the last time I cried.

I picked up the phone and hit speed dial #1.

"Yeah."

"You at Flap Jaws?"

"If you're asking if I am there now, the answer is no. If you're asking if I can get there before you, the answer is yes. Let me feed Vader and I will head out."

"Thanks, buddy."

"No problem, Tommy. The first round's on me."

•　　•　　•　　•　　•

It was near 2:00 AM when Roy Pura, the longtime bartender and owner of my downtown home away from home, announced the dreaded last call. Craig Carter, my sergeant and off-duty psychiatrist, stood and slowly walked to meet Roy at the bar. A few minutes later, Carter appeared at the table with me and Franky holding a bottle of Wild Turkey 101.

"Last call is last call, Sergeant," I said through slurred speech.

"When you just wiped away a bartender and owner's outstanding parking tickets, last call gets extended."

I didn't always like Carter. In fact, I would say it was a 40-60 split on liking to disliking, but tonight, he was on the 40% side. I smiled, cracked open the bottle, and poured another over my remaining ice. Over the last five hours, we had already talked through everything going on at work, we had talked through everything happening in our lives, and we had even talked through the issues Franky had with the amount and sheer size of Vader, his enormous black Newfoundland's bowel movements. What we hadn't talked about was Tammi.

Carter put his hand on my shoulder. "We haven't had a night like this since Stephanie moved out with the kids."

Franky nodded. "Nope, kind of the same situation tonight, ay Tommy?"

I downed my drink and poured one more. Before I could speak, Carter added, "I assumed that's what this was. Not because I thought it would happen, but this is the first night you've gone more than ten minutes without mentioning her. What happened?"

"Ah, nothing really." I shrugged. "New job in San Francisco. She said she wanted to try to make it work, but I decided to go into jackass mode and basically threw her out."

Carter smiled. "Shit, Tommy, you must have six weeks of unused vacation. San Francisco is better than Chicago this time of year. Just go and figure it out."

I looked at him and for a split second, I thought, *that is one hell of an idea.* Then I remembered. She set this up for more than a month. Six weeks ago she said she needed to go out west to a restaurant show but she was really interviewing. She gave notice at her old job. All this without saying a word to me. "Fuck that, Sergeant."

Nothing more on the subject was said. I don't remember getting home. I don't remember much of the evening. I remember the last bottle. I remember it being empty. I remember being at home in an empty apartment.

• • • • •

Seven a.m. came too early. When I got up, I found I had made a pizza. By that I mean I had put a frozen pizza in the oven and it cooked for nearly four hours. I guess I had also decided I would watch some TV. It was on Cinemax and very loud. What a loser. That's why I showed up at the department at 8:30. Normally Carter would have ripped me a new one. Today he said nothing. The last time that I showed up that late was the day after Clark, my longtime friend in Vice, was killed. Franky and I found his body. It's funny how the mind ties things together. As if I wasn't depressed enough as it was. My new partner was bright and chirpy as I walked by. She appeared eager to talk to me. However, I think my appearance or maybe someone clued her in, but regardless, she understood the message that today she may want to take it down a notch. She let me pass and arrive at my desk without comment. After several minutes, she slid a note to me as she passed. It read simply:

I have the addresses for all the other school employees on that evaluation team and Nate Kittleson's father will be in by 1 PM from Minnesota.

I reached out and grabbed her arm before she could scuttle on by. "Give me twenty minutes to run through things and then I'll be ready to go. Work with Franky and Karen on the schedule today. We need to meet with everyone and then maybe go back through any witnesses at the accident scene."

"No problem," she replied. "And if you have not seen your e-mail, it was a positive ID on the Wells woman."

I nodded.

•   •   •   •   •

Thirty minutes later we were in a car from the pool with Dr. G's full report in hand. It included all the forensics on both murder scenes including medical and physical information. I asked Patti to drive so I could take a little extra time to review the file. We were headed to the school to meet with Eric Graham, the physical education teacher and boys' soccer coach. We were going to try to meet with each of the faculty members that were on the committee that evaluated the bullying complaints from Nate Kittleson and the rape allegations from Leah Malecha. Franky and Karen planned to spend most of the morning going through all the information collected at the two scenes and find whatever they could that tied the two together. We knew we had the mysterious envelope which basically locked them into being related, but we wanted forensic evidence as well. I knew we had good footprints at the accident scene, but I hadn't read if we recovered any DNA or related items that could tie directly back to the perpetrator. The same at the Dawn Wells' site. Why would a killer be so careless with a footprint but not leave anything else? Killers were stupid, I thought.

"If we can get through the interviews by noon, we can grab an El Famous Burrito before heading back to the station to meet with Jack Kittleson, Nate's father," I stated, glancing toward my partner as we drove.

"Sounds fine," Halterman replied.

Basically, I was fishing with the burrito comment to see if she even knew the place, but I got nothing in response. She waited a bit in silence before continuing. "So, are you going to tell me what's going on today?"

"Going on?" I asked.

"Yeah," she replied. "I admit I don't know you well, but in less than twenty-four hours I have seen you go from hating everything I represent as a partner, defining it in detail to our sergeant, actually working fairly well together for the balance of the day, and then showing up late and looking like hell the next morning."

"Seems like a busy twenty-four hours," I said.

The silence that engulfed the car after that statement was deafening. I should have said more, but I really didn't know her that well and she was right, less than a day ago I did hate everything she represented. I hated having her thrust on me like I was not capable of taking on a partner. We were about a mile from the school when I stated flatly, "My girlfriend left me last night. She didn't give any warning and took a new job in San Francisco. She informed me minutes before she took off for the airport. Tie that to seeing a kid cut in half and a woman in a barrel, I just felt like having a drink or two was in order. Unfortunately, I felt that way about six times taking the drink count to closer to twelve or fourteen."

She shrugged. "Thanks for telling me. Next time if you need someone to drive or someone to talk to, why don't you call? I could have used a drink last night as well."

She said it flatly, without any goofy inflection. She held no negative judgment. I hadn't thought about what she might be feeling after yesterday. She had been a street cop a week ago and now was being thrust into murders, and her first two were some of the most gruesome I had seen in years. "I will keep that in mind."

That was the end of the conversation as we were pulling into the school. We did not need Principal Bale's approval to meet with these teachers any longer. They were part of an active investigation. I was going to enjoy telling him as much.

Marci was immediately on the phone the moment we entered the front office. Within seconds, without even having to ask to see him, Principal Bales was standing in front of us. "What do you need, Detectives?" He said it questionably as he was looking at my partner but had no idea who she was since I was here with Franky before.

"This is my partner, Detective Halterman, and we will be setting up meetings with the following people today," I responded. "Eric Graham, the physical education teacher and soccer coach, Herb Whychoff, the senior English teacher, and Bill Ronin, chemistry."

"As I said before, I will be glad to allow that but I would like to speak to them first."

"Principal Bales, this is not a request. Dawn Wells is dead. Mark Schulman is dead. Mark Schulman was killed by a car that was owned by someone who registered a complaint against him in this school. Right now, the only thing linking these deaths is your bogus committee that from my perspective was more interested in burying bad press than helping your students. So forgive me if I am not interested in whether you have warned these individuals. Bring them all to this front conference room immediately. If their classes need an instructor while they're gone, then find someone on break, because we're going to be a while."

Bales seemed about to protest, and in truth, he should have. I just told him that the primary requirement for a school and more specifically a principal, was to protect the students and he did not do that. I took a shot at his most core value, and he said nothing about it. He stuttered a bit before answering. "I will have Marci call them. Graham is out on the soccer field because the weather was nice so he took his class out there. The others are nearby."

"That would be perfect," Patti interjected. "Perhaps I could go meet Mr. Graham on the soccer field and talk to him out there."

I liked the divide and conquer attitude, but I didn't know what type of interviewer my new partner was. Trusting her to ask all the right questions was something I did not immediately want to do, especially on a case of this magnitude. However, this was not the time to shut her down so I let it pass. "That would be fine, and..." I stopped in midsentence as a loud bang rang through the school.

"What the hell was that?" asked Bales.

"*Gunshot*!" I shouted. "Outside. Bales, call 911. Let them know there are officers on the scene."

I unbuckled my gun as I ran back toward the front door. The shot had been in the distance. It sounded like a rifle but the echo off the buildings left the source in question. We got outside and stopped on the front steps allowing all our senses to take in the environment. There was silence except in one direction. "Toward the fields." I pointed. "Voices."

We ran full speed around the corner of the building. To the south were the football fields, a soccer field, a baseball diamond, and two tennis courts. We were within a hundred or so yards when we could make out a group of students around what seemed to be someone on the ground. We arrived at the group and saw a middle-aged male missing the majority of his face. The back of his head had been blown away and he was clearly already dead. The students had a variety of emotional responses. Most seemed to be at the point of vomiting, many were crying, and a handful were around him attempting some sort of CPR.

"Stop, kids. He's gone," I said.

Patti got on her radio and was calling it in. We could already hear sirens in the distance, most likely from Principal Bales' call.

"Who is this?" I asked the group, not centering on any one student.

A girl stepped forward. "It's our teacher, Mr. Graham."

Patti and I looked at each other, then back to the kids. Then we both changed into "secure the scene" mode. I pointed and began directing traffic. "Okay everyone, please back away. We don't want any evidence lost or inadvertently tampered with. I need everyone to remain here but off to the side. We will want to talk to everyone who saw what happened."

Patti then took over and began moving everyone over to some nearby bleachers, except one girl who was still crying and had spots of blood all over her face. Patti recognized the blood spatter and assumed she must have been close when it happened. "Excuse me, can I ask your name?"

"Cindi. Cindi Dimmitt."

"Hello, Cindi, I'm Detective Halterman, but you can call me Patti. With me is Detective Tomas O'Malley, but you can call him Tommy. I'm going to guide the rest of the students over to the stands, but would you mind if Tommy asked you a few questions?"

She was still crying and answered through her broken breaths. "No, that would be fine."

Patti motioned to me and then headed to the sidelines with the group of students. The sirens were right on top of us now and although I didn't see the lights, I believed they were at the front of the school. I moved around so Cindi could speak to me without having to look at the body of her teacher. "Cindi, just from your appearance, I can make the assumption you were close to Mr. Graham when it happened?"

She began crying harder again as she tried to speak. "Yes, we were talking about soccer."

"Can you tell me what happened?"

She shook her head and her voice got louder as if arguing. "I don't know. We were just talking and then there was a loud bang and he fell backward."

"Where did the loud bang come from?"

"I am not sure. It kind of sounded like it came from all around, but I first thought over there." She pointed across the open fields toward some buildings in the distance, and when I say in the distance, I mean, really in the distance. I glanced down to the body and based on where it was lying, her direction seemed true. There was nothing over there for more than one thousand yards at least.

"Good information, thank you. That is very helpful." I paused and let that small praise settle in which seemed to pacify her just a little. "Is there anything else you remember?"

She shrugged again. "No, just what I saw with Mr. Graham. It was awful."

"I know," I replied. "Nobody should ever witness something like this. "But no other sounds, smells, or did you see anything?"

She again started to shrug then stopped.

I interjected. "What? Do you remember something?"

"I heard a car."

"What do you mean, you heard a car? Was it loud, or different in some way?"

"It squealed its tires. It was coming from the same place." She pointed in the same direction as she had previously.

Just then, Principal Bales arrived in the area. "What happened?" He paused when he saw the body of his physical education teacher on the ground with his skull opened up spilling its insides on the turf. "Oh my God. What happened?" His head fell and he repeated it. His first words were confused and pained. His second sounded filled with fear.

I looked right at him, noticing the anguish in his face. "What do you think happened, sir? It seems someone feels your committee did not do their job, and they are taking a very serious step in bringing attention to it. Is there anything more you want to tell me about it?"

He did not answer. I actually thought he was going to be sick. No matter what I felt about how Bales had handled the complaints, this result was not his fault. I knew that, but it still chapped my hide. He took the law into his own hands to protect his school's reputation with no care for the students involved. All of this was tied together, I could feel it. The bullying. The potential rape. All of it. Now, however, I had to find out who else was taking the law into their own hands but had upped the stakes considerably. It was no longer about hiding the truth. It was all about throwing the truth out for all to see.

"The paramedics are here, Tommy," stated Halterman from the side. "I also called Sullivan and Huston and let them know."

"Thanks for calling the others, but the only thing the paramedics will do is pronounce him dead. We need Doc G here. Once everything is secure, we need to find where that shot came from."

"I spoke with several of the kids," replied Patti. "They all say the same thing. The shot came from over there." She pointed the same direction as Cindi had originally shown. "Based on what I see from here, that was a shot Chris Kyle would struggle with."

Christopher Scott Kyle was the United States Navy Seal veteran and sniper and basis for the movie, *American Sniper*. It was a slightly obscure reference but just like quoting lines from *Caddyshack*, *Ghostbusters*, *DodgeBall*, or any of the other great movies, she instantly gained some respect. Above all, however, she was correct. The shot was from at least 1500 yards and the bullet struck right between the eyes. There was not much wind but enough. It wasn't just the shooter that was impressive, it was going to be the gun and site. *Find the gun, and I find the shooter*, I instantly thought.

"Nice reference. With that, what does it mean?" I posed the question on purpose. My thought was, does knowing the shot was made from this distance change the perpetrator?

She looked across the sports fields toward the buildings in the direction of the shot. "I don't see a high school kid making the shot."

"Or even having access to the gun," I added.

She shook her head. "I would not automatically rule it out. There are exceptions to every rule, but this just feels like it came from someone more experienced."

I agreed. "This whole situation seems like it came from someone very organized, non-emotional, and mature."

"Are you saying a professional?"

"I am saying we check the finances of everyone involved and see who can afford three professional hits and if anyone has large sums of money moving around."

As our discussion continued, the number of people present continued to increase. Even Sergeant Craig Carter was on the scene and just as I saw him, two news vans were pulling in. I leaned closer to my partner. "This is about to get crazy. Let's go check out where the shot came from."

She did not answer and simply started walking. A nice perimeter had been established around the body. The coroner's van had also just arrived and drove straight up across the field toward the large group of people and the body. Officers were taking down statements and information from those who were in the area, most of which were students. As we got safely out of range for our conversation to be heard from anyone nearby, we both saw the black Suburban pull up in the distance.

"Is that the FBI?" Patti asked.

"No, it looks like GiST?" I replied.

"What the hell is GiST?" she asked.

"It's the governor's special task force. He calls for them on larger cases, usually homicides. It's a group of hand-picked detectives. They are well-connected and well-supported."

"Are they going to take the case from us?"

I smiled. "No, we will still do all the work, but they will take all the credit if we find the killer. If we don't, they will not be tied to it at all." I smiled a little at the comment. Although it was 100% true, it just sounded funny hearing it out loud.

"You mean they get all the glory with no risk."

I saw she was now smiling a little as well. "You hit the nail on the head on that one."

We could now see the two individuals who had gotten out of the cars. She motioned her head toward them. They were about 100 yards ahead of us. "Do you know them?"

"Yeah, I know them. Most of them came through the department either before or after me."

"How about those two?" she asked, not hiding her raised hand pointing their direction. They both stood by their car with their eyes fixed on us.

"Yep, I call them Ass One and Ass Two."

"Ass One and Ass Two? Do you mean that figuratively?" Her pace had slowed a bit as she wanted the information on these two before we arrived. They clearly were waiting for us to reach them before they continued.

"Detective Adam Only, AKA Ass One, and Alan Toose, AKA Ass Two." I stopped and turned to my partner. "They started in the department three years behind me. Never met an ass they would not kiss. Worked with Internal Affairs for two years before leaving together to join GiST. They collectively have cleared fewer cases than detectives with eight years less time, but they knew the right cases to clear at the right time. They are great in front of a camera and are the smartest guys on the squad, just ask them."

She nodded understanding. "So, their heads barely fit inside the car."

I smiled. "Yeah, they would do better in a convertible."

"Which one is which?" she asked.

"The tall one is Toose. He's okay. The pipsqueak is Only."

They started walking slowly again. "So," she said, "you don't like Ass One much, do you?"

"Nope," is all I replied.

We arrived at the Suburban. Toose was first to speak. "Hey Tommy. How have you been?"

"Fine, Toose. You?"

"You know, I can't complain." He shrugged as he turned his eyes to my partner. "Been busy though. Where is Franky?"

I understood the real question. *Who the hell was this little number with me?* I reached my hand out causing him to do the same. I ignored Ass One. "This is Patti Halterman, my new partner for the better part of twenty-four hours now. Franky is working the same case, just in another direction."

"Been a crazy morning, hasn't it," Detective Only broke in.

I ignored the comment. "Detective Halterman, this is Detective Toose and Detective Only. They go by Ass Two and Ass One..."

"Fuck you, O'Malley."

"Fuck you, Only."

"Hey," broke in Toose. "Let it go, you two. We have a case to solve and although it's clear the two of you don't like or want to work together, the governor says we have to. Therefore, let's make the best of it."

"Best of it, my ass," Only replied.

Halterman pointed behind the two. "Based on the trajectory, the shot came from over there. We stepped it off. We have already crossed fifteen hundred yards making the shot more than two thousand I would estimate."

All our heads turned and this statement alone seemed to pull all of us out of the playground name-calling. Without another word, we started walking toward the point of origin. We had crossed a baseball field, a lacrosse field, and were now on what I believed was a Frisbee golf area. On the other side of this area was a row of bushes and on the other side of the bushes was a street.

We arrived at the bushes and noticed they essentially formed a wall or fence. They lined what I assumed was the outskirts of the school property, and although any car could run through them, they did provide some sort of barrier to prevent someone simply driving onto the property through the fields. There were a few breaks in the bush line where a person could cross and all four of us slipped through one of them to end on the other side. We looked back and could still see the commotion around the field where the teacher had been shot.

"It would take an extremely skilled marksman to make this shot. You are talking two thousand plus yards in a light wind with really nothing to rest against." Detective Only clearly thought he was dialed in on what took place.

"You spend anytime signed up, Only?" I asked, referring to the armed forces.

"Signed up?" he said questioning the phrase.

"In the armed forces? Army? Navy? Air Force?" I paused and hesitantly added, "I'm sure not the Marines."

"No, I went to college instead."

"Yeah, I went to college too, but that didn't keep me from the Marines."

Only pushed his lips together. "What's your point, O'Malley? Need to show off or something?"

"No, jackass, just want to show you where the shooter sat." I pointed to the next break in the bushes. "See here, no shooter from this distance is going to freehand make that shot. They laid on the ground here. It kept them out of sight and allowed them to tripod their gun in a settled position. They sighted their shot and waited. See how the grass is pushed down. Notice the two marks in the dirt where the stand rested. They probably parked their car right behind to protect anyone from seeing them, took the shot, and exited immediately. They probably didn't even turn their car off."

"See those tread marks," Halterman said pointing. "One of the witnesses said they heard a car take off. You would not noticeably hear an engine that was already running take off, but you would hear tires squeal if the driver was nervous and in a hurry."

I looked back to Only and Toose. "Good thing you guys are here. We would have struggled without your help."

Although I am certain Only wanted to throw out another *Fuck You, O'Malley*, he also knew he had no leg to stand on. There was no doubt what the evidence was showing us.

Toose immediately got on the phone and called for their forensics team to head over. "We will section this area off, get imprints of the tires, and have the car identified in a few hours."

I rolled my eyes but didn't speak again. I knew my work here was done. We had all the evidence we needed. They would determine the most common type of car quicker than we'd be able to, so that could help us. I knew the real value here. Not only could no kid make this shot unless they were the luckiest shooter in the world, only about ten to fifteen people in all the Midwest could have made that shot. Our suspect list just got significantly shorter.

My partner broke the silence as we started walking back toward the victim. "It looks like our suspect list just got significantly less."

"Really? I hadn't thought about it. Why do you say that?" I asked.

"What? Are you stupid? Who the hell could make that shot?" She stopped almost surprised at my response then saw my smile. "Now I know why everyone hates you. You mess with everyone at every opportunity."

"No, just the people I like." I'm sure she took that as a compliment because she smiled slightly and then didn't speak again.

We arrived back at the coroner's van and Dr. G was sitting against the back bumper completing some paperwork. She looked up as we approached. "Hello, Tommy. Patti. This was a pretty clean one to investigate."

"How so?" I asked.

"Your victim was killed by a bullet directly through the brain. Based on the initial measurements, I would estimate the shooter was more than 2200 yards out and was using a Barrett M82 Sniper Rifle."

"M82 sniper rifle?" questioned Halterman. "How can you tell that?"

"Two reasons," replied Doc G. "First, it was a 0.50 BMG cartridge which is why your victim's head was completely blown off. Second, and probably most importantly, it's the only rifle I know of that's readily available, shoots a 0.50 cartridge, and has the ability to shoot that distance."

I noticed a hesitation in her statement. "But what are you *not* telling us?" I asked.

"You should know," she replied. "It's not the M40A5."

I shook my head but it was Patti who questioned the conversation. "What do you mean?" she asked. "What is the M40A-thing?"

Elise glanced to me telling me without speaking that the conversation was now mine to finish. "The M40A5 is the rifle used by the US Marine Corp. It's basically a modified Remington 700 hunting rifle. Combined with the Schmidt and Bender Police Marksman II scope, under good conditions you can repeatedly hit a 3-inch target at 800 yards. In short, it's extremely accurate, but its maximum range is 1200 yards. The M82 is built for large cartridge, long distance, but you lose accuracy. It's made to take out electronics, antennas, radios, and so forth. It's not built for taking out people because after 800 yards, you're losing several minutes of angle per hundred yards."

"Minutes of angle?" she asked.

"Let me say it this way. If when I walked over here I thought there were ten or fifteen people in the Midwest that could have made that shot, I now say there are probably ten to fifteen people in the United States that could have made that shot with that gun, and that may be inflated."

"What are you thinking then?" she added.

"I am thinking Marine, and a gifted one."

9 WE STAYED AT the scene for another thirty minutes. The plan was to question the remaining teachers that were part of the complaint committee, but before we could do that, they had cancelled school indefinitely. With the murder of a student, a counselor, and now a teacher, the ability to continue classes had ended, regardless of the support the school provided. The story was making national news and even with the GiST squad on it, I was sure the FBI would be involved. They were probably on their way from Quantico now. We basically had less than twenty-four hours to close this case.

I checked my phone and saw it was still just before noon. I placed a call to Franky without even posing the question to my partner, an action I would most likely have to change. Twenty minutes later we were pulling into Summit, Illinois, and El Famous Burrito. El Famous is not a place to go at night unless you're comfortable in bad neighborhoods, or you're a police officer, but even a police officer may be a target. However, at lunchtime, there were no issues. We slid through the door on the corner, walked up to the counter, and I ordered. Without missing a beat, Patti ordered as if she had been there a million times. Five football-sized burritos were quickly placed in bags before us and ready to be taken out. There were three chicken burritos for Franky, Huston, and Carter, a beef burrito for Patti, and I had my traditional refried bean and cheese. It probably had twenty ounces of beans all through it.

When we got back into the car I finally had to ask the question. "Okay, I'm trying to catch you with all my idiosyncrasies—arguing with Carter, Mr. J's for breakfast, and now El Famous Burrito—and you don't blink an eye. What gives?"

"Let's just say I have two older brothers and a father that all would be friends with Tomas O'Malley if given the chance."

That answer was good enough for me. I nodded, smiled slightly, started the car and headed to the department. When I arrived, Carter, Sullivan, and Huston were all in the Bulls Room. I handed the burritos to Patti, walked into the room, picked up all the papers and files spread across the desk, stacked them neatly as I grabbed them, and then left and headed three rooms down.

"Damn it, O'Malley, we had those all in a certain order," shouted Carter.

"I told you," added Franky.

"Then you can re-order them in here. We are not going to be cramped in the Bulls room when there's plenty of room for everyone in here."

"The Goddamn Royals room is the same size as the Bulls room," replied Carter.

"Right, then you should have taken it in the first place." I paused, then added, "And if you want your burrito, you better get your ass in here as well or I may just eat it myself."

They really didn't care which room they were in. I knew that. Carter just liked to make a big deal about the name. He most likely caught shit about it when the brass came through plus the room intentionally rarely got used. Some cops even thought it was cursed and when used, helped bad guys get out of charges. This came to an apex in 2015 when the Royals actually won the World Series. Nobody used the room for months. Now that they were back to losing 100+ games, occasionally someone stumbled inside. I used it exclusively, and today was no different.

"Patti and I will put a report together on the school shooting this afternoon, but we want to run through it with everyone before that. We also what to hear what you guys found in the forensic reports."

"Any quick conclusions you can draw from the shooting?" asked Carter. "I filled them in on what I saw."

I glanced to Patti and motioned for her to take the floor. She was clearly ready with a response. "We think we can significantly limit the pool of suspects to a very few. That does not mean we can make any assumptions on the other two murders as it's conceivable that there's more than one perpetrator. However, we feel the high school shooting could have only been performed by someone with extensive shooting ability. The shot was estimated at 2200 yards and used a 0.50 caliber shell. Tomas can speak to it better than I, but a rifle able to shoot that distance with that caliber shell has a very large target range expanding as the distance increases in feet instead of inches even with a high-powered scope. This individual hit a two-inch spot between the individual's eyes nearly blowing most of his head off. If we didn't have witnesses, he would not have been identifiable except by DNA."

"Are you serious?" asked Franky. "A 0.50 caliber at 2200 yards? That is not possible. What gun could do that?"

Patti looked toward me as she didn't remember the gun Doc G suggested. "Barrett M82 Sniper," I replied.

"Shit," said Carter, who, like me, spent several years in the armed forces, though he was a Navy dog. "I have been around some of the best shooters in the Navy, and I don't know any who could have hit that target on one shot."

I shook my head but did not respond as Franky was ready to ask another question. "So, we've been talking and we didn't see anything to make us believe there were two perpetrators. Do you actually believe that?"

Patti shook her head. "I don't think we know. We just didn't want to rule it out because the potential shooters are so limited. If you guys are able to link the first two murders together, then I think we're comfortable saying there are one or two perps."

Carter swallowed a large bite of his burrito and followed with a comment that was stated more like a question. "Yes, I think we are comfortable tying the car accident and the woman in the drum together. We have the note left on the car which is a clear tie and we have clear footprints at both scenes. The shoes, however, appear to be the exact same shoe, size, brand, etc., but the molds have very faint differences. It's almost like the person bought several pairs of the same shoe and used a new pair at each place."

"Or it could also be two different people, but working together." Karen had been quiet until this comment but it did catch us.

I thought about that as I took another bite then decided to add my two cents. "You know, I have a buddy, E.Z. Zimmerman, out of Minneapolis that I talk to now and again. A homicide detective there working in a special statewide division. He lives by one motto—the easiest answer is usually the right one. What is the easiest answer here?"

"Well," started Halterman. "It's much harder to get multiple people to perform a series of murders."

"I'll agree with that," added Huston.

"Unless one is a copycat, I suppose," Patti added.

I shook my head in agreement. "Correct. I think we have one killer with the only exception being if that killer got someone else fired up enough to commit a third kill. However, I think there's more of a chance of the same person killing all three people." I paused waiting for someone to ask why.

"Why do you think that, Tommy?" asked Carter.

That's why they call me the best detective in the department. I control what everyone says and thinks. "Because, although the shooter at the high school was extremely skilled, so was the driver of the car and the use of the chemical in the barrel. Think about it. We have no evidence to identify this killer. Other than a shoe size that fits, I don't know, close to 250,000 people in Chicago alone, we have nothing."

They all seemed to agree with the statement. Carter still wanted the floor. "Then what do we have? Who could have done this? Are we ruling out the Kittleson kid and the cheerleader whose car was used?"

I nodded agreement. "For the shooting alone, I'm ruling out anyone under the age of twenty-five. The person who did this was disciplined, trained, and patient. And for the other murders, I don't know. The individual waited in the bushes to steal a car to be used as a weapon. They acquired a controlled chemical, kidnapped a woman with nobody knowing, had her call the school to delay any search, and then murdered her and destroyed all evidence of the murder but had no fear of giving us a roadmap to the body. Then, if we had any doubts, they laid down like a cougar stalking its prey for an unknown time in the middle of the day to make a shot that only a handful of people in the world could have made. The shot alone would have taken the maturity and experience of someone who has been in that position before. If you have never drawn a gun on a person, especially a sniper rifle, you have no idea the pressure that goes into holding steady for that length of time."

Now there was no argument. The silence alone provided the support. It was Franky who then posed the question. "Who then? One of the parents? Another teacher?"

"Or maybe just a random vigilante that heard the story and had had enough," added Karen.

"What do we know about Kittleson's parents?" I asked.

Franky answered. "Becky Kittleson has primary custody and lives locally. She works in the finance department at a food company. I will have to check on the name. Jack Kittleson is her ex-husband. He lives in Lakeville, Minnesota. That's a suburb somewhere south of Minneapolis. He's a former Marine but now runs a food company in Lakeville. They met here in Chicago at Becky's place of employment. According to her, their marriage broke up because he couldn't let go of Afghanistan."

"Or it couldn't let go of him," I replied. "However, if he was a Marine, he would be knowledgeable of guns and most likely skilled. When is he arriving?"

"Any minute now, according to his wife," Karen answered. "She called him immediately yesterday when we started questioning her and their son."

"I want to know where he was stationed, what he did, and I don't care who you have to call to get it. Find out if he owns any guns and where he's been for the last thirty days." He was instantly my primary suspect and the fact he was coming in voluntarily to see us only added to that belief. If he was who I thought he was, he was pompous enough to feel he was untouchable. I was going to change that.

"I'm on it," stated Karen, "but why thirty days? The events just started."

"Because these are well-planned-out murders. Nobody from Minnesota could have come down here and worked these out without a ton of significant planning. In fact, it would be nearly impossible."

She shook her head but it was Halterman who spoke next. "Come on, I'll join you." Both women disappeared through the conference room door.

"What else do we know?" stated Carter before they were even through the door.

"The other thing I wonder about is *how* they were killed." My tone showed a mix between being puzzled and maybe even impressed.

Franky nodded. "Yes," he added hearing my tone. "Who kills someone in a barrel of chemicals?"

"Someone who wanted no evidence left," added Carter.

I raised my eyebrows. "But that is the clue. The evidence left is the chemicals. You can't go to Walgreens and buy a chemical that melts flesh. We need to find out where that came from." I began flipping through the lab reports. "Look," I said pointing. "I knew I read it somewhere. They broke out the entire chemical makeup of the compound. This is not like a single chemical that is 100% liquid nitrogen or something. This is a mixture. The percentages are as accurate as a fingerprint to identify the source. We find the source, and we find the person who used it." I handed the page to Franky. "Doc G listed some companies that use caustic in their process."

Franky took the list. "Interesting."

"What's that?" asked Carter. "You know one?"

"One of them is the pharmaceutical company that Doc G's husband essentially runs."

"Good, get on the phone with him. He might be able to help or have people that can help distinguish something special about the compound, or who might be using it or have access to it." I was actually starting to feel just a touch of the jazz. In this case, things were not coming together, but things were moving. I turned to Carter and saw his eyes locked on someone or something through the conference room window. I followed his gaze.

"Jesus," he whispered. "You just never know what to expect."

"I walked to the doorway of the conference room and in as strong a voice as I could muster, even deeper than I thought possible, I said, "Mr. Kittleson, I presume?"

If we were having a contest for the deepest voice, all I can say is, he won. "Yes, I am Jack Kittleson. You a Marine?"

He went straight there, without hesitation. "Yes," I replied.

"Semper Fi," he replied.

I nodded understanding, however, this exchange actually made me push more toward his guilt, as did his 6'6" build and his brick shithouse arms and legs. The guy was an easy 320 pounds and it was all muscle. However, he was looking for a connection, and from my point of view, a friend to keep the heat off. That was not going to work for me. *Semper Fi* was one of the most important phrases in my life, but it would never be used to help someone who didn't deserve it.

"Come on in and grab a seat," I said. "Can I get you anything?"

"You can get me an explanation of why you are giving my son the beatdown on this jackass kid who got killed. Just because this kid bullied my son at every corner, and you and that school did nothing about it, does not make my son a killer. You above all should understand what it takes to kill someone."

He was not beating around the bush or hiding anything. In one sentence he simply said that his son could in no way have been able to kill someone, because he can say from personal experience you never get over something like that.

"Tell me, Jack, what were you in the Marines?" My voice was calm, trying to make some polite conversation to build on that initial exchange, avoiding talking about the events which brought us together.

He seemed to relax a bit, dropping his shoulders but still speaking with extreme pride, as did I when I spoke about my time in the Marines. "MOS 0317, American Special Ops."

Military Occupational Specialty Code 0317 was the same as mine, though I was several years older than my counterpart here. It could be earned by both infantry and reconnaissance Marines. I was in reconnaissance. "Same as mine, brother. Were you in Infantry then?"

He smiled. "Yes, scout sniper. You?"

"Reconnaissance."

Believe it or not, I was starting to fall into his trap. We were one and the same. We knew the same things, saw the same things, and lived the same things. I wanted to stay impartial, but I wasn't sure I could. I think Carter sensed that as he took the lead in the questions.

"We are at the stage of ruling out people who are related to the events that have taken place. You, by relationship that your son was bullied by the first boy killed, do have motive and therefore we need to eliminate you from discussion, as we are doing for your son and ex-wife. Because you live in Minnesota, we are assuming this will be easy to do. We simply need to know your whereabouts over the last thirty days, with particular emphasis on the last forty-eight hours."

Kittleson seemed to get hung up on one phrase. "First boy killed? You mean there are others?"

"I am not at liberty to comment at this time regarding other events that have occurred, but yes, the death of Mark Schulman is not the only murder we are investigating," answered Carter. "Now, back to your whereabouts?"

"Why do you need to know the last thirty days?" Didn't this accident which brought you to interview my son just happen?"

Again he was avoiding the answer. It could be just by interest. Sometimes innocent people are so naïve to what we are looking for and why they are there that they talk in a normal conversation mode rather than as an interrogation. However, I did not believe Mr. Jack Kittleson was naïve in the least. I took the lead here. "Listen, Jack, may I call you Jack?" He nodded. "Listen, Jack, you have to understand, we can't talk to you about the case. We can't provide you any information other than the questions we are asking, and it would do all three of us a huge favor if instead of seeking to know everything about this, you simply answer our questions so we can get you out of here. We need to know where you've been the last thirty days. More specifically, we need to know every time in the last thirty days you were in Chicago. Let's start there and see where things go."

I tried to shut him down a bit and it appeared to have worked, at least for the time being. He leaned back in his chair causing it to squeak. "I come to Chicago every other week as a rule. That may change if Nate has something going on that I need to attend to or schedules just work out. In the last thirty days, I was in Chicago last weekend and two weekends before. Prior to that, I would have to check to be sure."

"We will want you to go back and verify the weeks prior, but for now, let's focus on the weekends you were here. What do you do when you're here? Where do you stay? When do you get here and when do you leave and anything else like that?"

All of a sudden he seemed to understand this was not a courtesy visit. I sensed that in one set of questions, he went from making sure we left his son alone to, *wait a minute, am I a suspect*?

"Wait a minute, do you think I did this? Do you think I could hurt a boy, even if he was picking on my son?"

Carter now responded again. "Mr. Kittleson, we do not think anything. As I said initially, everyone is a suspect until they are no longer a suspect. For you to join the 'no longer a suspect' crew, you need to answer our questions."

He stood up and I can say without question, I do not fear any man. I am one of the most highly skilled black belts in the country and although I rarely show it, I train to stay in that form every week. This man when he stood was simply foreboding. He stood like Thor above the table looking down on us like we were children. I instantly stood to match his position but fell well short of his size.

"I don't have to answer shit, Detectives. I have done nothing wrong and the same goes for my son. I suggest you take me and him off your list of suspects and do not bother us anymore."

"Sit down," I said. "Nobody is calling you a suspect, or even thinking that way." I was lying. "A boy was killed. Two other people at that school have been killed. Rather than have people close to the situation get defensive and possibly not tell us something that will help us catch the person responsible, we need everyone to support the process. I know this is not what you intended to hear, but goddamn it, we need to rule you out. I can tell you that learning you were a Marine put me completely at ease knowing I would finally get support from one person. Now, I see you are just the..."

He cut me off with his hand and retook his seat. "Don't play the Marine card with me, sir. I will answer your questions, then I will leave to check on my son. If there are any future conversations, you will need take them up with my lawyer."

I was not sure how to take that, but I was pleased to see him back in his seat. I glanced at Carter and he gave me the go-ahead to continue. "Back to the questions then, and let's take them one at a time. Where do you stay when you come down here?"

I could tell by his tone he still had attitude about the discussion. I also think that although we had this Marine bond, he was contemplating if he could take me. Not that he would consider it, it was just something guys did, at least something Marines did. After all, I was doing it to him. Suddenly I thought about the last individual I had these thoughts about. His name was Marco Filini and he was the hired henchman for Joey Polino and Ross Moretti, two crime bosses in Chicago. He was also skilled in the martial arts and itching to test those skills against me. When the bosses went down, he disappeared into the night as we had nothing on him. However, he was the first person in a long time that openly did not fear me, and in fact, wanted the opportunity to match me. I think Jack Kittleson wanted the same. He stared directly at me as he answered. "Not that it's any business of yours, but I stay either at a local hotel, occasionally with my niece and her husband, or even once with Nate and his mother."

"You stay with your ex-wife?"

"One time, and my wife knew about it from the start."

I smiled. "I was not implying anything. I'm just impressed as there's no chance I would be allowed to stay with my ex, even if it made sense." He acknowledged the comment but did not reply further. "For our discussion," I continued, "where did you stay last week?"

"That was the week I stayed with my ex and Nathan."

"That is great news," I replied. "They will be able to corroborate your timing." In my mind I was thinking, that's horrible news. I thought back to what Patti had said earlier—it is much harder to get multiple people to perform a series of murders. *Unless they are family*, I thought. They will cover for his ass. "Did you guys talk about Mark Schulman during this visit?"

Jack's face hardened. "We talk about that asshole every visit. Despite what you might think, I teach my son to be mindful of everyone's beliefs. I fought hard for this country and for our freedom, and just because I don't hold to the beliefs of those I fought to protect, it does not mean I do not respect their right to have those thoughts."

In my face. This guy absolutely may have killed that teacher on the soccer field, and hell, he may have killed the kid and the counselor, but he knew every answer to give that hit me like a rock. I stood up, paced around the back of the table, and just thought for a minute. I needed to trip him up. I needed to smack him in the face just like he was slapping me. I turned back and put both hands hard on the table. "Why did you kill the teacher? Why shoot him from 2000 yards? You know it would point to you. Why, damn it?"

This created two things. I put the ball in his court to be surprised, and it still showed I was on his side. I gave him evidence as to why we would think it was him. He slammed his hands on the table and stood up. However, he didn't run or say he was getting his lawyer. He heard the bait in my comment, where I was on his side. "What teacher? What points to me? What are you talking about? I'm here to talk about my son and that kid who was murdered."

I got to hand it to him, he was good. He either was not behind this or was one of the best actors I had ever seen. I was betting on the acting. Just as I started to go at him further, Carter broke in. "Hey now, aren't you jumping the gun a bit?"

Thank you, Sergeant, I thought.

Turning to Jack, Carter continued. "As I said before, you are a suspect, and the fact that you are a sniper for the Marines does make you of particular interest in one of these murders. That murder took place today. In fact, it took place this morning. Can you tell me when you got into town?"

"I got in this morning, early. I left Lakeville at three in the morning, arrived here before nine."

"Interesting," Carter replied. We were both thinking the same thing. Plenty of time. "Did you see anyone or go anywhere that you would have been seen? How about pay for anything with a credit card? Did you do anything to define your whereabouts and timing?"

He shrugged. "Not really. I bought gas on the tollway coming into town. When I arrived, I drove by the school but didn't go in. I just drove around."

"So you were driving essentially all night and didn't even stop for food?" Carter asked questionably. "And at the time of the murder, you were near the school?"

"I told you, I stopped at the oasis on the tollway because I did not want to exit and get back on and have to pay twice. I didn't have any change. The gas station there had breakfast burritos so I grabbed one. From that point on, I was on my own till I got here."

Yep, Jack Kittleson was good for the shooting, everything in my gut told me as much. He is trained to make that shot, he was in town with no alibi, and the one time he stayed with his ex-wife and son, all this unfolded. My immediate answer, the ex-wife and kid orchestrated the first two murders, and Dad came in to take the attention off them. There's no way they could have made the shot, and now a second killer would throw questions on the first two being related to the third.

"Where is your wife in all this?" I asked.

"Becky, my ex-wife?"

"No," I replied. "Where is your current wife?" I flipped through some pages in the folder. "Kim Kittleson."

He seemed surprised at the question but didn't hesitate to answer. "When I married her, she already owned a small bed and breakfast, the Albion Hotel, in Bayfield, Ontario. She lost her manager there several months ago. She's going up there almost every weekend and at times throughout the week. She's there now."

It was quick and to the point. We would check out the Albion Hotel, but from personal experience, I don't believe a stepparent by definition was involved. I used it as a transition, and it seemed to work. "Do you know any of the following individuals: Robert Bales, Dawn Wells, Eric Graham, Herb Whychoff, or Bill Ronin?" I left out Mark Schulman because we had already established he knew the boy bullying his son.

He nodded. "Bales is the asshole principal we met with. I don't remember all their names, but the others all sound like the committee we talked to. That fucking Wells should have stuck up for Nathan. She was the goddamn counselor."

Wow, by saying that, it actually makes him sound less guilty because had he done the crime, he would have never offered that he hated our victim in the barrel. You never know what you're going to get in an interview. It's almost as if admitting he blamed Wells for lack of action makes him less a suspect. "So, you didn't like this committee, specifically Dawn Wells?"

"Not like them?" he stated, his voice getting stronger as he spoke. "They were there to protect kids. They were there to give kids an education and prepare them for their lives ahead. All those assholes wanted to protect was their precious school's reputation."

I glanced to Carter and we both clearly were thinking one thing: motive.

Carter replied. "You know, Dawn Wells went missing a few days ago. Would you know anything about that?"

The comment was out of left field, but I liked it. Jack noticeably was surprised. "No, but a few days ago I was in Minnesota. My wife was in Canada so I had to be there not only for work, but to take care of our son and the dog."

"I assume there are several that can confirm that?" I asked.

"Well, I scan in at work and both the dog and my son were fed all week, so I guess there's that too."

I liked his sarcasm. "Fine, let's go ahead and get your travel schedule over the last four to six weeks and then we can call this a wrap for now."

He immediately seemed agitated. "Wait, you haven't told me why you're harassing my son. He had..."

I raised my hand and cut him off. "At this time, we do not think your son is involved. Further, we believe there are plenty of traffic cameras that will confirm his whereabouts. He said he was alone that morning but gave us the route he drove. As long as we can confirm he was where he said he was, he is off the person of interest list. Now"—I pushed a legal pad and pen over to him—"please pull out your phone, or calendar, or whatever you use to keep track of your schedule and jot down when you came to Chicago, how long you were here, where you stayed, and any other information that seems pertinent. And if you can include whenever you met with this school committee, include that date and an overview of the discussion."

That seemed to satisfy Jack Kittleson and he proceeded to pull out his phone, open the calendar, and begin jotting down some information. Although he definitely had motive and was the first person who may have the skill to commit the shooting, he seemed very forthcoming with information. However, I also knew Marines. They were never short on confidence. He may feel he was untouchable, a trait I often wore proudly as well.

Just then Franky knocked on the door, cracked it open, and waved me to come over. He had an expression I didn't like. He refused to tell me even by the doorway and escorted me outside shutting the door behind. In a soft voice, he said, "Guess who used to work at US Ingredients in Joliet?"

"I don't know," I answered questionably.

"Jack and Kim Kittleson," he replied. "It is where they met."

I tilted my head. "And why do I care where one of our suspects met his new wife?"

"Guess what they do there?"

I was actually getting a little annoyed with the twenty questions game. "I don't know, make ingredients?" My sarcasm was so clear I should not even call it sarcasm.

"You are not so dumb after all," he added proudly. "It's a spray-dry facility that takes chemicals such as soybean oil and glycerin and turns them into powders and fats."

I still wasn't getting it but I let the pause sit so he would continue.

"Guess what chemical they use in their process?"

"*Bingo*!" I slapped both hands across his chest knocking him back several feet with the excitement making my voice change from its previous whisper. "Please tell me they use caustic."

"Bingo," he replied back proudly.

"Great work, Franky. Keep looking into the other sites that use, produce, or sell the chemical, but I think a visit to US Ingredients is warranted. We need to know the controls they have around their plant and if any caustic has gone missing in the last thirty days. However, right now, I'm going to ask my new friend a few more questions."

After re-entering the room, I could tell that Jack was ready to be done and felt that the previous conversation had brought him close to being let go.

He pushed the legal pad back my direction. "So, can I go now? I want to go see my son and it was out of courtesy I came here in the first place."

Again, best detective in Chicago. "Well, why don't you just sit tight for a minute more," I answered. "I have a few more questions."

Reluctantly and seemingly to even Carter's surprise, Jack Kittleson remained in his seat. He was about to ask something but I broke in first.

"So tell me about US Ingredients."

"What about it?" he asked, clearly surprised at the question. "I worked there for five years after returning from the Marines. Actually, I met my current wife there."

"Oh yeah. Must have some good memories and contacts there still?"

"Is that a question?" Jack asked.

"Sorry, Jack, let me rephrase it." I actually did not mind the question back. I really didn't know how I wanted to ask about his work there, so any added time was fine by me. "If you worked there five years and you met your wife there, you both probably still have ties with some of the employees, don't you?"

He shrugged. "A few I guess, through Facebook. We don't talk on the phone or anything and unless I run into them at a store or something, we don't see each other when I'm back." He paused, and before I could break in again, he turned it back on me. "Why do you need to know about US Ingredients?"

I ignored the question. "How about your wife? Kim, wasn't it? Does she have any friends back there?"

"Same as me for all I know. She doesn't talk about any." He paused then out of nowhere he added, "There was one gal on nights she was close with at the time. They did everything they could together when their schedules allowed. Shona Williams I think was her name."

"Nice," I replied. "Still good friends are they? Your wife and Shona?"

"Like I said, maybe on Facebook. I bet they haven't spoken in years."

I could tell he was getting frustrated but I was really only getting started on this line of questioning. "What do they do there? At US Ingredients," I added to avoid any confusion of talking about her friend Shona.

Jack seemed proud to answer. "In layman's terms, they make powdered fat. Through a variety of chemical reactions and a distillation process performed under vacuum, they strip off monoglycerides and di- and triglycerides and then spray-dry them into powders. They are used in nearly every food industry. In fact, their products can be found in every loaf of bread you buy."

"What chemicals do they use?" I asked.

He listed off so many chemicals and oils my head began to spin. However, he did not mention one I particularly cared about. Purposely avoided – possibly I thought.

I stood and paced around the table. "What about caustic?"

The question hung in the air for just a second, then he answered without further hesitation. I couldn't tell if the question bothered him or not. "Caustic? Of course they have caustic onsite. But it was used between runs, as a sanitizer. It was not part of our manufacturing process."

"Is it harmful?" I asked, trying to see what he knew about it.

"Harmful?" he replied with a slight laugh. "Why don't you stick your hand in it and see what you think." When I didn't respond understanding he added, "Yes, it is extremely harmful. It will eat skin, for lack of a better explanation." I took a few pretend notes on my legal pad. "What is with all the questions about my old employer and caustic?"

"Really nothing," I replied. "I'm just trying to build a history for each family. The caustic question was just for my own interest."

He stood. "Then if there's nothing else, I assume I can go."

"Sure," I replied, reaching out my hand to shake which he took. As he moved toward the door, I shot one more question his way. "Say, Jack, when was the last time you or your wife were back at US Ingredients?"

"Well, I have not been back since I was asked to leave. My wife, two weeks later."

"You were fired?" questioned Carter, who had been for the most part quiet during the entire interview.

"I was asked to leave," Jack repeated, but stopped in the doorway. "If it matters, you can easily find out. They thought I was stealing money and burying it in our budget. I found out after I left that they discovered it was the vice president of manufacturing. However, by that time I had moved on and so had they. They had given me a nice severance package so all was good on my end, but I would never go back."

He left the room without another comment. I turned to Carter. "What do you think?"

"He has motive and opportunity, and he has the skills necessary plus access to unique chemicals involved in the murders. We would be foolish not to follow up on his alibis and check out US Ingredients."

"Let me rephrase. Do you think he did it?"

Carter shrugged. "Everything in me says it's too neatly packaged, but some of his responses make me think yes."

10

AFTER JACK KITTLESON left, Franky was eager to find out what we learned. I was equally interested in anything he had dug up with Huston. It was almost 3:00 PM. We had been with Kittleson for two hours; no wonder he was ready to go. We weren't even holding him for anything so the fact he stayed that long was something. Again, it could mean either he had nothing to do with it and was basically just sharing openly, or very often, narcissists stayed as long as they could believing they were not only untouchable, but wanting to share all they could just to show how untouchable they were. I was on the same page as Carter when it came to Kittleson. He had all the makings of someone sharing info, but damn it, he sure could be guilty.

I met Franky and our two partners by my desk when Carter waved us all into the same conference room where we had questioned Jack Kittleson. "Okay, folks, what do we have?"

Franky stood. "We have four locations using caustic at levels that would allow a barrel to go missing and they may not report it."

"What do you mean, they may not report it?" I asked.

"It's not a controlled chemical or even restricted. The chemicals that make it up are readily available. However, I spoke with a professor of chemistry at Northwestern and he clearly stated that nobody but a skilled chemist would mess with compounding it on their own. Therefore, going back to my original statement, the majority of these locations hold such a small volume of it, if half a barrel went missing, they would have called and reported it as a theft. The other four, however, keep up to two hundred gallons onsite. If half a barrel was drained out, it would be within the error range of the measurement of the tank, and it would not have been reported, and most likely would not have even been known."

"Unless the person taking it was a former employee and he had help?" I added.

"Well, if you're asking if US Ingredients is one of the four, it most definitely is. When I spoke to the plant manager, he informed me they keep caustic in a 350-gallon tank in their tank yard outside. But it is not on the new more accurate load cells, whatever the hell those are. Usage is measured with a long rod they stick down the tank to see how much is left in it. The depth of the liquid in feet and inches is recorded on a form. If it were half a barrel, or four full barrels off, nobody would know the difference."

"Then is US Ingredients a dead end?" asked Carter.

Franky smiled. "They have more than a hundred cameras all over the plant. Entrances, building grounds, the production lines, and tank farms."

"Tank farms?" I repeated smiling. I glanced down to Carter who I knew thought the same. We simply needed to get proof. "If we can put Kittleson at US Ingredients anytime, then we can catch him in a lie." When asked, Kittleson had not expected the question, and although his answer was solid saying he left under duress and would not be welcome back, that didn't mean he did not have friends. Shona Williams comes to mind.

"Yes," Carter replied. "Putting him anywhere at the plant, even if it is not the tank farm, puts him right at the top of the list."

Franky continued to smile. "The plant manager is waiting for us this afternoon. He is having his security guy stay as well to walk us through the cameras."

Carter now stood. "Sullivan." He turned to me, "O'Malley, get down there now." We both looked at each other causing Carter to catch our uneasiness. "Ah shit," Carter continued. "O'Malley, get with Halterman and chase down any of the other teachers on that committee. Sullivan and Huston will take the food plant."

Although I wanted the food plant, I did like the sergeant's error. Franky was still my partner at some level. Something told me this case being so large, however, would probably be one of the last we handled together, at least for a while. But with everything turning as it does, it would be just a matter of time before partners move on and Franky and I ended up together again. I looked toward my partner who, by her expression, I believe also wanted the food plant. "You ready?"

"I already have the addresses," she replied. "Herb Whychoff and Bill Ronin are frickin' neighbors, if you can believe that. They both live in Downers Grove."

"Neighbors?" I replied questionably. "Can this situation be more bullshit? And Downers Grove? How do private school city teachers both commute from Downers Grove and end up on the same committee?"

"Check it out," stated Carter. "And don't be such a pussy with your questions. Two of their colleagues are dead and they might be next."

"Will do, Sergeant," I replied. "And the report will be on your desk this evening."

Carter paused in his tracks and smiled then he replied, "It better be."

Halterman and I exited the room leaving both Huston and Franky alone with Carter. I assumed there would be a short discussion on the tactics of handling the food plant and then the two would leave. To my surprise, as I stopped briefly at my desk, I saw the three exit the conference room together.

"You really want to join us?" echoed Franky's voice off the office walls, intentionally loud enough for us to hear.

"Yes sir," replied Carter. "I'll drive. That way we can carpool back to the station and discuss the interview and findings as we drive."

Although they did not physically roll across his forebrow, Franky's eyes clearly showed his displeasure. However, he also knew there was no arguing the fact, so after another few seconds, off they went. I turned to Patti. "I don't think Franky will be back in time for dinner."

I meant it as an analogy that he would be back late. What I got back from my partner was, "Oh, great, we're going to dinner? We can talk through the case then. Will they meet us later?"

I didn't respond but just grabbed my things and left.

•　　•　　•　　•　　•

It was about a forty-five minute drive to the neighboring houses in Downers Grove if done late at night or early morning. In the afternoon, GPS said we were looking at two hours. Therefore, I did what every good cop does. I put my flasher on my roof, hit the siren, and proceeded down the inside shoulder of Interstate I-90, the Eisenhower. We were back on the forty-five minute timeline. I am a damn smart cop.

"You know that's not legal," Halterman stated.

"Yep," I replied.

"Good, I didn't want to think you were just stupid."

"Nope, I'm a damn smart cop." I was pleased with my answer.

"Proud of yourself, are you?" she said sarcastically.

Too pleased evidently. "No, I just want to get to these two guys before they end up like the soccer coach."

"I'll call ahead and make sure they're home." She paused, then added, "You know, we haven't done anything about Bales, the principal."

"Shit," I replied. "That's right. After you call the two teachers, call the station and send someone over to his house. Just have them keep an eye on it and him. No questioning. We need to visit him as well."

She didn't answer but I could tell she heard and agreed. She went straight to making her calls and quickly we learned both Whychoff and Ronin were home; in fact, they were both at Ronin's house so she told them to stay put and we would be right over. She put a call into Bales and got voicemail. She then called dispatch and got a uniform headed over. Bales lived in an affluent neighborhood in Naperville. It was actually further west than Downers Grove so swinging by his place was going to be a short jump from our first stop. I was getting hungry but I had already decided if my partner was coming along with me, then a pizza at Flap Jaws was in my future. After a short jaunt down to the I-88 tollway and then a quick exit into Downers, our GPS put us only five minutes from our destination which meant we had made even better time than I had hoped. I turned my flasher off and pulled the magnetic light in.

"I guess we don't need that anymore," Patti said with a touch of tone.

"Nope, I shall follow all the laws from this point on." As I said this I made a right turn on a red light without using my signal. She saw it. I knew she would, but she said nothing.

We arrived at the house about the same time I thought Franky and crew would be arriving at US Ingredients. I wondered whose visit would go better. I wondered if Ronin and Whychoff would take us seriously. I wondered if they would care about what their decisions and inaction had caused. When I met them, I immediately learned all those answers and then some.

We began walking toward the house. I glanced back at the car and then tripped over a flexible sign stuck in the ground and almost fell. "You okay?" asked Patti catching my arm.

In a slightly embarrassed voice I replied, "Yeah, just not paying attention. Damn lawn care company leaving their flags in the ground. Must have been that white truck leaving the road as we pulled in. You can smell the spray."

Patti led the way to knock on the door and instantly I pulled her back. "I'll do it." My action would have been odd to anyone not in the know, but the stories of my former partner being shot through the door in front of me were well known. She took it without question and stepped aside. Immediately rustling could be heard from inside. A well-groomed, short man wearing an Oklahoma State Cowboys polo opened the door.

"You must be the officers who called?" he said, in a higher-pitched voice than anyone would have thought would come from his stocky frame. He looked like a wrestler carrying a low center of gravity, short hair, and definitely in shape. I think it's my black belt training and previous time in competitions when I was younger that always had me size up individuals. Regardless, he did not seem to be returning the evaluation.

"Yes," I began, "we are the detectives who called. May we come in?"

"Oh, sorry, Detectives." He said it as a child would say it when mocking his parents. "Listen, we know what's going on." He motioned to an individual in the back that was either Ronin or Whychoff as we still didn't know who we were talking to. "We know there seems to be someone targeting our discipline committee. We do not need your help or your bullshit questions."

"Bullshit questions?" interrupted Halterman. "Aren't you a teacher?"

"Listen, I appreciate your concern and yes, I am a twenty-five year teacher at Fenton Northwest. I have seen everything. We did not make any decisions that did not have facts and support behind them. We did not force any student to do anything they did not agree with. Whoever is committing these heinous crimes is a deranged individual, but with school indefinitely cancelled, we will just lay low until you guys do your job and catch the son of a bitch."

I stepped in front of my partner clearly showing my agitation with this asshole. "Here's how it's going to go, teach. My partner and I are going to come inside and ask you and your buddy some questions. If you refuse, one of two things is going to happen. We are going to take you downtown by your own choice as a material witness and possible suspect, or we are going to take you in for questioning, the latter of which makes you look a whole lot more guilty than the first."

His face dropped. "What the hell do you mean? You think we could be behind these murders?"

It was clear he never thought that was the direction we would be thinking. In truth, I was not thinking that either, but if I shut him up, I was good letting it go that direction. He stepped aside and swung his arm over inviting us in without actually saying it. As we walked into what was a small living room, the other man stood and walked toward us with an outstretch hand. "I am Herb Whychoff, the senior English teacher, and this is Bill Ronin. He teaches chemistry." We both shook Herb's hand but Bill did not return the gesture. Herb continued. "Please excuse our abruptness. We are shook up about these events and although one direction is to be defensive, perhaps we should be more passive. Eric Graham was a friend of mine, a very good friend."

"I appreciate your words," I responded. "The goal here is to stop this killer before anyone else is harmed. That's why we need to speak to both of you."

"Then what is all that talk about how we could be suspects?" replied Ronin.

I turned back to the chemistry teacher who still stood with a grimace across his face. "Listen, Mr. Ronin, everyone is a suspect. At worst, the two of you are deeply involved. Over half of that discipline committee is dead. Our first victim is at the source of that committee's discussions. Trying to play innocent with me right now is not going to serve you at all. My partner and I need answers, not bullshit. So I suggest you knock this crap off and let's sit down and talk through what the hell is going on. We may just save both your lives in the process." Hot damn, I was on a roll and I could tell in Patti's eyes, my partner knew it.

Whychoff motioned for us to take a seat. "Let's sit down. We want to help. Ask us anything."

"Thank you, Mr. Whychoff," Patti responded quickly. I think she was preventing me from going off on another tangent.

We all took seats and I decided to take over the questioning. "Tell me, Mr. Ronin, why should I not consider you a suspect?"

He was instantly on the defensive again, and I liked it. I didn't think he really was a suspect, but it never hurts to keep witnesses on the edge. He probably was going to say he couldn't hurt anybody.

"Because I couldn't hurt anybody," he stated firmly. "I liked Mark Schulman. He was a student of mine and a good kid."

Right when he said it, he knew he opened up a door he should have left closed. "Is that why your committee ignored the complaints of a boy being bullied by Mr. Schulman and a girl being raped?" *Bingo*.

"Wait just a minute, sir."

"It's Detective," I interrupted.

"Wait just a minute, Detective," he replied snidely. "We met and discussed both those cases in detail. We didn't tell either student not to press charges. We heard their complaints and provided the families with feedback on what we could or could not substantiate. There were no witnesses. No evidence to support their claims." Without speaking, I stood up and looked behind me, shrugged, and then sat back down. "What?" he replied, staring at me.

"I just thought you called me Detective. I didn't realize your committee was filled with detectives as well."

"What do you mean by that?" he asked.

Oh, I was about ready to explode. My partner stood and placed her hand on my shoulder. Why do people do that to me? Franky does it all the time, and now this woman who barely knows me does it. Do I scream, *this guy is out of control but a soft touch on the shoulder shuts him down?* Patti held her hand in place but took over the comments. "He means you had no business even investigating or saying anything to the family. These are felony charges. A girl was potentially raped. The first thing you should have done was call the police. Further, we have already recovered text messages, Facebook posts, and many other examples of social media bullying from Mr. Schulman's web presence. The evidence was readily available. We don't think you even looked."

"We had our entire IT department on it. We..."

"Shut up, Bill," Herb Whychoff interrupted. "We did nothing of the sort. Bob wanted this to go away. He pushed us to talk to the family about the hard fight to prove anything and how the evidence just wasn't there."

"Damn it, Herb, you need to keep your mouth shut."

"Both of you knock it off," I interrupted. "Who is Bob?" I asked toward Mr. Whychoff.

Herb didn't even acknowledge Bill Ronin's request to remain silent. "Robert Bales."

"The principal?" I asked.

"The very one," he answered. "Bob did not want the bad publicity, especially the allegations of rape."

Patti's voice was softer and more caring. "So you guys pushed them to bury the charges and take your advice. How did they accept that?"

"They were very disappointed at first. I still remember when we told Leah and her parents. She broke down in tears. She couldn't believe we would not support her. Especially Dawn. She was very upset at Dawn Wells."

"The counselor?" I confirmed.

"Yes. Leah had gone to Dawn before even telling her parents."

I glanced toward Bill Ronin and he just looked down. Then he lifted his eyes to lock on mine. "Dan was furious. Herb may never forget Leah's reaction, but I can't get Dan out of my mind. He looked at me like we failed him. Like we failed his family."

"Didn't you?" I asked, but said more like a statement. "Didn't you fail them?"

When there was no answer, Patti asked, "Who knew about the charges and the decisions?"

Herb took over the conversation again. "We did our best to keep things quiet. I can't say who the kids or families told, but internally we did a decent job of minimizing the spread. Bob did not want us talking about it to anyone."

"Well, since you didn't even do an investigation, you didn't have to ask anyone any questions." It was clear I was patronizing and pissed, all in one. We interviewed the two for the better part of the next thirty minutes. Outside of implicating everyone even related to the committee, the families, and the school, they didn't provide any real information. Their main use was confirming what we already knew. Their concern was simple—they wanted protection.

"Protection?" I said to Patti as we pulled out.

"They probably deserve it," she replied. There is definitely someone targeting that committee. I think we need to speak a little longer with Dan Malecha. I did not like the way he referred to Dan's level of anger and disappointment."

"I was thinking the same thing," I added. "And why don't you call in and have a car watch this house as well." I was basically acknowledging they needed it, but I hated wasting taxpayer money on people that were the source of the issue. "Right now, however, we should swing by and talk to Robert Bales while my anger is at its peak."

She smiled but did not reply. Instead, she had the route mapped on her phone in minutes and we were very close to his Naperville home. She then dialed dispatch to request another car to go to the teachers' houses.

•   •   •   •   •

"What is the plant manager's name?" asked Carter.

"Dominick Redding," Franky answered. "He goes by Dom and he wants us to ask for him when we arrive at the gate."

"They are gated?" Carter asked. "Is there a security guard?"

"Yes, on the gate, but no on the guard. They have a call box."

"But even with a gate, we can determine if anyone came in and got a barrel of chemicals?"

Franky nodded to the statement, the tone making it a question. "We should. They are pulling the chemical records from the last two months, and camera footage. He thought they would have most of the answers we need by the time we arrive."

We pulled into the driveway of a huge blue building. It had four big towers coming out from one of the buildings as well as two huge tank farms on each end. Rail lines came up to the back of the building and there was a huge distribution center about two hundred yards away separated by a single road and another gate. We pressed the call button. "Dominick Redding please."

"This is Dominick. Is this Detective Sullivan?"

"This is," Franky replied.

"I will buzz you right in. Please park out front, and I will meet you at the door."

"Seems helpful," Huston said as the gate made a loud metal-on-metal noise and then slowly started to slide open. Carter and Franky looked at each other but didn't answer. "What?" she added.

"Usually when people are too helpful, you have to be careful they're not trying to appear open, but in the end only really providing you information you already have or don't really need. We will want to keep an on eye on him and what he allows us to see."

True to his word, he met Franky, Carter, and Huston at the front door and guided them in. He was a small man. When Franky first saw him, he immediately thought about Steve Jewell, the late general manager of A-Tas Uniform. He was tied up in the Polino case several months ago and ended up in my trunk. That was the event I still needed to tie back to Teflon Marco Filini. The hired killer at that time working for Polino and Moretti that never had any of his crimes stick. I had to admit, however, the dead body in my own trunk was a solid move.

Franky was first to speak. "Dominick Redding I assume?"

"I am very pleased to meet you, and please, call me Dom."

"I am Detective Frank Sullivan, and"—motioning to the others as he introduced them—"this is my boss, Sergeant Craig Carter, and partner Detective Karen

Huston."

Dominick shook each of their hands but stopped when he got to Carter. "Must be pretty important to bring the three of you out, and one of you a sergeant."

"If solving several murders and theft of some hazardous chemicals is important, than yes, it *is* fairly important I would say." Carter's words were said with just enough sarcasm to shut Dominick up where he stood and push him immediately to the reason they were there.

He stuttered just a bit as he started to speak. "Uh, yes, we have pulled everything from the last sixty days. Let's go into the conference room and I will show you what we found. We may have something, but it's not as clear as I would have hoped."

They entered a conference room in the front of the building. It was becoming dark outside as the days in March were still fairly short when it came to total daylight. Franky could still see the car parked in front, but thought he would soon not be able to. Immediately Dominick opened up a laptop that appeared to have been preset and connected to an overhead projector.

"We found a few discrepancies that are worth discussing. First, however, I want to explain how our system works. We do not use caustic for every product or every clean. Therefore, there are times after or during a run when the level in the tank does not change. Secondly, the tank is 350 gallons. Some of our cleans may use only five to ten gallons. In those cases, both the weight measurement and the level indicator have acceptance ranges that are larger than the change that would occur. Does that make sense?"

Franky nodded. "Sure, what you are saying is you are not using enough caustic in your process to register a change in the two methods you utilize to track your running inventory level."

"Very good, Detective."

Franky smiled and looked to both Karen and Craig for approval on his expert summary. Neither provided any such support.

"There is more, however," continued Dominick. "Even though it may be within the error level, we will still record whatever result we have. So if prior to running we measured thirty-two feet and after running we anticipated measuring based on the required usage thirty-one feet and ten inches, but we actually measured thirty-one feet and nine inches, we would note that but not be alarmed because it was within an acceptable range."

All three were tracking this line of thought but nobody commented at this time, just chose to nod understanding instead.

"Well, to cut to the chase," Dominick added as he moved his mouse on the computer to open up a document he had previously saved. "There were three times in the last sixty days when discrepancies occurred. All were within our acceptable error ranges but one does stick out rather significantly."

Franky's interest immediately piqued.

"These first two occurred on days when we were running products or performing cleans where larger amounts of caustic were used. Seeing a variance there is not surprising. What I did not tell you before is we perform and record a measurement on all our tanks every night, whether we use them or not. And on the third occurrence, we never used any caustic, but the level in the tank dropped by an eighth of an inch and the total tank weight went down by the equivalent of about twenty-five gallons. Although it was within acceptable error ranges of the equipment, there is no other time in history that shows that type of change, as minor as it was."

Now all three detectives were deeply focused on each word he was saying. Franky started to speak but Dominick raised his hand. "Wait," Dom continued. "There's more. We then used that date and time to correlate to our security cameras and something truly strange came up. Here's a video of the camera on the gate between our distribution center and the main plant. This is not the gate you came in but one directly to the south."

He clicked on a video box that he had previously minimized on his screen. The box opened and it showed the picture from a camera pointing directly toward a gate. There was a streetlight above the gate providing some illumination to the area. Everything was still, and if not for the headlights of a car flashing off the building in the background, there would have been no movement.

He stopped the video. "Did you see that? The lights."

"Yes," Franky replied. "A late delivery or something?"

"Good thought," Dom answered, "but I checked and we didn't receive any deliveries that night for another two hours, and we were between shift changes so no employees would have been driving around." He let that sit in then hit play. Nothing happened for more than two or three minutes then all of a sudden, the picture went bright white and then turned to a snowy screen, like turning on a TV channel with no reception.

"What happened?" Craig asked.

"That night was the night that four of our cameras where shot out."

Although I was not there, if I had been, I would have just said, "Bingo!"

Franky stood. "You had four cameras shot out and you didn't report it?"

Dominick leaned back a bit not expecting that to be his first question. "Detective, with all due respect, the police force has made it clear that every time I've been vandalized, they don't want to hear about it. I have spray paint, eggs, toilet paper, you name it, every month. We are not in a great neighborhood. The plant is still secure, and we had nothing stolen. The cameras are lit so they are an easy target. We passed this off on kids. Kids that are a talented shot as some of the shots were at a fairly good distance. To be honest, we were more impressed that they even knew where the cameras were. They are not hidden, but they are not in the open either."

"What cameras were they?" Franky asked.

"That's the other piece that is strange. They are all cameras that would show a car from that gate to the tank farm with the caustic."

Franky appeared more agitated than he probably should have. He wanted to blame this plant manager for putting a murder weapon in the hands of a killer, whether there was intent or not. "So you're telling me someone cleared a path by blowing out cameras all the way to your chemical tanks, you had chemical missing, and you didn't put the two together?"

"That is what I'm telling you. There's no way those two pieces of information would ever be considered and linked."

Sergeant Carter now stood. "You said a minute ago you did not notify the police about the cameras being shot because it was simple vandalism, and that you had nothing stolen. I think you need to change that determination. You did have something stolen."

Dominick was now becoming slightly defensive and his helpful demeanor with that defensiveness was starting to fade. "There is one problem with that theory, Sergeant. None of our gates were ever opened. Those gates are opened from this office. There's a camera in the office and that camera was not damaged because it's inside. Nobody that entire night pushed that button to allow anyone in, and according to my facilities mechanics, the gate was not tampered with. That gate and the opener that runs it are over a thousand pounds. Unless your perpetrator is also a gate installer with equipment to handle that weight and size, nobody drove on this property, and I don't see anyone moving a fifty-five gallon drum by hand. Therefore, although the actions that night are suspicious, I don't see how anyone came on the campus and removed half a barrel of caustic. The easy answer is that our measurements are off, which happens all the time."

That did stop the three a bit, but they all knew there was too much circumstantial evidence involved to not have the source of the caustic that melted Dawn Wells' body come from this plant. The issue, solving the last obstacle. The killer solved that issue, but how?

Franky took the lead. "Listen, Mr. Redding, I do appreciate your last comment, and it does shed some level of question on the situation. However, there is just too much stacked up to believe the caustic did not come from here. The individual responsible for this is too good. They have performed three murders and left no trace of evidence behind. If they have the ability to shoot out key cameras plus access this building and know what to do, then I think they have the ability to open the gate." He paused, glanced to both his colleagues who showed in their expression they too believed in his summary, then Franky continued. "On a separate note, I would like to discuss two of your former employees."

"Former employees?" asked Dominick. "I can't really talk about former employees."

Franky instantly went into what he likes to call *ass-mode*. "You know what, we are very busy and we don't have time for this crap. You can answer a few simple employee questions now, or you can come with us, spend the night at the station while we obtain the necessary documents, get the necessary human resources people called in, and we answer the questions then. I suggest now, and we then simply go about our business. Don't forget, I haven't decided if we are going to arrest you for failure to report a crime or not."

"Accessory after the fact," added Carter.

"Arrest me? Accessory after the fact in a murder?" He didn't seem mad or defensive, he seemed scared. Franky believed Dominick Redding was simply a good guy, someone who followed the rules and tried not to make any waves with anyone. There were not many of these guys left, but when you found one, they were easy to scare, even with false threats of being arrested. His voice cracked as he continued. "Listen, ask me what you need to. I will answer everything I can that won't get me fired. If you cross a line, I will have to make a call to get some guidance."

"Fair enough," Franky replied. "Jack Kittleson?"

Dominick's eyes widened in surprise. This was clearly not a name he expected to hear. "Jack? He was the former plant manager. He was let go because the new vice president thought he was embezzling money. Then, after he was gone, it was found *another* vice president was doing it. Nice guy, always treated me well. I used to report to him and took his job when he was let go. He called me a few times to answer questions and help out. He was very supportive of me."

Franky had a little interest in the embezzling money comment, but it really wasn't what the discussion was about. Might be something either he or I could use the next time we had Kittleson at the station. "What about his demeanor?"

"Demeanor?" Dominick asked in return.

"You know, did he have a temper? Did he fool around with the staff? What kind of person was he?"

"No, no, and he was extremely smart. This job is complex and there's some science to it, but he had multiple degrees and experience. This site is really a glorified refinery. He could do much more than what was needed here, which is why he landed on his feet so quickly. As for fooling around, I can't say he ever cheated with anyone if that's what you were implying. But he did meet his wife here. He was divorced when they met and to the best of my knowledge, they are still together. When he was let go, she quit shortly thereafter. She remained friends with a few individuals here, but I don't think he stayed in touch with anyone, at least not that I heard."

"Tell me about his wife, Kim Kittleson isn't it?"

"Yes, Kim. She was in quality. Reliable, good worker, easygoing, pretty—just an all-around good employee. In fact, her departure had probably more of an impact than his. She did the daily job of two to three people and we had no bench strength there. I stepped right into his role so it was simply smoother."

"Would you believe either one of them could steal the caustic?"

He smiled almost as if he didn't believe Franky was really asking the question. After a long pause where Franky didn't change his expression, Dominick answered. "Sorry, I just didn't think you were serious. Both would know where the tanks were and because of each of their previous jobs, both would know where the sample port was and could conceivably fill a barrel. So if you ask me if they physically could have done it, yes, they physically could have. If you're asking me if they did, my answer is no."

"Thank you, Dominick," Franky replied. After taking a deep breath, he began again, "Just one more question, if you don't mind."

Dominick looked up to him but did not reply, just lifted his eyebrows as if to say, *whatever, just say it.*

"Did you know that Jack Kittleson was a sharpshooter in the armed forces? A sniper?"

"No, but I don't know much about any of the current employees' backgrounds either," he replied.

"Right, right. No, I get it. That's not my point. My point is, Jack Kittleson had the ability to shoot out those cameras. Jack Kittleson had the ability to offload half a barrel of caustic. Are you telling me Jack Kittleson didn't have any way to get through that gate?"

His eyes changed when Franky said that. Carter and Huston saw it too. Franky immediately drove at the nonverbal response. "You just thought of something. What?"

The plant manager pressed his lips together. "I told you nobody opened the gate from this room, but several of us programmed the gate receiver into our car garage door opener. I use it myself. I can't believe he would still drive the same car or have saved the program, but if he had programmed it in when he worked here, we have not changed that operator in fifteen or more years."

"Good information," Franky replied, a smile growing on his face. Craig Carter clearly thought the same as he too showed a slight grin.

The three continued to ask a few questions and get formally shown the gate operator room and camera. Although everything they heard was all circumstantial, it pointed clearly to Jack Kittleson. He had motive. He had the skills to commit one of the murders and the previous knowledge to obtain the chemical to commit the second murder. The vehicle murder was simple planning. Furthermore, the shooting out the cameras tied all the murders together. All we needed to do was confirm Jack Kittleson's whereabouts the night the cameras were shot and the chemicals stolen.

11

WE ARRIVED AT Robert Bales' Naperville house ten minutes after we left the two teachers. There was an unmarked police car out front and two officers seated inside. I walked up to the driver's side window and the officer had already lowered the window to talk. I recognized him but could not place his name nor could I read his uniform.

"Hey O'Malley, nothing much going on here. The house has been quiet."

"Is anyone home?" I asked.

"Yeah," he replied. "We have seen a light or two go on and off. We think we saw shadows through the shades. We think there are at least two people home."

"Very good," I said in return. "Why don't you boys go get yourself some food? Detective Halterman and I are going to spend at least thirty minutes talking to the homeowner so we'll be here. Once we're done, we'll determine if we need to keep you guys here all night."

They seemed pleased to be able to leave for a while, though the last comment quickly took the pleasure down from being too great. Stakeouts seem romantic in movies and on television. In real life, they suck. "Hey," he began as we started walking toward the house. "I would not walk on the grass. A Pest-Go Truck was here a short while ago spraying the outside of the house. Probably don't want to get that stuff on your shoes."

I nodded in return but really didn't care. A little bug spray never hurt me. I checked my phone and it was going on 6:30. Where had the night gone? Franky, Carter, and Huston should be finishing up at the food plant. I had no idea what I was going to say or what the conversation was going to be with Bales. Patti and I had discussed it briefly in the car. We already knew his role in this thing. He was basically the kingfish asshole. Probably not guilty of anything other than being a complete jackass. Was he indirectly responsible for the three deaths? My answer was yes, but the law didn't have anything I could charge him with. At this point, my only direction was to talk to him and see if something comes out that can help us determine who was behind this. We had a handful of suspects, some better than others, but all circumstantial. I needed something to tie it all together. Our second purpose, I suppose, was to let him know we would keep a car outside for protection if he wanted. I hope he didn't, but if I were him, I would take it.

I walked up and rang the doorbell. I did notice the spray marks on the edge of the sidewalk from the lawn treatment, but I didn't smell the normal odor. However, I had no time to think about it as the door immediately cracked open. I actually tripped over my tongue when my eyes fell across the woman before me. She was thin, sexy, and appeared to be closer to a lingerie model than my vision of a principal's wife. Her hair was long and blonde, her cheekbones high and well defined. Her skin was soft. I could tell that without even touching it, though I wanted to. I'm not even going to mention her breasts—but they were perfect. She was wearing a long, almost see-through gown. I don't know if it was a dress or some sort of evening casual wear. I didn't care. What the hell was she doing with him?

Patti did not cover for me well. Clearing her throat and speaking around me, she asked, "Is Mr. Robert Bales available?"

The woman smiled. "Yes, my husband is here. Is there something wrong?"

I now had gained my composure. Who am I kidding? No, I hadn't. "Um, we met him at the school. We need some follow-up to the recent murders." My voice cracked and I sounded like I was going through puberty.

"Way to go, stud," Patti whispered.

"Oh yes," the woman replied sadly. "What a horrible situation. I can't believe all that has occurred. Bobby is just devastated, absolutely devastated." She paused and moved aside the door lifting her arm to lead us in. The movement caused her gown to slip across her leg revealing everything from her thigh down to her bare feet. Holy shit, it moved, and I don't mean her leg. "Please, come in. I'll go get Bobby."

Patti and I walked into the house. It was a beautiful home. It was pricey, but everything in Naperville had a bit of price to it, as I understood it. However, it was not what I would call out of his means if he was good with money. I had no idea how much a principal at a private school in Chicago would make, but it was obviously enough. She led us into what I would call a den but she called it a study.

"Please wait here in the study. I believe he went upstairs. Can I get you anything?"

"A cold shower," Patti whispered.

"What was that?" she asked.

"A cold glass of water would be great," I replied. "Patti, did you need anything?"

"No, thank you," she replied in an overly sweet voice. "I feel a bit sick."

"Very well," Mrs. Bales answered. "My name is Dani. I will fetch Bobby and that water in just a jiffy."

She left the room and I tried to turn to Patti but I had to look toward the ground.

"What in the hell was that?" she asked. "What are you, thirteen?"

I couldn't even answer, and I think I began to blush.

"Jesus Christ, Tommy. That was beyond a shadow of a doubt, pathetic."

I slowly moved my eyes up to hers. "Yep, I know. I just was completely caught off guard."

Patti continued to shake her head. "Don't worry about it. She obviously shows what she has for a reason."

I really just wanted the conversation to end. I was embarrassed, but part of me was thrilled that the little guy in my pants still had the ability to move. I thought Tammi might have taken that with her on the move to California. I still could not believe what she was doing with a fifty-plus year old, crabby-looking principal. I thought that even more when I saw him entering the room, completely disheveled and appearing as if he just rolled out of bed.

"Detectives?" he began. "I'm surprised to see you at my home. I thought we talked through everything at the school."

I turned and instantly I was back to my old self. "Well, Principal Bales, I guess with all that has happened and still happening, we felt some follow-up was called for."

"Follow-up?" he replied questioning.

"Yeah, follow-up." My tone instantly went to annoyed. "You have some issue with additional questions? I mean a committee of five people investigating allegations put forth on a boy in your school has gone from five down to three and if you add in the boy, that's 50% of the people involved are dead. Probably worth some additional discussions, don't you think?"

"Please, Detectives, I am on your side. Perhaps originally I was trying to protect the school, but it's all over now. The time for making more bad decisions has long since passed."

For the first time, I heard actual regret in the man's voice. Maybe he was human, or maybe he was just saying what he needed to now. I took a seat, as did my partner and Bales. "We just left your other two committee members. They shared a great deal of information with us. They say you pushed them to deny the claims and make the allegations go away." That was a bit of a stretch, but I never gave an oath to tell the truth, the whole truth, and nothing but the truth.

His head fell. "I suppose they did. It's not a lie." His voice trailed off slightly, but he was on his own now, I was going to let him go. I hoped Patti did the same. She did. "I mean, I didn't come out and say it, but they knew. I kept talking about the good of the school. What the hell was I thinking? Bullying? Rape? I keep thinking, what would I want if it were my daughter?"

Not what I expected. "Principal Bales..."

He held up his hand. "Please, call me Robert. Who knows, I most likely won't be a principal tomorrow anyway."

Just then Dani returned with three waters. "Here you go. I knew Bobby would want one as well, and I assumed you were just being polite," she added glancing to Patti.

We all nodded a thank you and then she took her place behind her husband. "Uh, Robert, it might be better speaking to you in private," I said.

Dani smiled. "I will leave if you want, but Bobby already told me everything. He told me how much of an ass he was, how he made horrible decisions for the wrong reasons, and how he was responsible."

Again, not what I expected.

Dani continued. "If you are wondering if I was disappointed in him, absolutely. Those actions were not the actions of the man I fell in love with. However, I also know that I have made a ton of mistakes in my life as I am sure you have, Detectives. That does not make anything right, and I am sure there will be some horrible things coming our way, but nothing can be as bad as what those kids and teachers have already faced."

I thought it was interesting she said "kids." Only one of the murder victims was a student, but she was already including the kids who were bullied and brutalized in her comment. Beautiful and Classy.

"You see, Detective," Bales added. "I get it. I'm fifty-five years old. I have been in education my entire life. I have been principal of Fenton Northwest for the last twelve years. When I started, I would have never made the decisions I made this past year. I was an idealist thinking I could change children's lives, and boy did I do that. I just never dreamed I would have changed them for the worse. I don't deserve any forgiveness. I don't deserve any further thought. I am indirectly responsible for the death of a student and two teachers. What do I have left but regret?"

There was nothing more to say on the subject. I did not expect it, but Principal Robert Bales got it. It simply took this to make him see it. He was fairly deep in depression, but it didn't mean I could let my questions go. We had to stay focused. We had to know if he could help us. "Robert, I hear your pain and I'm actually glad to hear that you're feeling what you're feeling. My fear was you would still be fighting against all that had happened. Seeing you as you are now, maybe you can help us find out who's behind these murders."

He shrugged. "I don't know who is behind them. I told you what I knew. Of all the parents who showed any emotion, Peggy and Dan Malecha simply showed disbelief. They stared at me like they couldn't believe I would not help their daughter. I will never forget that stare." He wiped his nose which had started to run. "And Jack and Becky Kittleson held similar reactions. Becky cried and called me and several on my committee some names, but it was simply her emotions. We never heard from her again. Jack was different though. He just stared at me. Not at the committee, just me. I think he was in the armed forces, and he was definitely in shape. I remember thinking he was going to simply charge me and what I would do. Then he just stood and walked out, never saying another word to me."

"What would you have done?" I asked. "If he had charged you?"

"I don't have an answer for that," he replied. "Taken it, I guess. I think even then I knew what we were doing was wrong. Him beating me up seemed like an acceptable result."

Now I was beginning to understand the man I had despised thirty minutes earlier. "Do you know anyone else who could have done these things? Another student who had brought complaints against Mark Schulman maybe? Any rumors of other students with issues? Anything we can follow-up on?"

Bales again looked down and Dani placed her hand on his shoulder. He moved his other hand to rest on top of hers. I actually felt guilty for lusting after this woman in my mind. They were either great actors, or they truly cared for each other. On that note, he had hit the home run–kind of like me and Tammi Hutchins. Bales turned back to us. "Schulman was a jackass. Take any undergrad on the football team, the debate team, the chess team, or fill in any less cool subject and you will find someone he bullied." He paused again and gripped her hand tighter. "But do I think any of them or the parents could have done this? My answer is still no."

I glanced to Patti and she nodded back to me. There was nothing here. I stood and placed both hands on the side of the desk allowing me to lean a bit closer to the man sitting in the high-back chair but shrinking into it as if he wanted to hide. "My only other question for you is about protection. We do believe there is someone killing everyone on your committee. Therefore, we do believe your life is in danger. I have a car outside watching your house. If you have any concerns, just run out and talk to them."

He was about to protest but a flexing of Dani's fingers into his shoulder ended his comment before it started.

"Very well then, Robert," I started. "We will stay in touch. I would suggest you keep a lower profile over the next few days and if you see or hear anything out of the ordinary, let us know." I dropped another card on the desk and Patti and I moved toward the door. I turned back to the man who had not gotten up and actually held his head in his hands. "Bales, there's never a situation where I will believe you acted appropriately. However, I am pleased to see that you do understand. I would not do it today, but a call to the families involved may help create some healing, for all parties involved."

Patti nodded and we both turned back to the door. Dani walked over and met us as we began to pull the door shut. "I know you think my husband is a horrible man, Detective." She was clearly speaking mainly to me. "I'm not going to argue he made some terrible decisions, but the thing I hope you saw tonight is he knows he made some terrible decisions as well. I don't know that he will recover from this. I'm not looking for any pity, just understanding."

I didn't speak and just turned and walked out. Patti pulled the door shut behind us.

•　　•　　•　　•　　•

"Jesus, Roy, just give us the bottle."

The Flap Jaws bartender shrugged. "Tommy, trade me your keys for the bottle and you have a deal."

Patti lifted her Diet Coke. "I'll be in charge of his keys," she stated grabbing them off the table as she spoke.

Roy Pura looked to her, saw a verifying nod from Carter and Franky, and left the bottle on the table.

"Thanks," I said to Patti. "But you don't need to worry about me. I'll take an Uber home."

"No," she replied. "You will take an Uber to the precinct tomorrow and I will drive your car. My car is still at the station."

I nodded understanding and Karen smiled at her counterpart's quick response.

"What are we drinking to?" Carter asked.

Clearly not the question I wanted to hear. "Well, Sergeant, why don't we drink to Tammi leaving me for the fuckin' restaurant in San Francisco?" The sarcasm was flowing so thick in that comment a few of us had to duck. "Or how about a teenage boy getting run down without a clue to determine who did it?" I used that break to pour and take a shot of Wild Turkey. "Or no, I got it. How about drinking to a teacher being melted to death in a barrel followed by another having his brains spread across a soccer field." My voice was slurred and the alcohol was already getting to me.

"Tommy," stated Franky. "Enough."

I grunted, stood, and walked to the bathroom. I needed to be away from the table. I was being an ass and I knew it.

"He takes on his cases, doesn't he?" asked Patti when I was out of earshot.

"Probably more than any of us," Franky replied. "Tommy has a knack of getting into the heads of people. He told me once he tries to feel what they feel. He believes if he can enter their positions in the world, he can help see the answer."

"Does it work?" Karen asked.

"Tomas O'Malley has solved more cases than any detective in the history of

Chicago homicide. If that does not answer your question, I don't know what will." Carter poured himself a shot and slammed it down as did Franky in his wake.

"What do you guys think of this case?" asked Karen.

Before any could answer, I had made my way back to the table. "Sorry, Sergeant, I didn't mean..."

"Knock it off, Tommy, and sit your ass down," interrupted Carter. "Before our minds are completely gone, we need to discuss this case. I don't want to wait until morning. I'm sure I will be up most of the night anyway."

We proceeded to compare information from the day's activities putting everything out in chronological order.

"So," I began. "According to Doc G, Dawn Wells, the counselor, was killed first, then the Schulman boy and the soccer coach."

"Right," answered Carter. "What are you getting at?"

"I'm not sure yet, but it definitely means one thing."

"What?" asked Karen.

I turned my eyes to Patti. "These were all premediated."

"Absolutely," I replied. "These were not only premediated, they were premediated almost to a professional level." I pushed the bottle of Turkey aside and instantly began to sober up a bit, though I really was not sobering at all, just thinking clearer for a short minute. "Maybe we are looking at this all wrong. Maybe the person or persons behind this is not a parent, but a professional."

"A killer for hire?" asked Franky.

"Who else would be so precise? So regimented?" I leaned in just a bit and spoke softer. "Think about it. This was well planned. The person obtained twenty-some gallons of a custom chemical. They kidnapped a woman with nobody knowing and days later stole a car and committed a hit-and-run murder before the car was even reported missing. Then the accuracy of the shooting goes without saying."

"It makes sense," interjected Carter. "But who would have had the ability to hire a professional like this?"

I leaned back in my chair. "I think our list of suspects has not changed. The same people that would have wanted to take revenge on the committee and the boy remains intact. We simply now need to follow the money. A professional committing one hit is expensive. Three or more hits, significantly more."

"And who would have the connections to find a hit man?" added Carter. "It's not like you can go through the yellow pages?"

"What are the yellow pages?" asked Huston.

"Jesus, you are young," stated Carter smiling and taking another shot.

Franky also smiled, but turned his comment directly toward me. "What about Filini? I hear he's still in town. Everybody knew his name after the Polino-Moretti case. We could get nothing to stick on him. We know he shot Polino in broad daylight in front of the police station and couldn't prove a thing. We also know he has some special hard-on for you."

I nodded. "It is not a hard-on. He's a black belt. I'm a higher black belt. He thinks he can take me. If he didn't feel this way, you and I would have both been killed four months ago and Polino and Moretti would still be running prostitution and drugs throughout the south side."

Both Huston and Halterman were taken by that comment. It was clear in their reaction. "That is a story I think I need to hear, but another time." Patti was staring at me strangely now. It was not an uncomfortable stare, but one of "you are full of mystery and I like that" stare.

Craig Carter poured another round for everyone except Patti who still was not drinking, though Karen Huston had downed a few beers and a shot or two now. "Listen, I like the discussion, but let's table it. I am sitting at a table in my favorite bar, with two of the best damn detectives I know, and Tommy and Franky are here too." He laughed at his own joke. "So let's just enjoy the liquor and talk shop tomorrow morning."

His voice had become slurred, which was funny that I noticed because I'm sure mine was also. I knew if I had a few more, it would probably be too much, but I didn't rightly care. I was feeling sorry for myself. I had lost a woman I thought I might marry. I picked up a case that included some horrendous murders. Individuals tied to one of the worst cases I have ever handled may be involved in this case, and my investigation may actually make their actions worse as they try to bring me out. Yeah, tonight I was going to have a few too many.

•　　•　　•　　•　　•

I woke up the next morning and felt like a truck had run me over. My head ached and I was absolutely confused. Also, I was naked. It was not all that surprising because I often slept naked, but the shower was running and I didn't start it. I tried to remember the night before but short of doing some shots and talking about the case, I couldn't remember anything else. I checked the clock–6:30 AM. "Shit!" I said.

I pushed the sheets off and saw my clothes from yesterday randomly thrown on the floor. I grabbed a new batch from my drawer and threw them on, then slowly walked over to the bathroom door. "Hello?" I said softly. There was no reply. "Hello?" I said louder.

The water turned off. "Tommy?" said a female voice from behind the door. A voice I knew well.

"Shit, shit, shit, shit!" I whispered. I was naked, in my apartment, in my bed, and my new female partner was showering. What the hell did I do?

The door opened during my stupor and she walked out wrapped in a towel. She did have a large smile and when her hair was wet and combed straight down, she was very sexy. I couldn't make a sound come out of my mouth, however, and I just moved slightly aside so she could walk by.

She placed her hand on my chest as she passed. "What a wonderful night, don't you think?"

"Uh, yeah. Wonderful." My voice was choppy and I could not hide it.

"How do you feel, big guy? You were something last night."

Again I stuttered. "Uh, I don't feel that well. My head hurts and to be honest..."

She sauntered up to me and did not let me finish. Still with her towel wrapped around her, she put both her arms around me and pulled our bodies together tight. She reached her lips up to my ear and whispered in a soft, sexy voice, "Don't worry, you big stud, you were drunk off your ass. I slept on the couch and nothing happened. You could barely walk, and I just wanted to make sure you were home safe."

She pushed herself away and I'm not sure what my expression was, but I'm sure her laughter was in response to it. She got me, hook, line, and sinker.

"Feel better now, Tommy?" she said, still somewhere between a huge smile and a full laugh.

"You have no idea," I replied. "Why did you stay at all? You could have taken my car."

She nodded and went to grab her clothes. "To be honest, you begged me to stay. Not inappropriately, but it was late and you didn't want me driving. Further, I did not want to drive that late and I was tired. You were going to make a late-night snack and then you were under your covers, clothes all over the place, snoring like a hog in heat. So I curled up on the couch and went to sleep."

"Jesus, I'm sorry. I should not have drank that..."

"Don't sweat it, Tommy. If we're going to be partners, we're going to see all sides of each other." She had walked into the bathroom now as she was talking. Shortly, she emerged in her clothes from yesterday. "However, I am not going to show up at work in the same clothes as yesterday so I'm headed home. You will need to Uber in."

"Done," I replied. "And thank you."

"No problem, partner." She was walking to the door and then turned back. "Hey, Tommy, sorry to hear about your girlfriend, Tammi wasn't it? Her loss." And she walked out.

What the hell did I say last night?

12 "WHAT IS THE PLAN today?" Franky asked after the morning briefing.

"Let's bring Jack Kittleson in and verify every moment of his whereabouts. Let's get his statements to those facts and then verify it against credit card charges, security cameras, etc. I want to know where he was during every murder and the theft at the food plant."

"Sounds good," answered Halterman who was listening to the conversation from her desk. "I will call him back in."

"Is he our only real suspect?" Franky asked.

I did not have to think long for a response, though he was my primary suspect, that was certain. "Let's get IT tracking all their finances. I still like the idea of a hired party doing this. The murders are all too clean."

"Too professional," Carter followed as he walked up.

"Right," I answered. "Let's check out all the Kittleson's, Malecha's, and even the Schulman's finances."

"The Schulman's? But their kid was killed? What could they have to do with it?" Patti asked.

I nodded agreement. "Right, but their kid was killed second. What if Dawn Wells came to them and let them know she was building a case against their son with all she was finding. To protect their son, they pulled off that elaborate murder of the counselor." I paused, still making this up as I went. "And then someone found out. Maybe their son was retaliation or maybe they were warned or blackmailed. We don't know anything about them. When we met with them, they were just victims. Let's give the Schulman family another run."

"How about the other teachers or the principal then?" Franky asked.

Carter now sat on the edge of my desk and seemed intrigued with the comment. "What if one of them didn't like how the committee voted? If they felt the kid was guilty, then that would support the murder. If they felt that the others on the committee acted erroneously in their voting, then that would support the other deaths. Absolutely let's take a look at all of them."

"I will get on it," Patti answered. "You don't need the IT guys, this is kind of my specialty. I will be able to tell you if they spent two dollars on a pack of gum in the last week, much less money for a professional hit."

Carter looked toward Franky. "Franky, I want you to update the board. Put each suspect up alongside a timeline and then let's rule them out based on confirming their whereabouts at any given time. How about the kid that was bullied. Weren't we checking his alibi on the hit-and-run with street cams? Let's do the same thing with each of them. O'Malley, work with Franky on it."

I shook my head. "I might have another avenue to follow-up on."

Everyone stopped what they were doing. My tone must have sounded more mysterious than I intended. "What do you have?" asked Carter.

"I am going to talk to Moretti."

It was like EF Hutton—you could have heard a pin drop. My history with Ross Moretti was not good. He had tried to have me killed. I had had him arrested and he recently had all charges dropped. His business had taken several million dollars of a hit because of me, but in all honesty, that was just a drop in the bucket. This case did not involve Moretti, so I assume my boss assumed I was going to see Moretti for some personal reason.

"Now just why in the hell would you go and do that?" asked Carter.

"I need to find Marco Filini, and he's the only connection I have to the man."

"You want to go speak to a crime boss who you tried to give the death sentence and you think he will help you locate someone he previously paid to have you murdered?"

I smiled. "When you put it like that, it doesn't sound like my best plan."

Franky interjected. "I have to agree with Carter on this one, Tommy. Didn't you have to commit to the court that you wouldn't center an investigation on Moretti without proper cause? Basically, you were to cease and desist investigating him."

"That is correct," I replied. "However, I am not investigating him. I am looking for an acquaintance of his to help on a case. I know Filini didn't do this. Vigilante stuff is not his style."

"Sure," Franky said with sarcasm flowing. "He is a murder-for-hire with a specification requirement."

"In some ways, he is," I replied. "For the same reason we are both alive. He kills by a set of rules, not out of revenge, but I bet he can give me some names of those who don't follow the same code."

"But do you really think he will give you any names?" Carter asked.

"Probably not, but just by asking I might stir something up."

Carter shook his head. "I don't like it, but I won't stop it either. However, you are not going alone. Take Huston with you."

"No offense, Sergeant, and please, Detective Huston, this is no reflection on you. I would love to partner with you for a short while to show you how a true detective operates, but I need to do this alone. There's no reason to give Moretti or Filini any additional ammunition to use against me, least of all a partner. They need to believe I still work alone."

Huston did not respond positively or negatively. It appeared she understood and agreed, but would still gladly go along. Part of her probably did want to partner with me instead of Franky for obvious reasons. Carter, however, stood and paced. "No, you are not going in alone. I will join you and sit in the car. They already know me. You will keep in radio contact and if you need backup, I will be there. There is no argument on this."

My eyes widened. "On second thought, maybe Huston should go with me."

Carter's face actually turned a bit red. His voice was short and firm. "I'll meet you downstairs. We'll take your car."

That seemed fine and I actually thought his reaction was slightly comical, until I realized I had no idea where my car was because I had not driven in. I also did not really want to ask my partner where she parked my car as it would open us up to several questions I didn't want to answer. Without missing a beat, Patti said, "I left my gloves in your car last night when I dropped you off. Walk down with me and I will grab them before you go."

"No problem," I replied. "Carter, meet me out front in ten."

As we went down the elevator, I could see Patti smiling slightly. "What?"

"I just wanted to say I was sorry. You should have seen your face when I hugged you this morning. You had no idea. You thought we..."

"I did not!" I exclaimed. "I may not remember everything, but I didn't think that."

"You can't even say it, can you? You can't even say that we didn't fuck like bunnies."

"First off," I said turning toward her. "I have never used the phrase, 'fuck like bunnies.' Secondly, no, I can't say it."

She and I both turned back toward the doors just before they opened. I was certain she was still smiling. Her actions were taking all the fun out of being drunk and I was going to have to re-evaluate my evening activities in mixed company.

• • • • •

We arrived at the Palomino Hotel and Casino which I learned had been purchased by Ross Moretti shortly after absorbing all of Joey Polino's holdings. Moretti still owned all the lowlife, drug-infused strip clubs and seedy hotels in the old Cabrini Green and South Chicago neighborhoods, but he had begun to drive his holdings upscale and now had the capital to do it. I hadn't spoken to Moretti since the day he was arrested. I had seen him several times in court but as the case began to unravel and all evidence clearly pointed to his partner, Joey Polino, whom Moretti had murdered, even the district attorney James Esson had to understand the case did not have merit. Moretti's attorney was a killer and left no stone unturned. By the time the grand jury finished, I was certain the case would be dropped. As expected, it was. Now Moretti was in a better position and I was coming to him for help. The strange twists my world took never surprised me, but often disgusted me.

"So, this is his hotel and casino now?" Carter asked as we drove into the lot, though he knew the answer.

"That's what I hear," I replied, "but as you know, I've kept my distance."

"When you go in, I'll keep my earpiece connected to your phone. I will hang in the casino. If you need help, you simply need to say my name."

"I won't need help, Sergeant," I replied. "Just like killing a man who was drugged is not Filini's style, Moretti has an opportunity to gloat with me today. He will not cloud that opportunity with anything below the surface."

"I'm sure you're right, but regardless, I will be here," he replied.

"Understood."

I turned off the car, climbed out, and handed the keys to the valet. "You gentlemen staying at the hotel or just visiting the casino?" the valet asked, implying my car would be taken someplace different depending on my answer.

"Just visiting," I replied. "And take good care of her, she's a classic."

The valet was polite but I don't think he was overly impressed with my 1974 shit-brown Camaro as there was a 2018 Tesla Model S P100D parked directly in front of me. Carter walked around and met me on the curb and together we made our way into the lobby. The hotel was left and the casino right. I opted for left to try to locate my old friend.

"How can I help you?" the concierge asked.

I pulled out my identification and replied, "I need to speak with Ross Moretti."

"Oh, excellent, Mr. O'Malley. Mr. Moretti has been expecting you." The concierge replied without hesitation and immediately picked up his house phone and dialed what looked to be three numbers. Both Carter and I were surprised by the quick response as well as the words used. Why was Moretti expecting me?

Carter leaned forward and whispered. "You sure you want to do this alone?"

"Absolutely," I replied. "Just keep your earpiece in."

Carter dialed my phone, which I answered. He nodded that he could hear me through his earpiece and then headed toward the casino. I placed my phone in my shirt pocket and glanced back toward the man in front of me on the phone. He was speaking but not toward me. It was probably intentional but I didn't care. I had only one goal—to determine how I could meet with Marco Filini.

"Detective O'Malley?" he said drawing my attention.

"Yes."

"Head straight down that hallway to the end. Go left and you will see some double doors. Go through the doors and take the elevator down one level. The offices and security are downstairs. A guard will lead to you to Mr. Moretti's personal office."

"Thank you," I replied and immediately headed in the direction described. It took about five minutes to actually navigate the hallways. The description was much easier than the actual path. Upon entering the elevator I felt my phone vibrate. I pulled it out of my chest pocket where I saw the screen reading "no service." *So much for backup*, I thought to myself.

The doors opened and I'm not sure what I thought they would open to, but what they did was not it. I felt like I was entering NASA or some other high security outfit. It was a large open room set up in a circle with computers and screens all around. There must have been two to three hundred individual camera screens and then a bank of extremely large screens on the far wall. There was a great deal of noise that reminded me more of an amusement park than a security office. However, I did not have much time to take this in before a hand grabbed my arm from the side.

"Detective O'Malley. We do not allow any guns in this area, but my boss has given you clearance to keep yours. I would ask that under no circumstances should you remove it from your person. If there is any security breach, my team will handle it."

I glanced at the individual before me and took in what I could. Truthfully, there was not much to see. He was in fairly good shape. He wore a decent suit and did have a badge but the only name I could read was "Brett." I didn't know if that was his first or last name. I nodded understanding but I didn't actually speak. I knew this was just posturing again. That was always what Moretti was about. By him allowing me to keep my gun it was as if he was saying, "even with a gun you cannot touch me." The man that still held my arm was the stereotypical head of security. He most likely was former Army. He was too rough around the edges to be Marine or Navy. He also most likely had no security training other than what he learned while serving. I respected anyone who served. They simply began to lose my respect depending on how they acted after their time was done.

I glanced down to where he held my arm. Again I didn't speak but I knew my message was clear. He did not release my arm as quickly as he should have, but he did release it. Point made by both. "Come with me," he stated. "Mr. Moretti is expecting you."

Hearing it from the concierge was powerful. Hearing it a second time was overkill. It lost some of its significance. Just like Moretti. He always took things just a bit too far. "Good, I've been looking forward to seeing him as well."

The security guard smiled as if to say, "Sure you have, asshole." We didn't have to walk far to reach another set of double doors. The guard pressed a buzzer on the wall outside the doors.

"Yes?"

"Mr. Moretti. This is George. I have Detective O'Malley here for you."

"Great, George, send him in," echoed a voice through the intercom on the wall. The door buzzed and opened about two inches.

"You can go on in. When you're finished, Mr. Moretti will page me to escort you out. You are not to walk unescorted at any time down here. Do you understand?"

I did not answer the question. "Are you telling me your name is George Brett? Like the baseball player?"

"Yes, that is my name. Not too bad having the same name as one of the greatest players of all time," he replied, his expression showing a mixture of pride and concern if I was going to make fun of him.

"If you say so," I replied and pushed by. Truth be told, I was a Kansas native and when I was a boy, my father fed me nothing but George Brett, Bo Jackson, Amos Otis, Frank White, and every other Royal great of the 70s and 80s. I had nothing negative to say about Brett other than he should be offended that this loser shared his name.

"Detective Tomas O'Malley. I would say it was nice to see you but since the last time we saw each other you were lying under oath, I think you would know my comment too was false."

"Hello, Ross, may I call you Ross?" His office was huge. I assumed he had to knock out some walls and combine several offices to create this space. It was also immaculate. Deep walnut desk and built-in wall shelves with wainscoting all around the bottom half. There was a built-in bar, not minibar but full bar to the far left and fireplace to the right. His desk was huge and clean. There was not a paper on it. I wondered if he actually worked or just sat in there and peed his pants. There was a sculpture of a naked woman wrapped on a pole on his desk. It appeared to be black marble. It was actually a very nice sculpture if not for the naked woman on a pole. That simply made it tacky.

Moretti stood. "No, I don't think you may call me Ross." He placed both hands on his desk. "I should tell you that I knew it wouldn't take long for you to come and see me. You wouldn't be able to obey the court. I really thought it would take you until summer, so you even beat my timeline. I have already called the authorities.

They will be here shortly to pick you up, and the fact that your sergeant is here with you only supports the harassment you're dealing to me. So Tommy, why don't you do yourself a favor and turn around and slowly walk out that door. I will have Mr. Brett come and politely escort your sorry ass out of my hotel. The hotel I own specifically because of everything you did to more than double my wealth."

I knew this rant was coming so I just let it flow. He had what he wanted to say ready to go so my best option was just to let it happen. When he finished, I calmly stepped forward and took a seat in a large leather chair in front of his desk. He remained standing. "Oh," I said drawn out in a tone of pure pleasure. "This chair is incredible." I meant it also.

He immediately softened. "You're telling me. They are something, aren't they?"

"Incredible does not cover it," I replied as Moretti took his seat. It was just that easy. One compliment to stroke his ego and he was back in my hand. "I don't even want to know what you paid for these."

"Six thousand dollars each," he replied proudly.

"Get out!" I exclaimed.

"Seriously. I brought them in from Italy. They were custom made to the size I specified. They normally build chairs to fit someone who is 5'10" tall. But I wanted chairs to fit someone 6'2" because I typically meet with men."

"Wow," I replied again. "Impressive." I paused and pretended to look down at the legs and the craftsmanship. I then lifted my eyes back up to him. "I am not here to harass you. I need your help."

If stroking his ego over a nice chair was good for me, I might as well have sung a song of praise to him when I stated I needed his help. He sat back in his chair and stretched his arms slowly over his head. "You tried to have me arrested for murder. Why in the hell would I help you?"

"Ross, with all due respect, you drugged me, put a dead body in my trunk, and tried to have me arrested for that murder."

He raised a finger. "I heard about that, but it must have been my old partner behind that tragedy. Thank God you were able to get clear of that mess."

"Moretti, listen to me. I have no desire to do some dance with you about all this bullshit. I am not here to get anything from you but a location. I need to speak with Marco."

His eyes immediately narrowed. "Do you think I'm a fool? Even if I wanted to help you, giving up any information about Marco Filini is something I would never consider." He shook his head and sarcastically added, "You may not have heard this before, but I think Marco is a professional killer."

"Yep, I heard," I replied. "And somebody out there is framing him, and I know there's no way he would have done the murders he is allegedly being accused of. I need to speak to him to clear him, but really I need to speak to him to know if he knows who the hell is really behind all that's going on. We are at a loss and all signs point to Filini." I was stretching the truth quite a bit but Moretti was right, giving up Filini would not do well for him. The only chance it would be worth the risk is if Moretti would be helping him by doing so. He was clearly chewing on my last comments, and he didn't reply and stalled for time by standing and pacing behind his desk.

"I have no reason to believe you, but I will at least make a call. On the off chance you're telling the truth, it may work out well for me, and if you're not, letting him know you're playing these games will also work well for me."

"That is all I am asking."

"You know, whether you're a detective or not, he will kill you without thought." Moretti was not trying to be dramatic, he was simply stating how he saw the facts.

I smiled. "I don't think so, Ross, but I appreciate the comment." I pulled out my card and grabbed a pen from a holder on his desk. I wrote my cell phone number on the back of the card. "Why don't you give me a call after you speak to him and let me know where we can meet, or better yet, have him call me?"

He took the card and I placed the pen in my shirt pocket. "Maybe we can all get together and break bread," he replied, taking the card.

"No, I really just need to speak to him." That was my way of telling Ross that a contract killer was more important than he was.

He didn't reply but reached up to press a button on his phone. There was a loud buzz then he said, "George, can you come and escort our guest out of the building please? And scoop up his friend on the way."

"On my way, boss," a voice returned.

Within ten minutes, both Carter and I were back outside waiting for our car.

"You okay?" asked Carter.

"Yep," I replied.

"Did you get the information you needed?"

I nodded. "Not yet, but I am one step closer. I'm not sure Filini will meet, but knowing him as I do, I think he will call."

13 CARTER AND I hit Mr. J's on the way back to the station picking up burgers for the group. I had called ahead to see what the team was doing, and Halterman told me they had broken down every individual remotely involved and in order of motive, organized them on the evidence board. She claimed it didn't tell much new information, but you never know what might come up with two new sets of eyes coming in after the fact.

When we arrived at the station, Franky was on the phone at his desk but his stare made me concerned. We dropped off the burgers in the Royals Interrogation Room which is where they had organized the suspect layout. The four of us were in the room with Franky still on the phone.

"Who is he talking to?" I asked Huston.

"I don't know," she replied. "I think another department, maybe in the suburbs."

"Okay," I said. "We'll see what that's about when he gets off the phone. Until then, why don't you run Carter and me through what you guys have?"

Huston and Halterman ran through all the work they had put together. They had in essence, put together a dossier on each person involved in the case. They had four tiers: highly suspect involvement, involved, ancillary involvement, and victim. I was most interested in the highly suspect and involved categories. In the highly suspect category sat Jack Kittleson, Robert Bales, Herb Whychoff, and Bill Ronin. In the involved category were Nate Kittleson, Becky Kittleson, Dan Malecha, and a question mark by Ross Moretti and Marco Filini. Now I didn't think either of the last two individuals were involved, but they absolutely could be individuals with information. Tapping into that information is where my challenge would be. What struck me, however, was that out of the first six people, half of them had the last name of Kittleson.

As I was wrestling with these thoughts, Franky hung up his desk phone and walked into the room. "I think we need to take a drive."

"Where to?" I asked.

"Downers Grove."

Instantly my mind went to the teachers and Bales in nearby Naperville. "What happened in Downers?"

It seems a house you sent a car to watch was burned to the ground early this morning. The car there said that one second it was just a house, and the next it was engulfed in flames. They called the fire department immediately but could do nothing but watch it burn. By the time fire and rescue got on the scene, the house was a total loss. There are two dead bodies inside. They said you met with them yesterday."

"Whychoff and Ronin. The teachers on the committee," Halterman said.

I walked up to the board and took their pictures down from the involved category and moved them to the victim category.

"How in the world did they get the house to burn so quickly?" asked Franky, now grabbing his burger to go. "We had the house under surveillance."

"They had to use some sort of accelerant," Carter stated.

"Yeah, but we had a car there the whole time. How did they get it in place without us seeing?"

"Shit!" I blurted out. "It's fucking March. How could I have been so stupid?"

"What, Tommy? What are you thinking?"

"It's fucking March." I repeated.

"Yeah, it's March. So what?" asked Franky again.

"When we walked up to the house, I tripped."

"What do you mean, you tripped?" asked Franky.

Patti added, "Fuck is right. Who sprays lawns in the winter? It was almost below freezing last night. There's no lawn winterization that takes place in March." She paused then added, "The killer was right there in front of us, and we just let him drive away."

"I even smelled it. I knew that smell too. My mind said it was fertilizer because of that damn sign. It was kerosene."

Carter now jumped in. "Are you telling me our guys watched a fake lawn service spray kerosene all over the lawn and the house so they could come and torch it later right in front of them?"

"That's exactly what I'm saying. Whoever did this somehow knew the teachers would be staying together in that house. They somehow commandeered a truck to make it appear they were a lawn service, but instead had the sole purpose of burning down a house with two committee members inside."

"Jesus, Tommy," interrupted Patti. "According to the police on the scene, there was a Pest-Go truck at Bales' house an hour or so before we got there. You don't think..."

"Who sprays for bugs in the winter?" interjected Carter.

"Nobody," I replied. "Patti, call Bales' house and get his family out of there." Turning to Karen Huston, I added, "Karen, call the Naperville Police. They should still have a car out front. Have them go into the house and clear it. Send additional cars there and prevent anyone from approaching the house."

Carter was listening to all the directions and didn't interfere, although it was really his place to make the call. As I took a break from issuing commands, he used the opportunity to speak. "Franky, once Patti is done, get your things and head to Naperville and gather up Bales. I want him in the station within two hours. O'Malley, Huston—you two get to Downers and gather any information you can on the fire. I'll stay here and help organize the efforts."

We began to break up when Ass-One and Ass-Two walked into the office. "I thought we agreed to share information, O'Malley," stated Adam Only. "My boss, the governor, will not be happy if I report otherwise."

"Shut up, Only," interjected Carter. "My team is following up on leads. I am sending them to a house fire now."

"Well, we don't care about any local house fire. We are only interested in the vigilante murder case." Detective Only smiled smugly and sat on the edge of Franky's desk pushing several things around the desk with his ass as he sat.

"Perfect," stated Carter. "We just laid out our suspect board in the Royals room. Why don't you check it out and come find me if you have any questions."

"Good," said Detective Toose, slightly surprised at the openness. "Only and I will review your board while they are at the fire and if we have questions, we can regroup after."

I was smiling slightly under my breath but didn't let it show. "Remember One and Two," I started, leaving the Ass title off in my boss's presence, "this is a two-way street. I am sure you have almost solved this case already so you will need to share what you know."

"Of course," replied Toose again. "We do have a fairly solid suspect already. We were looking to bring this person in."

Shit! They were going to bring in Jack Kittleson first, I immediately thought. I shook my head trying to appear surprised and impressed in one look. "Can I ask who?"

Toose looked toward Only and immediately Only took the lead. "I don't mind sharing. You will find out later today when we bring her in. We need the parents to be available because she's a minor. We immediately narrowed it down to a high school student due to the type of crime, which put Leah Malecha at the top of the list. The first murder, Mark Schulman, was a kid who was a well-known bully. We found evidence that Malecha was one of the many online victims of the Schulman boy. Further, there's a picture of her with her father and a trophy deer on Facebook, so she has grown up around rifles; and not to mention the obvious, it was her car used in the hit-and-run. Definitely too much of a coincidence."

I shook my head but didn't speak. I had reviewed the entire file we had built on Leah Malecha. She had been a person of interest for us, but only for about the length of one interview. Our notes were very clear to that effect on our evidence board. I leaned over and whispered to my partner. She smiled and without comment left the room heading toward the Royals Room. It took her only about thirty seconds to emerge with a file. If she did what I suggested, she left just enough information on Leah Malecha to not rule her out. I didn't want anyone, especially a rape victim, wrongly interviewed, but I did want her father brought back in for further questioning. I would free up any suspicion on Leah before Ass-One and Ass-Two could do any damage, but I would use the time to speak with Dan about his anger with the school committee as described by Bill Ronin. It appeared now that Bill Ronin was dead. Did that place Dan Malecha closer to the top of our suspect list?

I had allowed enough time to pass. I grabbed a file off my desk, a file I didn't need, I just needed to grab something, and waved toward Huston. "Come on, let's get to the fire. If the initial report is correct, we may have a victim or two in the remains." Turning to Carter. "I think Naperville is covered by the Joliet ME. Can you pull some strings and get Elise to take it?"

"I will see what I can do," replied Carter. "But you know, just like cops, medical examiners don't like to mess with jurisdiction either."

I nodded but was already mostly out the door. "Toose, Only—make sure you do not remove anything and if you have additional information, let's discuss it. We are working together on this."

●　　●　　●　　●　　●

Huston and I arrived at the fire thirty-five minutes after leaving the station. She had never been to the house, but there really was not much left to see. The house was a complete loss. There was about fifty feet on both sides between where this house had once stood and the two neighboring houses. Both neighboring houses were originally painted white and their walls adjacent to the burned house were now blackened with soot. I looked east and saw Herb Whychoff's house, still standing tall. Bill Ronin's house was reduced to items like refrigerators and a safe and a handful of other items that simply would not burn. I was pleased when I saw Doc G on the scene.

She walked over to me almost immediately. "Why am I here, Tommy? You know my counterpart. He already doesn't like you. When he heard you were behind the request, it only caused more friction."

"It's the same case as the hit-and-run boy, the counselor, and the teacher shooting," I replied, my voice lowered so as not to alert any news media nearby.

Instantly her expression changed. "You're kidding me. All the way out here?"

I shook my head. "My gut tells me there are two teachers in there. One is Bill Ronin and the other Herb Whychoff. I met with both yesterday. Both were on the same committee that gave oversight to the Schulman complaints."

She lifted her hand. "I don't want to know any more. Let my investigation do the work for me. Knowing this, the case would have been transferred to me anyway so I can handle Joliet. I already met with Johnson briefly. He will be handling the fire investigation. He already implied some sort of accelerant was used."

"Yeah, I think it was applied through a cover of a lawn company. Probably encircled the house." I looked down and saw the old lawn service flag I had tripped on previously. It had been trampled down by numerous feet working the fire. I bent down and picked it up. "Green-Go Lawn Service. We better give them a call to see if they had any service in the area."

"Find out what you can and I will speak to Johnson about your theory. Tough to provide lawn care when the ground is frozen." She began to walk away and lifted her radio to communicate the new information to her team in the process.

"That was our thought also," I added, speaking mostly to her back.

"Who is Johnson?" asked Huston.

"Tony Johnson. Arson investigator. He covers all the western suburbs but worked Chicago for over 25 years. Good man, and friend. He will shoot straight with us."

We gathered what information we could, but in all honesty, there was not much we could do here. Doc G in conjunction with several local police, did confirm the presence of two bodies. They were not identifiable other than the fact that they were both male. Doc G would not even estimate an age based on the remains. She said she would rush the autopsies, but it would most likely be tomorrow before she had anything conclusive. We also confirmed both suspected victims were missing. We were able to connect with Herb Whychoff's wife. She and their two kids had left to stay with her parents. She said Herb was going to remain at their house. He was not there at the time although his car was. I did not confirm anything to her and would not until we had made a positive ID. However, I already had made mine.

When Huston and I reconnected at my car, she confirmed that Franky and Halterman had obtained Robert Bales and he was being transported to the station. She also learned from Carter that Toose and Only had arranged for Leah Malecha to be brought in for questioning and both her parents were joining. Carter had also confirmed that Go-Green Lawn Care was a snow removal company in the winter and operated under the name Go-Snow Road Care. They had not reported any trucks missing but because there hadn't been any snowfall requiring plow service in more than a week, they wouldn't have known if there had been. All trucks were currently in their yard.

After briefly touching base with both Johnson and Doc G and learning their reports wouldn't be available at least until tomorrow, Huston and I headed back to the station. I wanted to be present before Leah arrived so I could douse the flame from Only and Toose immediately, though I knew A-1 and A-2 would not take my direction easily. There was no way I was going to let them dig hard into a victim that I believe was raped.

"Are you guys going back to Flap Jaws tonight?" Huston asked out of the blue.

I'm sure she noticed my stutter. Flap Jaws was Franky's and my place. Nobody else should call it their home away from home unless they were invited, and one invite did not automatically give you a pass going forward. "I doubt it. Kansas is playing in the sweet 16 tonight. I have an acquaintance on the team whose family lives up here. I was going to have them possibly come over if they were available." I paused, then added, "And we don't go to Flap Jaws every night. Last night was just one of those planets aligning scenarios."

She quickly recovered. "Oh, I know. That was just my way of saying I think we both, Patti and I, had a nice time seeing that side of you guys. You know, a human side."

I didn't offer any more talk about it. Usually I speak too much. Over the years I had learned that sometimes things just needed to settle.

14 HUSTON AND I arrived at the station at 3:00 PM. My partner and Franky were already there. My immediate concern was they were in a closed-door meeting with Toose and Only and their voices were definitely raised. Franky had dealt with these two jerks for several years so I knew they were in good hands, but there was no reason our new partners needed to experience this. Carter motioned with his eyes for us to go join.

I passed by the Bulls interrogation room and saw the Malecha family sitting quietly inside. Our eyes met and I could tell they held some concern. I wanted to tell them to remain calm but in truth, having them a little on edge usually meant for a better exchange. Leah simply held her head down low and again I knew my only goal was to free her from this burden. When I got in front of the Royals room, I could hear the voices behind the door going fairly strong.

"I don't care what you think, Detective Sullivan, this is our case as stated by the governor and we will handle it exactly as we see fit."

"Take it easy, Only," I stated as I entered. "As I said when we left, we are working together on this."

"Working together, my ass," he repeated. "Tell me, O'Malley, what was the fire you were just at?"

I smiled immediately though I should have hidden it. "A bad scene," I started. "Looks like arson. A house burned to the ground with two inside. Horrible. Just horrible."

He walked up to me. "Funny, you left out that the two dead bodies are part of the fucking school committee."

"Holy shit!" I exclaimed. "How in the hell do you know that? The ME told me her report would not even be done until tomorrow. Jesus, you GiST boys have connections."

"Cut the crap, Tommy," broke in Toose. "You requested Doctor Gerstenberger because you knew the case was related. We learned that from Joliet. Either we are working together or we are not."

"You tell us?" added Only, now only a few inches from my face.

"First," I began, "you need to take three steps back and remove yourself from my face."

Only pressed his lips together but complied with the request.

"Secondly, we are here to work with you. That is why we shared all our information. Our entire case is on this board, front and center. You were not needed at a leveled house any more than we were. My presence there was simply to confirm there were bodies inside the house I visited just yesterday."

"You were at the house that burned down yesterday?" asked Toose.

"My partner and I were, and we met with both individuals I now believe to be dead." I moved over passing right by Only and even brushing his arm slightly as if to say "get the fuck out of my way." I took a seat at the center of the table. "Now, if you will both cool your jets and listen, maybe we can solve this case."

Detective Only turned and leaned one hand down on the table so he could again get closer to me. "This is our case. As long as you understand and respect that fact, then maybe we can solve this. Otherwise, the 'we' in that will very quickly not include any of you."

I now stood. "How well do you know Governor Little?" He was about to answer until I raised my hand. "Let me rephrase. How well do you think I know Governor Little?"

Detective Only stared hard at me. Only was not the best detective, but he was not stupid either. He knew I had been around a lot longer than him. He knew I knew people and politics probably better than any other detective in the history of Chicago homicide. My question was would he call my bluff. Sure, I knew the governor. I knew his name and there may have been one or two people I knew pretty well that knew him. But the implication that I truly knew him was completely a bluff. Only was claiming he would get me kicked off the case. I was telling him without actually saying it, *go ahead and try.*

Only lifted his hand from the table and stood up. "Listen, the true goal is to solve the case. Let's get to it. We have wasted enough time as it is."

I don't know who crapped their pants first, me or Franky, whereas Huston and Halterman carried one hell of an impressed look on their faces. If I had my way, I would never tell them the truth.

"First off," I began, "Leah Malecha is a rape victim, plain and simple. She was not capable of performing any of these crimes nor did she have opportunity. She also does not have a temper or angry streak in her body. There is e-mail evidence that she was even considering taking the jackass back. Put all that aside and the physical evidence does not match. The shoe size, for starters. We obtained excellent shoe prints at the hit-and-run. Although it could be a woman, she would have to be a woman with incredibly large feet. Leah does not fit the bill."

"What the hell, O'Malley," stated Only immediately. "You are not going to tell me who I can and can't interrogate."

"When it comes to a rape victim who I'm sure did not have anything to do with this case, I absolutely will. However, I let you bring her in because we need to get some time with her dad alone. Dan Malecha presents a different position."

I went on to explain the information we had on the father, his anger, and actions. I also explained where we obtained that information and now suddenly those witnesses were gone. That fact only added to the circumstantial evidence warranting an additional conversation. By the time I finished, Leah was not going to be interviewed officially, but Toose and Only would sit with her and her mother while Patti and I pulled Dan into the next room. This provided A-1 and A-2 the satisfaction that they were still sitting with their "star" suspect but also got me in front of one of mine.

I walked into the Bulls Room to a somewhat tense subject in the form of Dan Malecha. "Hello again, Detective. To say I would like to know what the hell is going on here would be an understatement."

I nodded and took a seat across from him with my partner sitting to my right. "Hello, Mr. Malecha," I began. Peggy and Leah had already been escorted to a secondary room with Toose and Only so we could speak alone with Dan. "I'm sure you're wondering why you and your family are here."

"And why I am not with them?" he added in a very rigid tone.

I lifted my cheek muscles slightly causing one side of my mouth to turn upward showing I was choosing my words carefully. I had several options. I could be creative, try to work him into a mistake or a story, I could give some examples and talk about the murders trying to determine what he knew, or I could simply be honest. I believed he was more concerned about his wife and daughter at that moment and honesty seemed the best route. If I was wrong, I would severely damage any chance of gaining anything from him. However, if I was right, he would give us a few key clues that would help me verify his involvement, or lack thereof, once and for all. There was one zinger Halterman had found out in her investigation that only she and I knew. I would let her plant that seed when the time was right.

"To be completely frank, Dan," I began, "you are a suspect who warrants further discussion. Your family is fine and they are not being questioned in regard to anything about the case in particular, so I don't want you worrying about them, but I do want to speak to you."

He threw his arms in the air and then dropped them back to the table. His ears turned instantly red, I mean very red. Almost everyone had a *tell*–that involuntary action that occurs whether you want it to or not that signals something about you.

My immediate guess, red ears equaled anger. By the tone in his voice, it really was not a guess. "Well, that is just fabulous. You have half the damn police force working this case and you are spending all your time talking to a father who just wants the whole ordeal to go away. Do you think it is easier or harder on my daughter seeing this on the news every day? Hell, the school is shutdown indefinitely. All she's doing is sitting at home having friends call, text, and post every minute of every day about the whole fucking thing." He stood but kept both hands on the table. To be honest, he was a large man in fairly good shape, and he was at least fifteen years younger than me. I was not worried about an altercation, but the red in his ears had moved to his face and you can never be one hundred percent sure of an angry man's actions. "I am leaving and taking my family with me."

"What did you do with the twenty thousand dollars?" broke in Detective Halterman before Dan Malecha could take one step toward the door.

"Oh, that's your evidence. A twenty thousand withdrawal? Fuck off."

"Sit down, Mr. Malecha," I stated sternly. "You don't want us arresting you just to keep you here for questioning. I can hold you for forty-eight hours as a person of interest. You may be angry and you may be a lot of things, but I don't think you're a man that wants to look at your daughter from behind bars, even for two days."

His motion toward the door stopped and he turned to face me. "You're bluffing. You have nothing to hold me on."

"Listen, Dan," I replied. "Do I think you committed these crimes? I don't know, but the point of this discussion is for you to show me how *you* can prove you didn't. This is your chance to rule yourself out. Now you can use your profanity and play hardball if you like, but if you know nothing more about me, I never bluff." That was bullshit, I always bluffed.

The redness in his face began to fade, but his ears held their color. They actually looked hot. He slowly and reluctantly took his seat. "What do you want to know? I will give you five minutes."

Again he wanted to control things and the long-time interrogator in me just could not let that happen. "Actually, if it takes five hours, you and your family will still be here, but I think we can keep it closer to fifteen. I guess it all depends on you."

"His lips were still pressed tightly together and his words were short and concise. "Like I said, Detective, what do you want to know?"

"Let's start with the 20K," I replied. "What was it for and where did it go?"

"Westfield Ford, in LaGrange," he stated. "You may not have realized it, but we needed a new car. I put 20K down on a Ford C-Max for my daughter. Next question."

Yeah, he was really not pleased and the temper was still rising. "Okay, you know we will check that out."

"Really, based on the police work I have seen so far, I actually am not sure you will be able to find it."

Fair enough, I thought. "What was your reaction to the school discipline committee when they informed you that there was no evidence to support your daughter's claims?"

His face was now instantly red again. "You mean, when my daughter who was raped by another one of their students and this 'committee' as you call them did no investigation and came back to us pushing my daughter to reconcile with the creep and forget everything–is that what you mean about how did I react to how they handled my daughter's claims?"

I nodded. "Yes, when Principal Bales told your family just that, what did you do?" I wanted to know if this man would be honest with me. A guilty man would claim that it was hard to hear but that he understood. He would take all suspicion off of him by showing he could handle the bad news without question. An innocent man would say it like it was.

"I wanted to kill all of them, but especially that woman, the counselor."

Okay, by my theory he was innocent, but that statement took him from innocent to *holy shit, are you guilty?* "Wow, Mr. Malecha, you do know that Dawn Wells, the counselor, was murdered, correct?"

"I do," he replied sternly. "And if you think I spilled one tear about it, you're wrong." He paused and I saw something in his demeanor change. "Do you have kids, Detective O'Malley?"

"I do," I replied. "Two older children."

"Then, especially in your line of work, there have been times when they were hurting and there was nothing you could do about it."

"Of course," I replied. Normally I would not let a witness drive an interview, but Dan was becoming more emotional, and with that more honest.

"Well, that's what happened with me. My daughter was hurting tremendously— the type of hurt that lasts a lifetime. The type of hurt that will require counseling. I would have done almost anything to protect her, but in the end I couldn't kill anyone. I cry when I kill a deer but my wife's damn family makes me go with them." He paused and caught himself a bit. "So if you're asking me if I was mad, if I wanted to throw each of them through a wall, absolutely. If you're asking if I took my daughter's car and ran the boy down or murdered the counselor in that drum, then my answer is no, but I also didn't cry when I heard they were gone."

"Where were you Tuesday afternoon?" I asked.

"I was at work the entire day. I didn't even leave for lunch."

"Can anyone corroborate that for us?" I asked in response.

"Yes, everyone I work with as well as cameras throughout the site." His eyes raised. "Is that when the teacher was shot?"

I didn't answer that question. "What do you know about Bill Ronin and Herb Whychoff?"

He raised an eyebrow as he thought. "They were on the committee. To be honest, I don't even know what classes they taught. I don't think Leah had them for any class."

"Do you know where they live?" I asked.

His voice had lost much of its harshness. "No. Did something happen to them?"

Again I ignored the question. "Where were you yesterday afternoon and evening, including through the night?"

"With everything going on, when I am not at work, I am home."

I smiled and leaned back in my chair. "I assume your family can confirm that?"

"They can, because they were all home with me," he replied.

Halterman got up and walked out of the room. I assumed she was running down the hall to ask them that very question. It was a moot point for me. Dan Malecha was either one of the best liars out there, which was possible, or he was not guilty. I had criminals like this in the past that could speak with passion, change their demeanor, and basically make me feel like they were not the killer only to find them sitting over a body in their home two days later. I did not feel Dan was that guy.

Within moments, Patti re-entered the room. "Sorry, just had to step out for a second," she said. "Did I miss anything?"

"No," I replied. "Everything on your end check out?"

"It did," she stated.

"Dan," I began, turning back to him. "How would you like to go back and join your wife and daughter?"

"I would, very much," he replied.

Without another word, I stood and motioned him to get up as well. The three of us walked back to the conference room where Toose and Only were still grilling the mother and daughter. "I trust you four had a nice conversation?" I asked, looking toward the Malechas for a response to make sure these two assholes didn't cross any lines.

I was disappointed when I saw Leah's face clearly had signs of recent tears. However, her response was borderline acceptable. "I think it was fine. They just wanted to know about Mark. It's just hard to talk about it sometimes."

I turned to leave the room. "Well, you are all free to head home now. I do truly appreciate your flexibility in coming down."

Dan Malecha pressed the back of his hand on my chest, and then turned his hand out to shake. "Thank you, Detective."

"Thank you, Dan. I wish only the best for you and your family."

After several minutes, the three left, and my collective team sat staring at each other like children in front of a campfire. "Where do we go from here?" asked Detective Halterman. "Dan Malecha surely is not guilty."

"Are you serious?" questioned Only. "What better motive than a daughter hurt, and revenge on the people that refused to help her for their own well-being. Further, Carter told me there is a question about his finances."

"Halterman is right," I responded. "The finance issue was a cash withdrawal for a car. He told us where, and we will follow the money and check it out. Everything else about him screams hurt father but not murderer."

"But he has motive?" Only replied again.

I turned to him. "I know it would be easy to call him guilty, but I just talked to him. The guy is not the killer, and he has alibis that will be easily confirmed, and if it is motive you want, check out the Schulman boy's social media. There are dozens of families with motive."

There was pause while Only let out a deep breath that he wasn't buying it. I don't know if he didn't believe or trust me, or if he simply just wanted to arrest somebody so he could tell the governor, my good friend, that he had arrested someone. I believe mostly the latter.

Patti broke the silence. "What if there is a suspect we have not considered?"

All eyes turned to her but it was Carter who replied, "What are you talking about?"

She waved everyone to follow her back into the Royals Room. She pointed to the board. "We listed out this group here of social media victims as a group of unknowns we have not followed up on."

"Right," I said, supporting her direction but not sure where she was taking it.

"You," she pointed to me, "just said there were dozens of families with motives. I think we have all agreed that just being bullied on Twitter is a big leap to murder, but I think we also know that usually rapists don't rape just one person."

Now I was tracking her thought.

She continued. "What if one of these social media victims was also raped, possibly before Leah Malecha? Then, the rumors get passed around about Leah and the committee and that triggers the person."

I stepped forward and added, "In that scenario, let's say the individual was dating Schulman first. They would not only have the previous rape as enough motive, but then add to it Schulman had broken up with them or cheated on them with Leah."

"Pretty thin," stated Franky.

"Yep, but worth some follow-up," I replied.

Franky reached down to the table and grabbed a large file. "IT put together a full packet on each of his social media accounts. I have scanned it but not good enough to determine a primary victim list."

The file was not a file but a three-ring binder that was packed at least four inches thick. "It looks like we have some reading to do tonight," Halterman said looking at me.

Huston asked, "Did you get in touch with your friends who want to watch the basketball game?"

Carter interjected, "Ah that's right, the Kansas game is tonight. You mentioned that last week. Are the Jacksons coming over?"

I began to see the writing on the wall and I was not sure I liked it. "They are," I replied reluctantly.

"Are we all still invited?" interrupted Franky.

I knew I either had to act like an ass or open my arms to this before it went south. I chose the arms.

"Sure, everyone head on over. The game is at 7:00, come by any time before that."

They all seemed pleased until Franky remembered, "Hey, where is Bales? When we brought him in, we told him to wait in that conference room, and it's empty."

Carter smiled at the instant reactions from everyone, including me. It was as if we had just realized we had lost something so important that it now completely consumed our mind. "His wife drove up and got him. They went to grab some food and then he said he would come back."

"Were you able to meet with him at all before the Malechas arrived?" I asked.

Franky looked toward my partner who had joined him on the drive. She nodded back to him to continue. "Well, Patti gave him the third and fourth degree on the drive, but I think our takeaway was the guy was just a flipping jerk at the time of the committee decisions. If I believe what he says now, he realizes his mistakes. He received notice from the school board that he's on temporary unpaid leave, so he has a bit of personal depression on top of the tragedy of the whole situation. Do I think the guy is possibly one of the worst principals I have personally run across? My answer is yes. Do I think his life could be in danger? My answer is absolutely yes. Do I think he knows who the killer is? My answer is no. He's just a scared former principal who doesn't know what direction the rest of his life is going."

I turned to Carter. "I don't need to talk to him if Franky is good with what he heard. Are you going to give him protection?"

"We already offered it out of our office," broke in Detective Only. "The governor didn't want another screw-up like the fire."

That last comment was directed at me. I took it. "You know, Toose and Only, you are both welcome at my house as well," I added, completely taking them by surprise. "The invite was for everyone." I was not serious and I hoped they did not accept it, but it was equally in their face as Only's last stab. Both Carter and Franky had to pick their jaws off the floor.

"Uh, no, thank you," Only replied. "We are going to run through the case over dinner and then head home. Thank you for the offer though."

"I think we all should just leave this case here tonight," Carter interjected. "We all need to take a break and let it sink in a bit. We have several suspects but no good suspects. I think we all agree we need to speak further with Jack Kittleson, but we also realize the challenges with these murders being performed by someone whose primary residence is in Minnesota and who works a full-time job. And so you are all aware, a job he has been at every day during this whole ordeal."

I think everyone was waiting for someone to give this type of guidance. It was getting late in the day and when you deal with murder after murder and you focus all on one case, sometimes you simply need to step back. Toose and Only walked over to a desk, presumably to wait for Bales to return. Carter headed to his office. I knew he would stay there until he headed my way. I grabbed my things as did Franky and our two partners, and we all left. We each went our own direction but agreed to be back at my house by 6:30. Andrea Jackson and her daughter Jessica would be over by six and I think even Rosalyn Clark, the widow of Tom Clark, my old friend in vice who died several months ago tied to the Moretti and Polino case, may also come by. Without intending it, I was going to have a party.

15 "HELLO, ANDREA, IT'S NICE to see you again," said Carter as he reached his arms out to embrace her.

"And you as well, Sergeant. Have you been well?"

"Very well, thank you for asking." He turned to Andrea's daughter. "Oh, Jessica, you look wonderful." He did not reach out to hug her as he knew she was sensitive to touching ever since her kidnapping and the horrible things surrounding it.

"Thank you, Mr. Carter," she said softly, a smile hidden well beneath her lowered eyes.

"Franky, long time no see," Carter said, turning to him as Franky had just taken a full tortilla chip covered in queso dip and plunged it into his mouth.

Unable to speak, Franky just lifted his head and smiled.

I walked over to Carter and shook his hand. "Sergeant, I'm glad you could make it. The game is just starting. I think everyone is here. Rosalyn, Karen, and Patti took over the kitchen so all we have to do is make sure everyone has what they want to drink." I handed him a beer which he refused to take.

"Do you have a McNaughton's?" he asked.

"I have stocked it ever since my first experience several months ago. I also got it permanently in place at Flap Jaws," I replied. "Start with this beer and I'll be back with one on the rocks."

"Perfect," he replied, turning toward the family room where the large screen television was. He walked into the room where both Andrea and Jessica had also made their way, Andrea taking the center seat on the couch in front of the TV. "May I sit next to you, ma'am?" he asked Andrea Jackson, the mother of Kansas' star forward Jamal Jackson.

"Absolutely, Sergeant, but I should warn you, should my boy make a bonehead play, sometimes I can't control what I strike so being within my reach may not be a good thing." She smiled as she spoke but it was clear there was truth behind it.

"She will," Jessica said from the single chair to the side.

"I'll take my chances. I have seen him play, and I don't think there's a bonehead play in him." Andrea seemed to like this comment but didn't take her eyes from the screen to acknowledge it.

The night went off without a hitch. My living room was not large enough for everyone, but we made due. The game was a great match-up and Kansas strolled into the Great Eight winning by double digits, Jamal Jackson being the high scorer at twenty-seven points.

It was a nice time for everyone. I'm ashamed to admit that both Patti and Karen fit in well. Further, they handled all the things I am not good at ensuring that glasses were filled, needs were met, and conversation continued. They were new enough that they could ask questions about the history, but knew not to pry into areas best left behind. It was clear to me, Jessica was still in pain. The young lady may never be free of it. Her case was one of those that brought me great pride in saving her, but also hurt like hell that I couldn't do it sooner. Those are the things that keep me up at night. I wake up sweating wondering what I was missing. Mark Schulman was that nightmare now. Regardless of what I thought about his actions, his parents deserved the same level of care in solving their son's murder. No killer is perfect, I knew that. I simply needed to find out what this killer did wrong.

•　　•　　•　　•　　•

It was 9:00 when everyone started to leave. By 9:30, it was Franky, me, and Patti. I think Franky wanted to run to Flap Jaws with me for an evening cocktail, but when it got down to just the three of us, I think he felt it was a crowd. There was also this BS about reviewing the social media file, which I did not feel like doing at all.

"Uh, Tommy, I think I'm going to head out. Vader needs a walk or I will be cleaning up another five pounder off my kitchen floor," he broke in, not part of any previous conversation.

"Vader?" Patti asked.

"My Newfoundland," he replied.

"You mean your significant other," I interjected.

"I would not say that. He is more like my roommate," Franky replied.

"Do you base all your timing and activities with him in mind?" I asked.

"Well, yes," he replied.

"Do you provide for him and make sure there's food and water?" I added.

"Well, of course I do, he's a..."

I cut him off. "Do you share a bed?"

"Hey now, I don't think that is..."

"Do you share a bed?" I asked again.

In a more somber voice, he replied, "Yes."

"Significant other," I confirmed.

Franky said nothing more but just waved his hand down at me with a grunt and turned to leave. "See ya, Halterman." He turned and pointed at me. "Tommy, get a life."

"Me?" I replied. "I don't sleep with a two-hundred pound dog."

Patti smiled probably larger than she needed to and added, "Good-bye, Franky. I will see you tomorrow."

In another huff, he slammed the door behind him.

"And then there were two," I said to myself.

"Well," Patti immediately stated. "What to do now?"

I was not sure what to do with that comment. Patti had definitely been flirting with me, at least I thought she had. I mean, what was all that crap with the hug and the towel. Yeah, she was flirting...or was she? I had no f'ing idea. I was not a ladies' man. I was barely able to speak to women. Tammi had been a fluke. And what about Tammi? She only left a few days ago, albeit she left seemingly without care. I mean, was it my fault she left? Absolutely not. I gave her three solid months of pure...

"What the hell are you thinking about?" Patti asked, staring at me from a few feet away. "You were looking right at me and didn't even blink. I could have been standing here naked and you would not have flinched."

I snapped out of my stupor and promptly went into not being able to speak stuttering over my words. "I, I, uh, I was just thinking."

"Thinking about what?" she said smiling.

I really didn't know what to say, and thankfully there was a knock at the door. I turned my head quickly. "Ah, what did you forget, Franky?" I hollered.

I ripped open the door about ready to make fun of him and then froze. "Tammi?"

In my doorway, looking incredible, was Tammi Hutchins, AKA my old girlfriend, AKA the bitch who took a new job half the country away without telling me. In my apartment looking fairly damn good herself was Patti Halterman, my new partner. This was a situation the best writer could not have dreamed up. This did not happen to twenty-plus-year divorced cops. Hell, this didn't happen to studs.

"Tommy?" Tammi said. "Can I come in?"

Again I stuttered over my words. "Ah, of course you may." I should have added-*oh my God it's so great to see you*, or *I can't believe you are here*, but I didn't. I stumbled over the five words and pulled the door open to reveal Patti, standing very casually in my entryway.

Tammi didn't see my new partner at first. She immediately began speaking as she stepped in. "I couldn't stay in California the way I left it. I handled it completely..." She stopped on sight. "Oh my God, I shouldn't have..."

"Relax, Tammi," Patti said as she stepped forward, hand outstretched. "I don't know much about you because Tommy here doesn't like to share, but I'm just leaving." Tammi didn't immediately reach her hand back in return. "I'm Patricia Halterman, Tommy's new partner. My friends call me Patti."

Tammi relaxed just a bit and turned away from Patti as if looking to me to determine if what she said was real. "New partner? You don't take on partners."

I shrugged. "Evidently the department doesn't see it that way. This case that started the day you left put Patti and I together." Part of me was thrilled that Patti dissolved most of the tension immediately by introducing herself and offering that she was leaving, but there was a part of me that did not want her to leave. There was a part of me that wanted the woman I loved just days ago to leave. I didn't realize how much she hurt me, or maybe I just didn't care as much as I thought I did.

Patti grabbed her coat. "I was going to help clean up, but I think I remember Franky saying he was going to Flap Jaws. That sounds like more fun. Tommy, I will see you tomorrow." Turning to Tammi, she said, "It was very nice to meet you."

She didn't give me a hug or even another look. She simply slipped between Tammi and me and walked out the door pulling it closed behind her. I looked to Tammi who looked away and took a few steps into the room but opposite of me, clearly showing she was upset.

"What?" I asked.

She shook her head. "Just not what I expected."

"What do you mean?" I asked.

"Well, you can't even say I've been gone days yet—you can still count it in hours—and you already have another woman in your house." She swung around with a look somewhere between fear, hatred, and tears. "Were you going to sleep with her?"

"Jesus, Tammi, I just met her. I had a lot of people over for Jamal's game. Both Andrea and Jessica were here as well. Franky left minutes ago. Patti was walking out the door as well."

"No!" she said sternly lifting her finger at me. "She was staying to help clean up."

"Damn it, Tammi. So what if I did have her over and I was going to sleep with her. You left me, remember?" Probably not the right direction to take this.

"Fuck you, Tommy. It has not even been three days. Three fucking days. I flew halfway across the United States to come see you this weekend and talk through how we were going to make this work, and you have a woman in your house. What the hell was I thinking?"

I didn't know what I wanted to say. Part of me wanted to grab her and hold her and tell her how thrilled I was that she was here. The other part wanted to add another layer to my wall and keep her out. She left me. She took a job on the coast without even discussing it with me. Until the words actually came out, I didn't know what I was going to say.

I stepped closer to her. "Tammi, you hurt me. I know we didn't know each other long but the hurt felt as if we did. I don't know if it was the decision, or the fact you never told me until you already had a plane ticket. That is not how I want to live my life." I am a tough guy. I don't cry, in fact, I don't remember the last time I cried. However, being a cop and having to deliver so many notices where you had to show empathy, right or wrong, I could make it look like I was close to tears whether I was or not. I wiped the corner of my eye, a move I learned when I was a rookie. "But when I opened the door and saw you behind it, my heart leapt." This was a line from one of my favorite movies, *For the Love of the Game.* We had watched it together. I hope she didn't recognize it, and hey, stealing a line from a movie may be bush league, but I did mean the words. "I don't know what our future holds, but right at that moment my heart felt things I wasn't sure I would feel again for a very long time."

She stepped closer to me and took both my hands in hers. "I have not heard you speak from your heart like that before."

I smiled. "Maybe you just weren't listening to what I was saying well enough. My feelings were always there."

She fell into my arms. Her head fit neatly under my chin and her hair felt nice as I held her. I looked with eyes wide open toward the wall of my living room, and although this embrace was nice, my mind slipped just for a second to my partner.

16 I SLIPPED OUT of bed the next morning, took a shower, and started to get dressed just as Tammi started to stir. She sat up on the bed. "Can't you stay home today?"

"Sorry, Tam," I replied. "I have a five-murder vigilante case that has all eyes on it. The governor's task force is already on it and I assume the FBI will show up today. We have made some progress, but there's no way I can take today off."

"Are you even glad I'm here?" she asked, a sad tone in her voice almost pleading for a certain answer. "You barely even put your arms around me last night, and I thought we would make love."

I was actually angered by the comment but I knew I couldn't show those feelings at that point. "Tammi, you left me. You set up another job and barely gave me a good-bye. You gave me the message that I was not worth even a discussion about it." I stopped, gathered myself because I could feel the tone starting to build. "I can't do this right now. To answer your question, am I glad you are here, absolutely. Let me ask you another question in return. Are you going to be here on Monday?"

She looked down in shame but did not respond.

"I thought so. Then what do you want from me?"

She stood up and moved over to stand directly in front of me. "I want you to tell me you love me, and we will get through this."

"I can't say that, Tammi. I'm sorry, but I can't say that." I leaned down and kissed her gently on top of her head. "Until a few days ago, I believed we would be together for the rest of our lives, and had you handled this differently, I would have believed we could even get through a long-distance relationship. I don't know now, Tam. I'm sorry, but I don't know." My voice trailed off and I broke from standing in front of her. I grabbed my holster and gun from the nightstand and turned back one more time. "I am glad you're here. If you weren't, we would have no chance, so thank you for coming back. I just don't know that I can put myself back out there."

I walked toward the door, and she grabbed my hand turning me to face her. She put her arm about my neck and pulled me down to her giving me a very deep and passionate kiss. We broke but remained only inches from each other. "Are you sure?"

I pressed my lips together. "No, I'm not sure of anything anymore."

I turned and walked out.

•　　•　　•　　•　　•

I rolled into the station and had not taken my mind off the previous night. It was a diversion from the case, a much needed diversion from the case, but really one that only added more stress. I would like to say I was a stronger man and stood my ground against the woman who left me only days earlier, but when she put the full court press on, I caved. I was her puppet the entire night, but I didn't like it, at least that's what I kept telling myself.

I don't remember parking or even getting in the elevator but before I knew it, I was walking into the questioning eyes of Detective Frank Sullivan. "So Tammi came back last night?"

I swung a hard stare over towards my partner. "What the hell, Halterman?"

"What?" she replied smiling. "Like I'm going to keep that a secret. We were supposed to go through Schulman's social media records last night, and because your girlfriend decided to grace you with her presence again, I had to do it on my own. There was no way I wasn't letting the others in on that."

"The others?" I questioned.

"Well, not everyone. Just most everyone on this floor," she replied, still smiling.

"And at Flap Jaws," added Franky.

"And just a handful of people at the White Hen Pantry across the street, but they didn't seem to care as much," Patti continued.

"Enough!" I interjected. "So everyone is clearly aware, Tammi showed up and surprised me last night. She was concerned with how she left things and wanted to talk through them, and we did." I grabbed some items on my desk as if I was busy before turning back to the two standing beside me who had been joined by Carter. "And no, we did not solve anything, and that is all I have to say about it."

"Wow, pretty defensive, buddy," replied Franky. "You might want to dial it down a notch if you want us to believe she didn't have you wrapped around her finger within ten minutes of arriving."

I glared toward my long-time friend. "I said enough, Franky." Turning to Halterman, "So you were able to review the report on the boy's social media presence last night without me?"

Her smile quickly faded. "Ah, not really."

"Not really?" I questioned.

"Well, I took it to Flap Jaws with me but I never really had the time to look too closely at it."

Franky smiled. "Especially since you left it in your car."

"Yeah, that might have been an important factor. Good callout, Detective." They were both smiling as she finished her statement.

"Oh, you guys are just precious. Do you really think you're that funny?" I shook my head grabbing the binder from her as I spoke. "I guess I'll go through it now and maybe I can solve this case while the two of you are pouring drinks." Carter coughed and cleared his throat. "What?" I said, somewhat sternly to him.

"Three," he replied.

"What?"

"Three of us poured drinks down," he added, now smiling broadly with the other two.

"Jesus," I added leaving the three of them in my wake.

"I will be right in to help you, lover boy," Halterman stated out loud. Then she softened her voice and whispered toward Carter and Sullivan. "Can I really say that kind of thing? I haven't known him long."

"Absolutely," Franky replied immediately. "Absolutely."

"Hey," I shouted out of the open door of the Royals Room. "Larry, Mo, or Curly, one of you needs to contact Jack Kittleson and get him in today. He has some explaining to do on his whereabouts during each of the murders, but especially the shooting and the night of the chemical theft at US Ingredients. I want him in today."

Carter slowly walked over to the doorway. "Did you just call me Larry, Mo, or Curly?"

We had been joking for nearly the entire time. I was a bit annoyed, but not really. However, I could tell right then that Carter was not pleased. Not pleased at all. "No!" I replied sternly.

"Then who the hell is the third?"

"Ah, clearly Huston," I replied, this time turning up to look at him to show respect.

He turned around to stare back at Halterman and Sullivan. "Well, where the hell is..." He stopped in midsentence. Standing next to the two was a smiling Karen Huston. He turned back to me. "You are damn lucky, O'Malley. Damn lucky."

My immediate thought was, *No, I'm just that good, Sergeant, now go fetch me some coffee.* You see, that's my problem. I think of 200-300 funny things to say each day. I actually say twenty-five of them. I should say about ten of them. Instead, I said, "Yep, Sergeant, damn lucky."

Shortly thereafter, Carter was back in his office and Halterman was next to me taking on half the book. Franky and Huston proceeded to contact Jack Kittleson to come in for an interview, and Toose and Only worked to find out what was going on with Robert Bales. The book of social media information was disturbing, to say the least. His Twitter account was the cleanest followed by Facebook and Instagram. In fact, if those were his only accounts, I would not have had such a strong view. Then we got to his e-mail and Snapchat. His e-mail was bad enough with everything from racial slurs, discrimination, and plain out meanness. However, his Snapchat was almost unreadable, I assume because he believed these messages went away forever once they were read, but the IT boys were able to recover everything. Although the messages disappear from the user, they are still logged and saved. Short of putting a gun in some of these kid's hands, I had to believe many battled depression up to and including suicide. He named a skinny girl who was battling anorexia and bulimia, Barf it up Barb. He named a larger girl named Elle, Ellie Fant, and his best work was on Nate Kittleson, AKA Gayte Straddle Your Son. He had volumes of material on "Gayte" all within the last year, which fit the timing we learned about when he came out about being homosexual. There were more than fifty kids called out for bad play, bad performances, their looks, or anything else that Mark Schulman could come up with. Although I didn't know any of the names but Nate's, I could feel all of their pain. All of us were young once. All of us know how mean kids can be, but social media had taken what happened in my high school to new levels. This was not unacceptable. It was deplorable.

"I wish this boy was still alive so I could slap him across the face," I said to Patti.

I believe she even had a tear in her eye as she reviewed her portion of the Snapchat section. "This is unbelievable, Tommy. I don't even know what to say." She wiped her eye when she saw me notice. "Sorry, I just don't know how anyone can do this. The kid was disturbed." She paused but before I could reply, she added, "I want his parents to read this. They need to know how bad their kid was hurting others."

I pressed my lips together. "They lost their son. They have paid the ultimate price already."

"I suppose," she replied, "but they want justice for a son who to me doesn't deserve it."

I looked toward her eyes. "Their boy was an asshole, but he did not deserve to be murdered."

She let the conversation die. We continued reading through the messages until Franky walked back in. "You guys all right?"

I think he could see Patti had been crying. "Yeah," I replied, taking the lead. "This stuff is bad though, Franky. In some ways, you could say our suspect pool is more than fifty because there are that many kids the Schulman boy tormented to a significant level, but as with our earlier thoughts, the number one target was Nate Kittleson. There is more hatred toward Nate than any of the others."

"How about other potential rape victims?" Franky asked.

I looked down to Patti and she shook her head. I didn't have an answer either and when she saw that, she took over. "There are several girls he clearly bullied, teased, made fun of, or whatever description you want to use, but none appear to have been in a relationship or physically assaulted by him. By these messages, they had to have despised him."

I nodded agreement and then continued where I had left off. "We need to speak with Nate's father. If Jack Kittleson knew the extent of these actions, he is definitely a good suspect. Forget having the means or ability, these messages would have pushed the strongest of fathers into protect mode."

"Especially one who already felt guilty about moving away," added Patti.

"And maybe even guilty about his son being gay?" Franky added.

"Maybe," I replied to Franky's comment. "But why would a father feel guilty about that?"

"How would you feel if your son came to you and said he was gay?" Franky asked.

"I'm not sure," I replied. "I guess if I were at all close with my son I would already know long before he had the courage to tell me, but regardless, it would not change anything for me."

Franky smiled. "I knew you would answer like that, but not all dads do."

"So, what is the story with Jack Kittleson? Can we get him back here today" I asked, changing the subject.

"He said he was in Naperville visiting friends. He would come by this afternoon," Franky stated.

"How was his demeanor? Was he angry about coming in?" I asked.

Franky shook his head. "No, to the contrary. He seemed pleased to help."

"Narcissist?" I asked.

"Could be," he replied. "Or maybe he just wants to see what he can learn from us, as much as we want to see what we can learn from him."

"We need to rule everyone else out prior to him getting here. That means we need to confirm the traffic camera video of Nate at the time of the car theft, and let's get a subpoena for the security feeds at Jack Kittleson's work. I want to see him in Minnesota at the time of any of these murders."

"I received an e-mail from IT," Franky said. "They have their report on the traffic feeds and Nate Kittleson's car. I will check that out after the debriefing."

Patti broke in, "If Kittleson is so willing to help, then why don't we call him on it?"

"What do you mean?" I asked.

"Why don't we ask him to give us approval for the security tapes at his work? If I remember right, Jack runs the plant. He could call and tell them to give us access.

You have a friend in Minnesota, don't you? Maybe he could go and collect them." She raised an eyebrow as she spoke looking for approval.

Franky smiled and added, "If nothing else, if he refuses, it will go directly against his *willingness to help* position he just took with me."

I nodded. "Get Jack back on the phone and pose the question. If we get the approval, I will call E.Z. Zimmerman in Minnesota and see if he can help us."

Less than a minute later Franky nodded. "He was hesitant as to why we needed them, but I think he felt cornered and authorized us to do it. He said he would make a call to the plant now. However, he also said he would be in this morning rather than this afternoon."

"How about that," I replied smiling. "We already ruffled his feathers a bit." Turning to Patti, "Nice work partner."

She smiled but did not respond further.

Carter appeared from his office, and we all started to make our way to the debriefing room. It was a packed house this morning as a couple guys from Vice had come up to discuss their case which was overlapping with another team's multiple homicides. It was good to see other cops when our paths crossed, but for some reason, anytime I saw anyone in Vice, I immediately thought about Clark. In my twenty-plus years on the force, I had seen nine police officers lose their lives in the line of duty. One was my partner, a mistake on my end that I will never forgive myself for. But in all those deaths, only one was a good friend. He called me the night before his murder, and I knew something was wrong. I have gone over the night a thousand times, constantly asking myself what I could have done differently. As a detective, you can always second guess yourself on the decisions you make, but those thoughts usually fade quickly. When someone dies because of your decisions, second guessing never ends. It eats at you like a cancer. Some guys don't recover. I was getting that way with Clark.

"You okay?" asked Carter causing me to jump.

"Fine," I replied, but I think he knew otherwise. I often went deep in thought. I think it really bothered Tammi, but for me it was a necessary normal.

Carter was unaffected and quickly moved on. He was pleased to hear that we had the video to verify Nate Kittleson's alibi. Halterman and I thought there was something he was hiding when he told his story about driving to the shore in the morning, but it was not about where he was. That being said, Carter was most pleased to hear Nate's father Jack would be coming in on his own this morning. He immediately stated he wanted to sit in on the interview. He also wanted me to push Zimm to get the video from Kittleson's place of employment in Minnesota. We needed proof the guy could not account for his time for some or all of the murders. We had built a timeline based on the reports from Doctor Gerstenberger. We knew he claimed to be in Chicago for the shooting, but we needed to see irrefutable proof he was where he claimed to be. Then we could extend that to the murders of Dawn Wells and Mark Schulman. We didn't need proof of all of them, just one to start bringing the world down around him. I could feel it.

By 8:00 AM, Franky was sitting in front of his laptop in the Royals room reviewing traffic video that was cut into about fifteen files from the IT group. Plain as day, we saw Nate Kittleson driving his car. Each video had a time stamp and location stamp and using the wall map and timeline we had built, we could quickly see he was telling the truth, all the way down to each road he took to get there. The last video, however, showed the one piece he left out. Nate Kittleson pulled up to a traffic light about two blocks from Navy Pier. Navy Pier is a tourist area right on Lake Michigan. It's very famous for its Ferris wheel, shopping, restaurants, and fireworks displays all summer. In all honesty, although I typically would steer clear of places like that, it was a nice area to grab a beer on a cool fall day.

However, on this brisk Chicago morning, Nate Kittleson was not going to Navy Pier or the small beach nearby for an early morning stroll. He pulled up and parked just on the edge of the Ohio Street traffic cam. After about ten minutes, another car pulled up. Both drivers got out and embraced.

The minute I saw it, I knew. "He was not lying about going down there. He was lying about *why* he was going down there."

Patti replied, "I know that boy."

I swung my head. "How? Who?"

"When I was looking through Schulman's Snapchat files. He's a football player." She grabbed the binder and began fervently flipping through the pages. "Here it is," she added, pointing to a page with about five entries on it. "Evidently he had a bad game and Mark was not pleased with his performance and needed to let him know. His name is Joe Bittol, and Mark preferred calling him Slow Shithole. Evidently he was too slow in the game to catch a guy breaking free, and in Mark's words, he cost them the game."

"What an asshole," I replied.

Patti continued, "It does not look like Mark knew Joe was very close with Nate. Had he known, he would have torn him up. A gay football player would not have had a chance."

"I agree," I said, with both Huston and Franky nodding as well. "But most importantly, we know Nate Kittleson did not run down Mark Schulman. We can use that as a lead-in with his father. It will possibly lower his defenses if he knows we removed his son as a suspect."

"Good call," added Franky. "Do we want to talk to this kid, Joe Bittol?"

I shook my head. "No, I don't think so, or at least not at this time. We don't need any more character witnesses regarding Schulman, and the camera is an equally good alibi for Mr. Bittol."

"What do you want to do now?" asked Halterman. "Just wait for Jack Kittleson to show up?"

I glanced to Franky to see if he had anything to answer and with his flat expression, I took the direction that the ball was in my court. As I started to reply, my phone rang. "O'Malley."

"So formal, Tommy," rang the familiar female voice.

"Doc G," I replied. "To what do I owe this pleasure?"

"I think you and your team may want to come down here. I have compared all the cases and found some similarities."

Instantly I got a shot of energy that was not present only a second before. "We'll be right down. The timing couldn't be better."

The three others were all within earshot and already knew what the conversation was. They were headed toward the elevator before I could even completely disconnect my phone. "What did she find?" asked Franky.

"I don't know, buddy, but for her to call us down, it must be significant. She said she was comparing the cases and found some similarities."

"Similarities," he replied. "Between the murders. Maybe this will tie everything back to Kittleson."

Halterman smiled and added. "We won't know till we go down and ask, gentlemen, so rather than just continue to give each other chest bumps on how awesome you both are, why don't we go down and see what the doctor has to say?"

You know, I've been called sarcastic. I've been called an asshole. Although I don't want a partner, having a smartass as a partner is not all bad. I snapped my head toward my partner and gave her what is from this point forward to be called, the "O'Malley Stare Down." Okay, dumb name, I'll work on it. Regardless, she was right. I wanted to know what Doc G had found. "Fine, Halterman. I was going to send you and Huston down for coffee for me and Franky, but I suppose you may both come with us."

That stopped her at the elevator door. She began to say something, stopped, and then began again. "You know, partner, I might get you a coffee if you solve this case before either Karen or me."

"Make it Turkey," I replied.

"Or a Goose Island," added Franky as the elevator doors opened.

"And challenge will be accepted?" I finished smiling.

We entered the elevator and Karen added, "And what do we get when we win?"

"I'm sure we can think of something," Patti replied. "Let's call it 'to be determined.'"

The doors shut and there was no more talk about it. I wondered what the women were thinking. First off, we would most likely solve this case together. Secondly, what the hell was to be determined?

We arrived at Elise Gerstenberger's office and she was actually working at one of her lab benches. Her office was simply a high-tech morgue. She heard us before she saw us and I believe she waved us over without even acknowledging for sure it was the four of us who had arrived. I suppose she does not get many visitors.

"Hello, Tommy," she began, "and friends."

We all nodded but I was the one who took the lead. "What did you find, Doc? As long as your work is done and you can tell me," I added smiling.

She did not acknowledge the shot at her normal requirement to resist speculation before all her work was complete. "The individual who committed the hit-and-run murder wears the same pair of shoes as the person at the murder in the alley and the shooting."

"Are you sure?" I asked.

"Well, I'm sure all the shoe prints are the same size, the same brand, the same style. There are extreme minor differences but within the error limits of the manufacturer. They are either the exact same pair of shoes or multiple pairs of the exact same shoe."

"If they are multiple pairs of the same shoe, it just further supports premeditated," Franky said.

"What size shoe?" I asked, understanding Franky's thought but more interested in tying these shoes to a person.

"Adidas cross-trainer, size eleven," Doc G replied.

"What size does Jack Kittleson wear?" asked Huston.

"We won't know until we ask him," I added. "Doc, do you have anything else?"

"Well, I believe the fact that I don't have anything else is also a clue tying them together. The ability to hide all DNA, all hairs, all fingerprints, or basically anything that would link back to any person is nearly impossible to achieve. This person achieved it three times."

"Wait a minute," said Detective Huston. "You're saying because you couldn't find anything else, that's a clue."

Her tone carried a level of skepticism that I didn't think would be received well by Elise, however, she took it in stride. "In short, yes. My team can always find evidence. Always. The person responsible for these crimes was able to avoid contaminating the scene to a level we couldn't find anything except footprints. I struggle to understand how a person so careful was so careless regarding their shoes."

Now I understood where she was going. "Let me ask you a different question. Do you suspect that because the individual responsible for these crimes was so careful, so precise, that the shoe evidence was a plant? You believe it was left there on purpose?"

She smiled that certain smile, and I knew exactly what was coming next. "It is not my job to tell you what the evidence means, only to tell you what the scientific evidence is." She tilted her head slightly and stared directly at me when she added, "I thought you understood that, Detective."

I shrugged. "No, I have never heard that before, Doctor. Please explain."

She didn't acknowledge my attempt at wit. "The evidence says the entire murder scenes were clean, except for a size eleven, men's Adidas cross trainer. This"—she took a few steps over to a lab bench where she had about fifteen different shoes with one pair set off to the side which she grabbed—"is the exact shoe which made the imprint. It's a common shoe that can be purchased at about half a dozen stores at any mall, but the tread pattern is like a fingerprint, one of a kind."

"How many of these are out in the general public?" I asked, also already knowing the answer.

"More than you could ever hope to count," she replied. "And with that, size eleven is the second most common size worn by males in the United States."

The four of us looked at each other and I think we all knew the same thing, we didn't have dick. We had a common size of a hugely popular shoe possibly not even worn daily by the perpetrator and only there to throw us off. We all turned to head out. Doc G handed me a file folder which I assume had her report neatly typed and placed inside.

"Thanks, Doc," I said as I took the file. "But sometime it would be nice if you would simply provide me everything I need to neatly wrap up a difficult case."

She didn't respond, but smiled nonetheless. "Good luck folks. Call me if I can help further."

We reached the elevator and it opened immediately giving the impression it hadn't been used since we exited previously.

"What do you think?" asked Franky.

I pressed our floor and then turned to the other three who appeared to be waiting for my response. I thought Franky had asked the question to everyone, but based on the blank stares, I believe he asked it only of me. "I think even if we are lucky enough that Jack Kittleson wears a size eleven shoe, a good defense attorney will simply ask our own doctor if it made sense that his shoe print was left, and when she says no, then they will immediately claim it's a plant and shouldn't be included."

"Yep," Franky replied, "we don't have squat."

"We need to catch Jack Kittleson in a lie. We need his whereabouts during all the murders and the surrounding days."

On that note, I pulled my phone out of my pocket and spun through my contact names to the very last one–Zimm. Now EZ Zimmerman was not a long-time friend. He was not someone I had worked with and had simply transferred to Minneapolis. In all honesty, he was a detective I met while sitting at Flap Jaws. He was on the stool next to me and we began talking. Six to seven hours later, we left Flap Jaws and had been friends ever since. We talked every week, sometimes more than once. We talked about cases and family and anything else that came along. He was a good person. He was no longer a detective, at least not in the typical sense of the word. He was more like Only and Toose, part of a special task force, but I didn't hold that against him. What I had learned about his history was that he had been through a lot on the force and at the time he made the change, it was really his best choice. I pressed the call button next to his name.

On the first ring, he answered. "Tommy, how's it hangin'?"

"Hey, Zimm," I replied. "Slightly to the left, but I don't know how that's important right now."

"I suppose not," he responded, a slight laugh carried in his words. "How about, 'hey Tommy, to what do I owe this pleasure?' "

The elevator doors opened on our floor as a smile crawled across my face. Our greeting was never the same, but always something similar. "We have a case here in Chicago where one of our key suspects works in your neck of the woods–Lakeville, Minnesota. Are you aware of it?"

"Sure I am," he replied. "Great little city. Growing fast. It used to be out in the middle of nowhere but now it connects as a major growth suburb. What's the story?"

"Well, to tell you the truth, we're not sure yet. A group of murders here in Chicago has a lot of noise around a boy whose parents are divorced. The dad moved up to Minnesota after the divorce and if not for living out of state, he would be our prime suspect. Basically, we have a multiple murder situation, and this suspect's alibi is his job, or simply being out of state in general. We need verification that he was in Minnesota at the time of the murders."

I was certain EZ Zimmerman smiled when he heard what was needed. "That should be easy to determine. There are cameras everywhere. Just give me his info, and we'll pull his car and address and be able to tell you how many times he went through any light by his house, shopped at Target, or multiple other options."

"I knew you would say that. However, I think we have authorization to get copies of all his tapes from the plant he runs, some food plant also in Lakeville. We get those tapes, and if they have card readers and cameras for entering or leaving, then we should have enough."

"Just send me what you need, partner, and I can get it today. Do I need to put together a warrant?"

"Nope, we have his permission and the company should provide you full run of the security. I will text you everything the minute I have it." I was sure Zimm was busy on his own cases, but every time we talked, he always made time. This was the first time I was asking for help on a case that would require him to gather evidence, but his response was the same nonetheless. I didn't expect anything other than what I received. We bid each other well and hung up.

I turned to the others. "All we need is Jack Kittleson to arrive, get written authorization for the video that he said he would provide, and we'll be able to rule him out quickly."

"Or rule him in," Patti added.

"Yes," I said smiling a bit. "Or rule him in."

I began drawing up the documents and to my surprise, it was less than fifteen minutes before Jack Kittleson exited the elevator in our hall and opened the glass doors leading into our department.

"Jack," I said, beginning to walk toward him. "Thank you so much for com..."

He stopped me in midsentence and his tone clearly showed he was not here to exchange pleasantries. "Keep your comments for someone who gives a damn. I know you're fresh out of leads and I also know you think I'm a suspect, or you wouldn't have asked for our security tapes. However, I have some bad news. The DVR is not working so we do not have any tapes. We simply have real-time video. So we will just have to identify some other way to show I was there. There are dozens of ways to identify me being present including calling some of my coworkers."

I guided him toward our wall of interrogation rooms stopping at the Bulls Room while he was talking. I let him finish before taking over. "Well, that is the catch, isn't it? People lie for each other, Jack. We really need the video, or any impartial electronic record."

"You know," he replied, still carrying an angered tone. "You are right, O'Malley. I killed these people and have forced my staff to lie for me. That is a foolproof plan all right. No wonder you don't have any clues."

I smiled. He was doing a good job playing the exact role I thought he would. The wronged individual who was being railroaded to an arrest. "Why don't we grab a seat in here and we can run through some things. In today's world, there's very little chance we can't find you on a camera somewhere if you were truly there."

I had placed my hand up to guide him through the door. As he walked in, he pushed my hand out of his way. "If I was truly there, my ass. So far you have accused me, my son, and I'm sure my ex-wife is not far behind. Why don't you stop harassing us and find the real killer?"

Now I was getting a little annoyed. "With all due respect, Jack, that's exactly what we're doing. I need to rule you out the same way we ruled out your son." That stopped him and his eyes swung to mine.

"What do you mean? You ruled out my son?" he asked. "Are you saying Nate is no longer a suspect?"

"Yes, that's exactly what I'm saying, Jack, and why you need to start trusting me. We tracked down traffic cameras that confirm your son was where he claimed to be. I know you may not like the fact we have to produce evidence to clear you and your family, but the sooner we do that, the sooner we can move on to others. However, you have to remember that you have motive. Your son was bullied by one of the victims and the discipline committee didn't do anything about it."

Jack appeared to soften a bit by his demeanor, but his tone remained hard. "If everyone who was bullied went around killing multiple people, we would have a mess on our hands."

I had no idea what he was trying to say there, so I thought I would go back to the previous conversation. "Regarding your son, he's no longer a suspect, but that does not relieve you of suspicion. In fact, freeing him probably puts more suspicion on you."

"Whatever, Detective," he replied, the frustration clear in his voice. "You guys have no idea who did this and are simply reaching for anyone with motive. Well, from what I understand with that jackass kid, there are dozens of families with motive."

We had not taken the time to count the number of comments Mark Schulman had made about other kids in the school, but based on the quick review I had given the file, hundreds was probably more accurate than dozens. "Jack, let's limit our talk to you right now. You said you would provide us access to the security video at your site to confirm your presence in Minnesota when the murders took place. Now you tell us that the DVR is not functioning so you don't have video support at your work. We don't need months of video, we need video at these three times." I presented a small piece of paper with several times written on it that I had jotted down. I read off the times of the hit-and-run, the shooting at the soccer field, and the estimated time of death Doc G provided for the first victim, Dawn Wells, in the barrel. I intentionally left off the recent fire. I didn't know how much Jack knew about any of the murders other than the hit-and-run so I wanted to watch his reaction.

He didn't miss a beat in his response. "Well, the first time, the time of the hit-and-run, I was in Minnesota because my ex-wife called to ask me to come down because you were harassing our son." He looked back down at the paper before continuing. "The other times, I have no idea without checking my calendar."

"Can you check your calendar now?" I asked.

He rolled his eyes at me clearly showing his level of annoyance was not going down. "I would love to, but I need a computer, and I'm not sure what I'll be able to tell you."

My partner had walked in during our talk and now she quickly left and came back with a laptop. "It's already connected for you. Pull up whatever you need."

He pressed his lips together and shook his head. "All I can do is look into Google Calendar and see where I was. Maybe some appointments or something."

We didn't answer and let him do his thing. Halterman motioned with her eyes for me to move to the side so she could tell me something.

She moved to where she stood between me and Jack Kittleson so her voice would be pointing away from him making it harder for him to hear. She stood on her toes to reach my ear and whispered, "Mike Schulman just lit up Franky on the phone. He says we, and I quote, 'aren't doing shit to solve his son's murder and if we don't do something soon, he's going to solve it on his own,' end quote."

"Jesus!" I replied, also in a whisper but louder than Patti and facing Jack causing him to look up.

"Everything okay?" Jack asked. It was clear he didn't really care, but just wanted us to know he heard me.

"Fine," I responded. "Thanks for asking." Turning back to Patti now in a much quieter tone, "What did Franky say to that?"

"He asked him to come down to the station so we could talk."

"Is he coming down?" I asked.

"I think so," Patti replied. "Franky took another call as he hung up with Schulman. I don't know who was on that one though. I came in here before much was said."

"I have something," Jack interrupted. "Here's the security at my house. It records anytime one of my doors is opened or closed. At the earliest time you gave me, you can see my garage door open and close when I came home from work. Since my wife was in Canada, you know this was done by me."

I didn't respond how I wanted, which was a fake sneeze in which I would say the word "bullshit" as I sneezed. Instead however, I walked toward him with Halterman in my wake. I was surprised how much he was smiling. I really think he thought he just proved something. "Is your security account still open?" I asked.

"Yep," he replied proudly. "Come take a look at it yourself."

"What system do you use?" I asked.

"ED Security," he replied.

"Electronic Doberman, same as mine." I said in return. I took a short breath and then added, "Let me show you something." When I got to the keyboard, I saw a familiar screen. I lie a lot when I'm interviewing suspects. Not because I'm trying to trick them or anything, but simply because I'm trying to get them talking, and to do that I often need to say something that's not true. Okay, as I describe it, it's clear that I'm actually trying to trick them. Regardless, in this case, I was serious. I mean, I didn't have a home security system now because I had nothing to steal, but when I was married, I did. My security system of choice was ED. I liked it because the initials also stood for erectile dysfunction and I liked telling everyone I had ED all around me or I paid for ED. Yes, it was juvenile, but I bet 10% of their customers signed up with them because of those initials.

I was very familiar with the system and after a few clicks, I did what I intended to do. "Is anyone home right now?" I asked.

"No," he replied.

"Then how did your garage door just go up?" I said as I moved away from the computer.

"Ah shit, but I would not have done that." He shoved the computer away from him.

"But you could have, that's the point." I had my misgivings about Jack Kittleson, but all signs kept pointing to him. The biggest circumstance was he was one of the only people in the country that could have taken and made that shot at the soccer field. Now, he was unable in a world of electronic surveillance to even come up with one camera that had him recorded, much less the suspicious situation with the broken DVR at his plant. Now his wishy-washy bullshit garage door excuse. Yep, this guy was guilty. I just needed to prove it.

"This is bullshit, Detective, and I'm out of here." Jack stood and was going to turn toward the door but stopped as I placed my hand on his shoulder.

"Jack," I began, "I am not going to lie. This does not look good for you. You are not able to account for your whereabouts during any of the times the murders occurred. Your garage door excuse does not hold water and the fact that your ex-wife called you to come down after the hit-and-run is also not a factor. She called your cell phone so there's nothing that says you didn't answer it here and just claim you still had to drive down."

"Well," he began. "I guess you just have it all figured out, Detective. I am going back to Minnesota now. I do not expect to hear from you again. If you want any other information or need to work a little harder to find a camera on me when another victim is being killed, talk to my lawyer."

Damn, I thought to myself. I was going to lose him and he already made the lawyer comment. I could read him his rights and keep him here, or I could just let him go. He was not going to flee the country, but he was going to leave the state. I would be able to get him back if he did these crimes. At this point, I was sure he had. His defensive play to cover and run sealed the deal. "Hey, Jack, don't run off. Your family needs you. You need to clear this up before you go."

"No, Detective, you need to solve the crime without me as a scapegoat hanging around." His tone clearly showed he was angry. He began walking toward the elevators then turned around. "And as for me needing to be here for my family, you already said my son was no longer a suspect. Therefore, the further away I get from you, the better chance I have to be there for my family." With that, he turned back and began walking between the desks.

"Are you the guy who ran down my son? I am going to kill you, you asshole!"

Mike Schulman's shouts were loud enough to be heard throughout the entire department. I had heard that tone numerous times before. He had been drinking and he was angry. A very bad combination. I moved as quickly as I could, as did every detective in the area, but none were fast enough. Schulman had done a full body blow to Kittleson similar to a middle linebacker hitting a standing quarterback, and instantly Kittleson folded. They crashed into Franky's desk and then both fell to the floor. Papers and other office supplies went everywhere. I think there was some yelling, but to be honest, I don't remember. With a quick roll, Jack Kittleson had switched positions with Schulman and had him pinned to the ground. Although Jack had no idea who this was, he was a former Marine and did not take lightly to being tackled and began punching Schulman in the face. It was as his second punch was heading down that I was able to grab his arm and secure him to the side. Franky grabbed Mike Schulman and pulled him from the ground and locked his arms around his pulling him backward into the first interrogation room. I grabbed Jack Kittleson and threw him down in a chair.

"What the fuck was that?" shouted Kittleson.

"Take it easy, Jack," I replied. "That was Mark Schulman's father. Evidently he thinks you might want to come up with some confirmation of your whereabouts also."

"You killed my boy, you asshole!" Schulman shouted from the conference room.

"Your boy was a bullying rapist, who hurt hundreds of kids, but I did not kill him." Kittleson replied. I was not restraining him any longer and he was standing now, broad-shouldered and staring right back at Schulman. As always, my mind went instantly to wondering in a cage match who would come out on top. Schulman was more blue-collar, rugged, and probably had been in a few more scuffles in his day, but Kittleson was simply in shape and a former military dog. I would give 85% odds to Kittleson, which would maybe have been even higher if not for the anger factor that was clearly driving Mike Schulman. Mike didn't care who he blamed or who he hit, but he wanted to hit someone.

Franky, for the most part, threw Schulman into one of the chairs and slammed the door, but because it was glass and had a special closer, the force he used was immediately absorbed and the door gently shut with far less emphasis than he had planned. I couldn't make out the words, but Franky was verbally giving everything he had to Schulman.

Kittleson turned to me. "Fuck him and fuck you, O'Malley. If you ever see Bales again, tell him to fuck off as well." He was still standing and took a step closer to me. When I looked at Kittleson, I had to hand it to him. He could appear threatening if he wanted to. He stared eye-to-eye with me. "And tell that jackoff Schulman if he ever comes at me again, I will tear him apart. From this point forward, do not speak to me or my family. You may talk to our lawyer."

I didn't back down, blink, or even acknowledge he was inches from my face. Instead I just smiled. In truth, whether he was guilty or not was immaterial at that moment. He was handling this exactly as I would. He was done. He and his family had had enough, and he was leaving. I still knew I could get him back if I wanted to, but other than a shitload of circumstantial evidence, I had nothing that firmly tied him to any of the murders. I still needed to catch him in a lie.

When Kittleson realized I was not going to speak and I was going to simply sit there and smile, he turned and headed toward the elevator without further comment. I hollered back to him, "Hey Jack, what size tennis shoes do you wear?"

He stopped at the glass doors and turned back. "You trying to build more fake evidence against me or my family? Well, I don't give a fuck. I wear size eleven, good enough for you?"

"Yeah, good enough," I replied.

Halterman walked up next to me, intrigued by the shoe size response but focused on something else. "What did he mean with the comment on Bales?"

"What do you mean?" I asked her.

She shrugged. "I don't know, it was like he knew something. The others he said f-you directly to, but Bales was, if you ever see him again, tell him f-off as well. Why not just say, f-Bales also?"

"Interesting thought?" I replied. "Why don't you track down Bales and see if he had any conversations with Kittleson."

She nodded and headed to her desk while I turned to join Franky and speak with Schulman.

"I don't want to hear a word from you, Detective," Schulman stated as I entered. "I know you suspect that asshole is the killer. I did some research. I asked around about him. Some of Mark's friends say Nate's dad is a Navy Seal or something. To me, that means he killed that teacher and if he killed that teacher, he killed my son also."

I motioned both Franky and Mike Schulman to sit. I tried to appear calm, but to be honest, the adrenaline was still flowing. We hadn't had that much excitement in the department since Marvin Springer, a former detective who transferred to Florida or someplace like that, slept with then Lieutenant Calderman's wife. He was thrown through a plate-glass window and never worked in Chicago again.

Calderman did not fare well either and ended up with an early retirement.

"Do you hear yourself talking?" I asked Schulman. "You just said the following: A friend of Nate Kittleson's—that by itself is third-hand information at best and from a minor. Then just because Jack Kittleson was in the armed forces he must have been the killer of the teacher on the soccer field. I'm a Marine. Maybe I am the killer."

"Do you have motive to kill my son?" Schulman shot back.

"Mike," I used his first name in an attempt to soften him and be friendlier. The same theory as always calling a waiter or waitress by name. It's a sign of respect and individuals simply respond well to it. "You need to take a step back and let us do our jobs. We are aware of everything you just said. We are talking to Mr. Kittleson and will stay connected while he's back in Lakeville. Without evidence, we will not be able to do anything and that is where we are today, gathering evidence."

I believe he only heard one word. "What!" he exclaimed. "You are letting him go back to Minnesota? He will be gone for good."

I smiled. "Last time I checked, Minnesota was part of the United States. It's not like he's going to the Middle East. He is not going to escape to Minnesota." I paused and tried to let that sink in but it did not appear that Mike Schulman was going to hear me. "Relax, Mike, we have this. We are much closer than you think." Yeah, that was a lie. "We have several leads we're following up on every day. With the weekend coming up, we could even have charges in place on someone before next week hits. Go home. Spend time with your wife. She needs you now probably more than she ever has."

Then Mike Schulman did something I would never have expected in a million years. He did not speak. He did not make any expression, deep breath or anything. He didn't even acknowledge us. He simply stood up, turned, and slowly walked out. He walked between the desks staring off into space with each step, and then through the glass doors to the elevator. He pressed the button, entered, and as Franky and I walked to the glass doors that faced the elevators in the hall, the doors shut and he was gone. I didn't know it at the time, but I wished that was the last time I saw Mike Schulman.

17

HALTERMAN APPEARED by our sides as we stared at the closed elevator doors. "What's up?" she said, following our eyes.

Franky answered for both of us. "That was a touch bizarre. I guess he was done."

I nodded. "Yeah, I suppose he came down here to yell and scream and then just leave, but I did not like his demeanor. He's a wild card. I'm actually glad Kittleson is leaving the city."

"Hopefully your comment on supporting his wife will set in," Franky added.

"Hopefully," I replied. Turning to Patti, "What did you find out?"

"I spoke to Bales' wife. He didn't come home last night. She checked his credit card bill and there was a charge for some place called Miss Kitty's Saloon. It sounded sketchy so I looked it up online, but it's just a dive bar in Naperville. Have you heard of it?"

"No," I replied. "But we should probably check it out. Not to help solve the case, but we should locate Robert Bales as soon as possible for his own safety."

"Didn't we have a car watching him?" Franky asked.

"They just wanted it on where they were staying, and Bales was more concerned about his family so unless they left together, the car would stay at the location." As I spoke, I could tell Franky was already following the thinking.

"Sure," he replied. "If those being watched split up, the car stays at the residence to ensure it's not tampered with. It's easier to attack those in a stationary place like a home, but I didn't think they were at their home any longer?"

"They aren't," replied Halterman. "They are staying with the wife's sister in Warrenville."

"Warrenville is close to Naperville and Miss Kitty's," I replied. "Let's go check it out and bring Schulman's social media binder you were supposed to review last night. We can run through it in the car and maybe find another victim that may have even more motive and opportunity than Kittleson or Malecha." We had already run through much of it earlier this morning, but I liked adding another shot about how she didn't run through it last night and instead chose to hang out at the bar with my friends.

•　　•　　•　　•　　•

We got in my Camaro and headed back to the western suburbs. We hadn't even gone one block when Halterman asked, "So, how did things go with Tammi last night?"

I did not know how to respond to that. The truth was, this was something very personal to me and for all practical purposes, I had just met Patricia Halterman. The other side of the coin was, she was my partner and we were homicide detectives. If something was bothering me or could possibly affect my performance in the field, she had every right to ask about it. On the final side—yes, it was a three-sided coin— two or three times when I was with Tammi last night I thought about Patti. She was my partner and I should not think those things, but I did.

"What are you thinking about?" she asked, breaking my thoughts.

I didn't answer right away and then glanced to her while we stopped at a traffic light. "I was thinking about how to answer your last question, because I don't know how things went with Tammi."

"That's a fine answer," she said, her voice soft. "I didn't mean to pry."

"You didn't," I answered quickly as I directed the car towards the Eisenhower. "You have a right to ask anything if you feel something that's going on with me may affect us in the field."

She had been looking at me when I spoke but looked away before she replied, "Maybe I wasn't worried about how you would be in the field. Maybe I was wondering for personal reasons."

Patti didn't speak the rest of the drive and I didn't either, mostly because I was scared as hell. My true bottom line—I was in love with Tammi Hutchins, and that love did not end because she hurt me. And now there was this simmer of electricity starting between me and my new partner. Something I know would be frowned upon tremendously by the department. I had never had a female partner. I did not think I was handling it appropriately, but I knew one thing for certain: Until I knew where things stood with Tammi, I needed to stop the electricity immediately.

We turned into a small strip of shops just off Ogden Road in Naperville. There was big sign on a building that said "Naperville Music." Then, adjacent to it were a few beer lights below a small sign that read, "Miss Kitty's Saloon." There were various posts on the windows about live music and specials, but for the most part, it looked like a small dive bar. A place I would probably like to go. It was late morning and to my surprise, they were open but I didn't know if that meant they were open to the public or just for deliveries and such. With a smattering of cars in the lot, they may even be open for business and have some clientele inside.

"What do you think," Patti asked, the first words she had spoken since her comment about Tammi.

"I think it looks like a place I could hang out and be comfortable. They even appear to be open."

She pointed to a sign on the far door. "Looks like they opened at 10:00 AM."

"Hey, throw a call into Franky and have him snap a picture of Bales from the suspect board and send it to us. Let's see if anyone remembers him being here last night."

We both climbed out of the Camaro and walked toward Miss Kitty's front door, Tammi placing a call to Franky as we walked. We entered the establishment and instantly I was in love. This was the Naperville version of Flap Jaws, only with a small corner stage added. It was one room, not large, but the bar ran the length of the wall. On the far end was a small stage and a handful of tables. One table had a group of ladies at it, there was one person sitting at the bar and a half-full glass left alone a few seats down. I sucked in deep and could smell the dive bar flavor. It was not as large as Flap Jaws and the bar was on the wall verses the center, but I imagined the same type of customers frequented both places. I would never consider moving to the suburbs, especially Naperville, but if I did, this could very easily be my bar of choice.

"You two may sit anywhere," a very pleasant voice said from behind the bar.

I looked up and was completely caught off guard. I expected to see the Naperville version of Roy Pura, a rough-around-the-edges ex-Marine who found his lifelong dream to own a bar in Chicago. What I saw was a phenomenally sexy blonde with numerous tattoos and piercings. The kind of girl that would scare the wrong man, but when I saw her, my immediate thought was, *Hello, my name is O'Malley, Tomas O'Malley*. I don't know what that means, but I was certain the right woman would think it was awesome.

I felt a slight pain in my side as Patti poked me back to consciousness. "Thank you, we are actually here to ask a few questions, if you have a minute. I'm Detective O'Malley and this is Detective Halterman. We're looking for someone who may have been here last night and is missing."

Her eyes raised slightly at that and she began to walk toward us. "Hello, Detectives, I'm Katie. I was working last night so I should be able to help you. We had live music playing but we weren't that busy."

When she moved out from behind the bar, I was simply taken by her. I was clearly fifteen years older than her but she was one of those women who the minute you saw her, you just knew she was a fit for what you thought was hot. Fortunately for me and the future comments I would get from my partner, my voice did not reflect my subconscious feelings. "We are looking for a man whose credit card showed some charges here last night. He never made it home, and he's potentially in some danger. His name is Robert Bales."

Patti began to lift her phone to show the picture Franky had sent but the bartender replied immediately, "Bob was here last night. In fact, he's still here. In the bathroom. That's his drink right there." She pointed to the empty spot at the bar.

"Thanks, Katie," I replied. "Do you mind if we sit and wait for him at the bar?"

"Absolutely, Detective O'Malley," she replied, somewhat ignoring my partner. "Can I get you something to drink? Club soda or anything?" She glanced to Patti. "You too, of course."

"I don't think so," Patti replied curtly.

"I'll take a diet soda," I added.

"No problem, Detective," she said smiling. She turned and slid back behind the bar grabbing a glass on her way.

I started toward an empty seat at the bar and Patti grabbed my arm. "Do you flirt with everyone?"

"That's Franky's thing," I replied. "I have no game so I don't flirt with anyone."

"Then what the hell was that? Your tongue was on the ground the minute she walked over."

I smiled. "I have to admit, she had a sexy thing going for her, didn't you think?"

"No," Halterman replied. "Not at all."

"Jealous?" I asked, smiling.

"Hardly," she stated releasing my arm.

"Let's go get Bales and see why he didn't come home last night."

She followed behind me. I took a seat next to Bales' vacant seat and Patti sat next to me. My soda arrived shortly thereafter and Katie brought Patti a water.

Katie stopped in front of me. "So, have you ever been here before?"

"No," I replied. "I don't get to Naperville much. We're from downtown. Does Bob come here often?"

"On occasion. He and Dani will swing by, but this is more his type of place than hers."

"Are you two together?" she asked.

Patti jumped on that one. "If you're asking if we are romantically involved, the answer is no. We are partners." Her tone was cold and words short and quick.

Katie was not phased. "I call them like I see them. You seem like you were a bit protective of your partner. Just seemed like there was more there." She tilted her head and turned. "None of my business anyway." Then she walked off.

"Bitch," Patti said under her breath.

"I'm sure she's saying the same about you," I replied.

We didn't say much more after, and Katie went about talking to the other individual at the bar. I could not hear everything, but it was something about her eleven year old that still believed in the Easter Bunny. First, I did not believe she could have an eleven year old. Secondly, I didn't have the heart to tell her that her child no longer believed but just pretended to because they still wanted to ensure they got the gifts and eggs. No eleven year old can make it through school these days and not know the truth. Just then, from the far end of the bar, Robert Bales emerged from what I assumed were the bathrooms. Our eyes met and his whole body seemed to go slightly limp. His shoulders dropped and he appeared like he was giving up.

"He's already drunk," whispered Patti. "It's not even 10:30 in the morning."

"I think it's more likely he is still drunk from last night," I added.

When he got near us, I was going to speak but he beat me to the punch. "Damn it, Detectives," he slurred. "What the hell are you doing here?"

"We are here to get you," I replied. "You did not come home last night. You need to remember your life is potentially in danger."

"What difference does that make?" he slurred again. "Somebody should kill me for what I've done."

"Stop talking like that, Bob," I continued. "Things will get better. Right now, we just need you to work with us. You need to stay at home with your wife, so we can help protect you until we get this mess cleaned up."

I don't think he heard everything I said, but he definitely heard the first part. "Things are not going to get better. That is not what that fucking caller said, and they are right. I don't deserve to live."

My ears perked. "What caller?"

"It doesn't matter," he slurred again in response. His voice was broken and he was barely speaking English at this point.

I used a stronger tone to try to bring him back to the present. Patti motioned to Katie for some coffee. "Bob, did someone call you? Did you know who it was?"

"Yes, I fucking knew who it was, and they were right. I'm responsible for all those deaths." He burped, and it looked like he was going to throw up. "I need some air."

"We'll come with you," I stated.

"Just sit your asses down," he answered. Now his voice was clearer. "Let me get some air, and I will grab my phone. I think I left it in my car."

I glanced toward Patti and she nodded. We would let him go outside but we would keep an eye on him. If he would go get his phone, then we could then see if he received a call and if he did, we could find out who was taunting him. He stumbled out the door and we walked over behind him, but didn't go outside. He stood on the front walk and simply stared into the sky, like he hadn't seen it before. It was dark in the bar so I was sure the light was an adjustment for him, but he was swaying so much I don't think he could focus on anything. We heard him yell something but it wasn't distinguishable. He then stumbled over to his car, unlocked and opened the door.

He leaned over and I imagined his phone must have been on the passenger seat floor. Then my heart stopped.

"Oh shit!" I exclaimed.

"What?" Patti asked, not watching as closely.

I bolted through the door as the shot rang out and blood exploded on all the windows of the car.

•   •   •   •   •

"Goddamn it, O'Malley! You guys were right there and you let someone we were protecting pull out a gun and kill himself." Carter was screaming at both Halterman and me and had been since we arrived back from Naperville.

"I know, Carter," I replied. "Damn it, I know," I repeated with my voice trailing off.

"We thought he was going to get his phone. Someone called him and we were going to trace the number." Halterman spoke softer, but her voice sounded more like she was making excuses rather than taking responsibility. Carter responded better to the latter.

"Listen, Carter," I broke in. "I fucked up. Just like with Dixon. I should have anticipated the possibility and not let him go to his car alone." Bringing up my old partner who was killed outside a suspect's house was not meant to draw sympathy, it was how I felt, and Carter knew it. His anger faded just a bit and the barrage of profanity ceased to be replaced with a *where do we go from here* discussion.

"Tell me everything. Tell me about the call. Tell me what he said, did, drank, etc. I want to know where this guy's head was that he would choose to take his life. He was a goddamn principal for God's sake."

"Before I do that, I need to call Zimm and have him collect Jack and Kim Kittleson's passports. Jack knew something about Bales. I think he made the call and basically talked him into suicide."

Carter grimaced but waved me to do it. "Make the call and then get back in here." Turning to Halterman, he added, "You start filling me in on the whole situation in Naperville."

I got on the phone with Zimm and gave him all the information needed and Zimm filled me in on where he was in the process. I then went back to Carter's office to see how Halterman was fairing.

"Sergeant," I began, taking the conversation in a new direction. "This is what Zimm has already. He had already been by Jack Kittleson's work and to Jack's credit, he had preapproved giving Zimm full access. Zimm confirmed that the archaic camera system the plant used was so old that he didn't even think a new DVR was possible, but definitely could understand why the one being used was not functioning. Zimm also routed a path between the plant and the Kittleson house and found three traffic cameras that could be used to confirm Jack's presence, assuming he went home via that route, the cameras were still working, and their clarity was sufficient to see the driver clearly. He also said that the Kittleson home is in a nice golf course community in Lakeville called Bracket's Crossing. There were no additional cameras in the neighborhood but the houses were close enough that neighbors could also have seen him. Zimm said he would start interviewing them after he confirmed the camera functionality and recovered the passports. He said he went by already but nobody was home."

"Nobody home, huh?" Carter asked.

"Well, this makes sense because his wife is in Canada at the bed and breakfast she owns and he's down here, though he's probably halfway back by now. I let Zimm know Jack's timing and plans."

Carter's face still held his displeasure. "Halterman filled me in while you were on the phone. Did you recover Bales' phone and what did you find out?"

Patti continued before I could speak. "There was not much evidence to collect at the scene," she paused, then added with a smile, "although I think O'Malley would have been willing to stay longer and interview the bartender." I didn't smile and she continued unhindered. "We do have the phone and went through it prior to it being taken back with the proper chain of evidence. There were two calls that were unknown. Both were from the same number." She pulled out her small three-inch notepad she carried with her at all times. "One was at 6:30 PM yesterday and another one was this morning at 8:00 AM. The first call lasted twelve minutes and the second lasted only three."

"That second call would have been right after we called Kittleson to come in here, and didn't you say he was staying in Naperville?" Carter was already drawing the same conclusions we had.

I nodded. "Franky talked to him this morning and said that. I will verify we heard it correctly. If he was in Naperville, I want to know the friends he was staying with. I think he was there to try to meet with Principal Bales and finish this spree he started."

Carter looked very seriously toward me. "Can we tie this to him, Tommy? It seems like all we have is circumstantial. Not being on camera in Minnesota is not enough. No DNA at any scene is a big gap. He, as well as dozens of others have motive, and the fact that he's an expert shot doesn't mean a thing in court. If one other person in the country could have made that shot, it is reasonable doubt."

"I don't know, Sergeant," I replied. "Patti and I talked about this our entire drive back from Naperville. Let's assume Jack goes back to Minnesota now as he said he is and let's also assume all the murders stop today, with the death of Robert Bales. This means there will be no new evidence out there to obtain. We will have let a killer come into our city, kill five people, and put a gun in the hands of a sixth who committed suicide, and then simply drive back home like nobody knew any different. These people may not have been the best or may not have made the best decisions, but none of them deserved to die because of it."

"Damn it, Tommy, what are we missing?" He looked to me and then to my partner extending the question to her as well without actually saying her name.

There was silence for a few seconds, which seemed like minutes. Then, Patti replied softly, "Do you think the son or ex-wife know?"

Both our heads turned. "What are you getting at?" I asked.

"Well, I'm trying to put myself in each person's position," she said. "They're aware of the other murders. They have to know that their father, or ex-husband as the case may be, is a sniper level marksman. Therefore, they too have to believe he could be the killer. They have to have some doubts. Do you think they asked him or even pursued this on their own? If so, could they have found something linking him or could they be hiding anything? I can't believe the boy would turn in his father, but you never know how you can push an ex in an interview."

Carter looked to me. "You are one of most manipulative interviewers I have ever seen. Can you make a run at her that does not put her on the defensive? Maybe the angle is that we know he is guilty and her son knows his father is guilty and what are you teaching your child to let this be the answer?"

I nodded. "I can give it a run, but I don't know that I would use that direction. I will need to think about it, but I like the idea." I looked to Patti when I said the last line trying to make it a compliment to her for coming up with it. "Patti, why don't you call Becky Kittleson and have her and Nate come in? She will probably call her husband immediately after receiving our call, so instead of telling her it's for questioning, let her know we have eliminated her and her son from any suspicion and simply want to let her know where the investigation is at and to see if hearing that information might jog something else from either of them. Anything we can do to keep Jack Kittleson out of the loop would be a benefit to us."

"I'm on it," Patti replied. She left the room and headed toward her desk.

"You know it's a longshot at best," I stated, looking toward Carter.

He nodded. "Yep, but you never know what you might find unless you're willing to turn over the rock and see what's underneath."

Just then my phone began to buzz again. I looked down and saw who it was. "Hey Zimm. What do you need?"

"Good afternoon, Tommy," he replied. "I took a flier and ran back by the Kittleson's house and the wife drove up as I was there. She was just getting in. I was able to obtain both her and Jack's passports without Jack even being there. She called her husband while I was there, and he didn't argue the fact or tell her to contact their lawyer. I don't have any warrant or document stating I had the authority to take them, but I did produce a form for them to sign saying they willfully submitted them to me and they would be sent to you. To be honest, based on what you said, how he was acting, I'm surprised I got them so easily. I mean, I could have gotten approval without issue, but the fact I wasn't asked to produce it was a surprise."

I thought a minute about what he said. "Maybe," I replied. "But maybe that's part of his narcissistic mentality. I think he truly feels he's untouchable, but..." I stopped and thought about what I was going to say then continued. "But unfortunately, he is probably closer to being right than wrong. We don't have much here, Zimm, so anything you can come up with would be huge."

"I will have the camera info by tomorrow morning. I already sent the camera locations in and provided the plate number we're looking for. The software will find it if it's there. Just send me the corresponding times to look for."

"Consider them on their way, Zimm, and thank you. If we could prove Jack Kittleson was not there, perhaps we would have enough for an arrest and from there who knows what case we can build."

I glanced up from my phone and saw three men in black suits walking in with my two favorite GiST team members. "Oh shit," I said, both through the phone and to those in the area. Carter and Halterman looked up when they heard my comment and followed my eyes.

"What is it?" Zimm asked.

"The FBI just arrived."

I could hear Zimm sigh through the phone. "This will be your case only through the night. I will get my team on the video. We will get it for you as soon as possible. Just send me those times."

"Consider them sent," I replied again, "but right now I need to go."

"Take care, buddy, and keep me in the loop."

• • • • •

I walked over toward the five men passing through the glass doors. I reached out my hands. "Hello, gentlemen. Can I help..."

"Are you Sergeant Carter?" interrupted the lead suit.

"No, I'm Detective..."

"Who is Sergeant Carter?" the man said loudly to the entire room.

"I'm Sergeant Craig Carter," he responded, equally as loud.

"Is there someplace we could speak privately please?" the head suit asked.

"My office is right over..." Carter was pointing but before he could finish, the three suits stepped right by him and clearly quit listening. Only and Toose were right in tow without comment, or even making eye contact. "Why don't you all just head right there," Carter added with a hint of tone as they passed.

I leaned in toward my sergeant. "Don't mess around with these guys. Just do what they tell you. We will fall in line. If you have to give up the case, then give it up. It's a career killer to do anything else."

He smiled. "Who the hell are you and give me back Detective O'Malley?"

I smiled in return. "I'm just saying, Sergeant. You have a career. This case is not worth it."

He nodded. I think he understood and agreed, but he would never say so in front of me. It went against everything we had stood for over the last eight years or so. Nobody took over our cases because we cleared more than any other department. However, we had six dead bodies and no current chance of making an arrest. I am sure Toose and Only were feeling the heat and pushed the governor to call in the feds. Carter walked in slowly behind the five men and began to close the door behind him when it struck my hand and I pushed it back open for Franky and me to fill in the rear.

When we entered his office, we saw the FBI agent who had asked for Carter sitting in his desk chair. I was sure this was just posturing, but I could tell from my boss's expression that enough was enough. Carter had heard what I had said before, but at some point you had to stand up for what you had worked very hard to become.

"So Carter, am I to understand that after the first two murders, the third one, the teacher on the soccer field, took place right in front of your team? Then, the next two burned down a house that your team had just been at *and* they had seen the truck that added the accelerant that caused the fire to spread so quickly making any escape for those inside impossible? And finally, did they just watch another victim leave their questioning to go out to their car and commit suicide?"

He then stopped speaking and stared directly at Carter in a patronizing stare that would have made the strongest suspect fold. Carter, however, remained stoic and returned the stare right back. "For starters, Officer..." His tone increased stating the bogus title in the form of a question.

"It is Special Agent, Special Agent Simpson," he replied.

"Like Bart or OJ," Carter stated. "I should be able to remember that." He paused and it took a minute for the reference to sink in, but when it did, the response was not positive in the least. Carter continued, "Now, Special Agent Simpson, I suggest you remove yourself from my chair and proceed to move to the other side of my desk. After you have done that, I would be glad to speak to you about this case."

The line was drawn. It was like two roosters in one henhouse, but there were no hens present and the other rooster out-ranked the one whose house it was. Slowly, Simpson stood and moved a few steps to the side. "Take your seat, Sergeant. I meant no disrespect. We will simply need an office to work out of as we go through this case."

"Great," Carter replied. "I will be glad to set you up in one of our large conference rooms. Now, in response to your comments, yes, my men were onsite when the teacher was shot. They were interviewing the principal when the shot was fired and were on the scene quickly. The fire took place the day after they were at the house and the surveillance car onsite did see the truck that we believe applied the accelerant to the house. The fire was set the next morning. Then, regarding the suicide, they had escorted the victim to their car to recover the phone. When the individual got into his car, instead of grabbing his phone, he grabbed a gun. End of story."

Simpson smiled but didn't acknowledge the description of events. "We need full access to everything you have on the case. We need a room to work and about thirty minutes with each member of your team that's on the case. We will want that time independently of each other. In groups, stories tend to become clouded. How does that sound, Sergeant?"

"Sounds perfect," Carter replied. "And let me know when you want to be done posturing and we will all get along better." Carter turned to me. "O'Malley, why don't you escort our new friends to the Royals room?"

"O'Malley? Tomas O'Malley?" Simpson asked.

My eyes swung to greet his. Having the FBI know my name could not be good. "Yes, Detective Tomas O'Malley. Why do you ask?"

His voice was strangely friendly and the condescending and posturing tone had vanished. "I have reviewed some of your cases. Most recently the Polino and Moretti case. We had been tracking Moretti for years before he moved into Chicago. We didn't understand the move until we learned through your case that he was working an angle against Polino. It made sense then. He was in over his head in New York and found an opportunity to take over a large market, save face in New York, but get out from under the challenges he had there. Nice work on Polino. We, the bureau that is, could not believe how close you came to bringing down both of them in one shot."

Carter was clearly agitated at the love falling my way, and I learned a long time ago to never let the compliments of someone from the outside cloud where your bread is buttered. My bread was buttered by Carter, and it would continue to be long after Simpson and his bullshit was gone. "Yeah, Franky and I just got caught in the crossfire. This was a case driven by Sergeant Carter and the boys in vice."

Simpson smirked just a bit. "Sure it was. Now, where is that room, and if you could point us to the coffee, that would be helpful as well." He glanced to his team and then back to me. "Then, when we're settled, why don't we start the interview process with you, Detective O'Malley."

"That sounds fine," stated Carter, answering the statement for me. "Sullivan, O'Malley, swing back here after you get them settled. I have a few things to run through before your interviews."

Not only Franky and me, but Simpson swung his head back to stare at Carter. I didn't know what this was about—more posturing this time from Carter, or setting up a plan for what we would share, but regardless, it was clear a private pre-conversation with my sergeant was not what Simpson wanted. However, to my surprise, he let it sit and exited the room with Toose and Only in tow.

Toose raised a hand to Franky and me. "We can show the FBI the layout. You guys finish what you need to and then head back over to join us, O'Malley first and then we will chat with Sullivan."

He sounded sincere. I never liked Only at all. He was an ass. Toose I think I didn't like just because I hated Only. In this case, Toose seemed straight-up and respectful. "Thanks, Toose, we'll be right with them," I answered.

When everyone had left, Sullivan closed the door, and we both turned back to Carter with eyebrows raised.

"What?" Carter asked. "Just look at me like we're talking about important case stuff. I couldn't let that asshole have the last word of *get us coffee* and not insert some other direction. They can get their own damn coffee."

Franky and I both smiled, before Franky replied, "You know, Sergeant, you have never been Mr. Politics, but it's good to know you're on our side."

Carter took his seat again and looked toward me. "O'Malley, thanks for seeing through that bullshit from Simpson on the Moretti-Polino case."

"No problem, Sergeant. You have our backs, and we have yours."

We stayed in the office for a few minutes and did actually talk about our plans before we both left and I headed toward the Royals room. The FBI had already set up camp and Toose and Only had joined them–*kiss-asses*, I thought as I walked in.

"Shut the door behind you and let's talk about Sergeant Carter," stated Simpson, before the door even latched.

"About Sergeant Carter?" I asked.

18

"TELL ME ABOUT Carter," stated Simpson.

"Is that a question?"

He let out a deep slow breath. "Listen, O'Malley, we have reviewed your entire career. Not just in Chicago, but you are among the upper echelon of detectives in the country. You solve the cases you are given and even have some highly notable ones under your belt. You even solve the ones you're not supposed to solve. However, you usually do it like a bull in a China shop so you end up standing in a pile of shit with a closed case in your hands."

"So what is this, the Tomas O'Malley story…in a pile of shit? I thought you were here to discuss our current case." Simpson looked to his team and then to Toose and Only causing me to continue. "Hey, eyes on me. You have a question for me on the case, then shoot. If there are some other games going on, then I can leave right now." I was starting to get pissed. "I never even got the names of your two cronies with you, so why don't we cut through the crap and you guys tell me what this is all about."

Simpson stood from the chair he had taken across from me and paced around the back of the table. "This is Special Agent Dixon, Jeremy Dixon, and this is Special Agent Bean, Joseph Bean."

They both stepped forward to shake my hands and the one introduced as Jeremy Dixon spoke as we shook. "We met several years ago. You worked with my cousin, David. You guys were partners."

Like a wave, face recognition kicked in and I remembered. My partner who had been killed outside that house had a cousin in the feds. I never knew him but did meet him at the funeral. He was angry and didn't mix his words. Words that had sat with me ever since—*You failed your partner. You failed my cousin. You were the experienced detective and you let him walk into a bullet. You should never hold a gun again and if I have anything to say about it, you won't.* At the time it was said, the events were still under investigation so I was limited to a desk.

"Yeah, I can see you remember now. When I saw you, I half expected you to punch me in the face, but I could tell you were caught by the suits and not the people behind them. Before we go any further, I wanted to apologize. Those comments were stated on emotion and held no truth."

I released his hand but did not speak. I don't think he knew how much his statement back then affected me. How much it still affected me, and no apology was going to wipe that away. I turned from facing him and stared blankly into space. Then back to Dixon, I replied, "I think about that afternoon every minute I'm on the street. Trust that whether you take your comment back now or not is immaterial. I did fail your cousin." Turning back to Simpson, "Now, can we get on with whatever this is, and don't tell me it's about Carter because I have nothing to say if that's the case."

Simpson motioned for everyone to again take their seats. "Let's all sit down and move beyond how this all started. We needed to get a few things out of the way, and we did." There was some shuffling around but in a few seconds, all were seated and facing each other. Simpson continued. "We are here for two reasons. First, the GiST team requested some help. They saw the case stalling and with multiple casualties, they didn't want it to go cold. Secondly, there have been some concerns coming out regarding this department. Concerns centered on the department's willingness to work with other departments, units, or law enforcement teams. We believe this starts with Carter, and we have been asked by the governor to assess that position. The governor was also very impressed with your performance on the Moretti-Polino case. Upon investigating your work history, it appears that the same individuals we feel may be keeping this department back are also keeping you back."

He stopped, creating a pause and ensuing silence that brought a level of discomfort to me and what appeared to be several others in the room. However, I had been an interrogator a long time and I would not fall prey to the silence-inducing panic. I simply leaned back and waited for someone, anyone, to say something.

"That was a lead-in for you to comment," Simpson finally said.

I then leaned forward. "Two comments: First, you didn't ask me a question. Second, the only thing I'm going to talk about is the case. I will not say a word about a man I respect as much as I respect my own father to fill some agenda for you or the governor. This department headed by Carter, of which I am a part, clears more cases than any other in the state and I would put our performance against any other department in the country. Therefore, if you want to ask me about the case, I will be glad to have a discussion. Otherwise, I guess I might as well get on with my investigation. I have another potential witness and suspect coming in today."

"You can play it any way you want, Detective O'Malley, but it will not change the outcome other than keep you where you are and move someone in around you."

I smiled. "Is that some sort of threat? Play ball or lose a promotion I don't want? Do your homework next time, Simpson. I am where I am because of me, nobody else.

I am an asshole and not afraid to show it. Ask Only and Toose." I glanced to Only and saw him nod. "Now, I will ask one more time—what do you want to know about this case?"

"So you are aware," replied Simpson. "Detective Only said you were one of the best detectives he had ever known." Simpson let that one sit in and I actually needed the time. I looked back to Only and he nodded again. "But he also said you were an asshole." I was still looking at him as he smiled just a bit, which I returned.

I lifted my eyebrow and placed my hands on the desk showing I was about ready to stand up and leave. "Is that all?"

"What are we dealing with? One killer, or multiple killers working together?" he asked.

My arms relaxed slightly and the two to three inches I had begun to lift off the chair collapsed back down. "One killer. Ex-military but not just military, Special Forces or simply an extremely skilled marksman. Also, the motive we believe is centered on two individuals: the first murder of the counselor Dawn Wells who was killed in the barrel of chemical, and the hit-and-run of the teenager. We believe the teenager was the focus but it was Dawn Wells whose job it was to help and she ignored the pleas from a student. The others are fallout from a simple need to destroy all who were a factor and should have stopped it."

Simpson shook his head, glanced to Toose and Only, and then back to me. "So you don't think this could be one of the students?"

"No way," I replied. "This is way too sophisticated. It's almost too well thought out to even be an emotional male. The planning is more female, but the action is all our main suspect."

Simpson seemed to be intrigued with this line of thinking. It was tied to my old experiences that the best planned murders were those planned by women. The best pulled off murders were those done by men. The most dangerous murderer was the man who could plan like a woman. Franky called my theory sexist but he couldn't argue with our history. We saw it time and time again. Simpson followed the short pause with the sixty-four thousand dollar question. "Who is your suspect then?"

"Jack Kittleson," I replied. "He's a Marine who operated much of his career as a sniper. His son had come out as a homosexual and has a heavily documented history of being bullied by the hit-and-run victim. He went with his son and ex-wife and complained to the discipline committee and was ignored. I have his son coming in this morning and I bet we'll find out that his son went first to the counselor to ask for guidance, just like another student had previously."

Simpson turned to Only. "Jesus, why don't you guys have a full workup on this guy? Why the hell are you looking at students?" Only started to speak but was cut off. "This guy is a former Marine or is active now?"

That question always sat wrong with me but I let it slide. "Once a Marine, always a Marine," I replied. "But he is not on active duty now. He runs a food plant in Minnesota. He was unable to verify an alibi for the times of the murders but we are verifying what he claims now using traffic cameras."

"Dixon, put a call into the Minneapolis office and let's grease the wheels for them. Who are you working with in the Minnesota homicide department?"

I stammered just a bit because I didn't know what I was going to get Zimm involved with if I named him, but I was too far out the door to turn back now. EZ Zimmerman, a friend of mine not in the homicide department any longer, is gathering the info. He's part of..."

"I know Zimm," Simpson interrupted with a raised hand. "Keep us informed with what he finds and if he can clear Mr. Kittleson. Where is your suspect now?"

This was the part I was not thrilled about saying. "As far as I know, he's back on the road to Minnesota. We didn't have anything to hold..."

"What!" Simpson exclaimed. "You let him walk?"

"There was no way the district attorney would have even held him on our current evidence. We cannot even catch him in a lie. He has admitted to not liking anyone on the committee, he has admitted to knowing his son was bullied by the Schulman boy, and he even said he was not sad about any of the murders we discussed. However, we have no physical evidence. The only evidence we have is a size eleven shoe print at every scene and Kittleson, like about 1/5th of the Chicagoland male population, wears the same size shoe."

"Who else are you looking at?" Simpson asked.

"To be honest, every one of our suspects after that is dead or a student. These are complicated murders. I just don't see a student being able to pull even one of these off, much less all of them. Our last lead is a mystery cell phone call that we think basically pushed the principal to suicide. Other than that, we are going to further interview Jack Kittleson's ex-wife and son to see if they can knowingly or unknowingly bring anything new against Jack. It's a longshot, but I have had longer shots than this payoff before. We have a few angles to work and they are already on their way in."

We exchanged a few more comments on the case, our findings, and what was up next, but in the end, the information they needed was already provided. I stood to walk out and Simpson grabbed my arm and turned me back to face him. "Regarding my original comments, I would ask you keep them to yourself, but if you choose not to, I would understand. I also understand your position and at some level I respect it. Defending your supervisor is critical to any officer ranks. However, you also have to be free to admit when something or someone is not working. At some point you need to start managing you own career, don't you think?"

"I am," I replied without hesitation.

As I walked out, he added, "Send in Sullivan please."

•   •   •   •   •

Franky, Carter, Halterman, and Huston all had turns in the Royals room. None took as long as my visit except Carter's, which went about thirty minutes longer. I did what any good detective would do and immediately went to Carter with what they had said. He was immediately steamed, and then just shook his head. He knew there were rumblings about him. There always were. It came with the job and he knew that to worry about it would only make it worse. He would control what he could control and let everything else fall where it did. Good advice, I always thought.

While Franky was in, Becky and Nate Kittleson arrived. They both appeared completely worn out, as if they had gone without sleep for days. I didn't know if this would make the interview better or worse, but my hope was they would have less barriers and be more susceptible to sharing. Basically, I hoped because they were tired, they would want the interview to end more quickly and be less protective about what they said.

I sat down with Becky and Nate Kittleson, handing them both a bottled water as I took my place across from them. "Well, I have some good news. We found the evidence we needed to confirm your son's story. He did actually drive down to Lakeshore that morning and could not have been anywhere near the hit-and-run." Their shoulders both dropped and I could see their whole bodies relax as if a stress had been lifted. Perfect, I thought. "Yes, we saw him all the way up until he stopped and parked through until he left. There was no way he could have stolen the car or committed the crime."

This statement served two purposes. First, it restated that at the time of the accident, we had irrefutable proof that Nate Kittleson was nowhere near the hit-and-run. However, and most importantly, I was trying to build some additional trust between Nate and me because I let him know we knew he met someone down there but I was not going to tell his mother that is what took place. I saw the concern in his eyes the minute I said it, then I saw that concern fade and understanding move in when I took the discussion no further.

"So, my question for you both is this. If you clearly didn't do this, who do you think did?"

They looked at each other and Nate looked down. The move was common with witnesses who were hiding something, but I wasn't sure if Nate was hiding something with the murders or still hiding his morning rendezvous the day of the hit-and-run.

"Why are you looking at me?" Nate said.

"Because I just asked you a question and you immediately looked away," I replied. "You are giving me a signal that you might have some ideas. Do you, Nate? Do you know who killed these people?"

"I don't know anything, Detective. Why would I?" He was becoming a bit agitated already. It seemed too quick to become so defensive but again, I was going to let it pass right now but keep pushing nonetheless.

"Well, let me ask this differently. Let me tell you both what we know, and you tell me if it sounds like anyone you know. "Our suspect is most likely male. We don't think it's a student because some of the murders are complicated to a level a teenager would not have the experience to plan. One of the murders required the ability to fire a weapon from a great distance. Only someone who had extensive training or an innate natural ability could have done it. We are thinking military background. Then obviously someone with a motive because of the victims involved. We believe the motive is revenge against the person who hurt multiple other students through social media as well as against the school's committee that evaluated the complaints and didn't act on them."

Nate instantly turned to his mom and she shook her head telling him "no" without speaking.

"Nate, what are you thinking? It's a crime to withhold information. It makes you an accessory. If you know something, you have to tell me now."

"Leave him alone, Detective," stated Becky sternly. "You know as well as I do what he is thinking. You just described his father to a tee, but his father is one of the gentlest individuals I know."

"That gentle individual just took down and beat Mark Schulman's father when his father came after him in the office out there. Had we not stepped in, he would have beaten him fairly well. That gentle man was a Marine who you know operated at a level that required him to make life and death decisions under the guidance of war. That gentle man just raised his voice to every detective within earshot standing firm on his ground. Are you sure you don't want to tell me more that your ex-husband has done? He is not the gentle giant you claim him to be."

"You don't know him, Detective. You see him as some gun-happy Marine who served and must be damaged goods and ready to take the law into his own hands anytime something doesn't go right for him. Well, you're wrong, and we don't need to stay to help you railroad him into jail." She stood and grabbed her son at the shoulder to pull him with her.

"Wait a minute, Mrs. Kittleson, it's worth noting I'm a Marine, just like Jack." She stopped and stared at me. "I would like to hope I don't think of anybody, Marine or not, as damaged goods. I am not here to railroad anyone. I simply asked if you or your son knew anyone who fit that bill. Have we considered Jack Kittleson as a suspect? Of course we have, but it should be easy for him to clear himself because he lives six hours away. All we need is to find one traffic camera or business that can confirm his location during any of the murders. Maybe my question for you is why did you get so defensive on the subject? Do you think he could be behind these murders?"

"I don't think anything of the sort, Detective. And don't you dare try to put words in my mouth." She was still standing and her son was looking up to her trying to determine if he needed to stand or not.

"I am not putting any words in your mouth or railroading your ex-husband." Trying to pull her back in, I moved from my previously open-ended question to one more directed at a subject. "Do you know any of the other children's families who were bullied or made fun of by Mark Schulman?"

She softened her grip on her son and moved to stand directly behind him with both hands on his shoulders. "Since all this started, I have learned that Mark bullied many kids, several in families we know and even know well, but until this happened, I had no idea it was occurring. Everyone kept it to themselves. I knew about the rumors around Leah Malecha, but the rumor I heard was that she made it up. I guess it holds more truth now with everything else." She paused, then looked back to me, and then remained quiet.

"What?" I asked. "You remembered something. I can tell."

She stumbled over a few words before finding her thought clearly. "I would never have thought anything of it at the time, but I ran into some girls I know through different school activities at Starbucks, and they were talking about a father blowing up at school one day over an incident. It was Dan Malecha, Leah's father. This is all thirdhand but he was incredibly angry from what I understand. I believe he was even said to have threatened Principal Bales, but you would need to check with him on that."

I did not want to dissuade her from additional feedback, so I wanted to support her feedback on Dan Malecha, although he was not a primary suspect at this time. "That is exactly the type of information I am looking for. You are making no claims of his innocence or guilt, just replaying some information you saw or heard. Is there anything else you can think of on Dan Malecha or anyone else?"

She shook her head negatively. "No, the only thing I can tell you is that since this all occurred, rumors have come out of the woodwork saying how Mark Shulman was horrible to different kids. The list of suspects from what I have heard will be extremely long and you would not be able to throw a dart in a room of students without hitting someone who was treated badly by the young man."

I was going to interject another question when Nate Kittleson opted to speak. "He treated everyone horrible. I would like to think I was the worst, but others were just as bad. The bottom line was, if his mouth was moving, he was tearing someone down. I don't know what made him so popular. It was almost like people wanted to be close to him to avoid being made fun of, but even that didn't matter most of the time. Sometimes, even his friends were his targets. It made no sense."

It was good to hear from Nate directly, but it really just reiterated my previous ideas. I understood their positions. They really didn't know any specifics and what they did know simply supported what I already knew. I could keep pushing. We could play a good cop/bad cop game, but in the end she was still in love with her ex-husband or in love with him to be there as a father for their son. There was no way she or her son would provide any information that could be used against him. I placed my hands on the table and stood. "I want to thank you both for your time and your candidness. We are checking every lead we can so if you think of anyone who was particularly upset at Mr. Schulman, made a scene, or anyone you just heard about, or even just a rumor, then please let me know." In police work you never know where your key lead will come from so leaving every door open was crucial. I knew where I thought guilt lied, and this interview didn't add any evidence to that case other than my main suspect's own family recognized it was possible for him to be guilty.

I remained standing, now not leaning on the table however. "You know, I don't have any more questions. Thank you for being so open."

"You're welcome, Detective, and sorry if I seemed defensive. I just know Jack had nothing to do with this."

"I understand." I paused and considered briefly one more thing to say before plowing forward with it. "On a side note, earlier you mentioned Principal Bales. I do have a bit of info for you."

"There's no way he is behind these murders. He was the reason Mark Schulman continued to stay out of trouble so he would never have killed him."

"No," I replied, raising my hand. "We know he's not responsible. He is," I paused to give it more emphasis, then continued. "He's dead."

"Dead?" questioned Nate immediately. "What happened?"

"At this stage I can't say anything more. It's already out in the news so you will hear about it shortly."

Nate stood and spoke softly. "That's all of them. Mark and the whole discipline committee. They're all dead."

"Yeah," I replied in a slow, solemn tone.

Nate continued. "Do you think the person behind them is done now?"

Interesting comment, I thought. "I don't know, Nate. What do you think?"

"I think he's done. I think he wanted to punish the person responsible and the committee that allowed it."

You do know something, I thought. *You are telling me I can cease and desist now because the person is done.* "Do you know who did these things, Nate?"

Becky began to protest again but I raised my hand and for some reason, she respected the action and did not stop her son from speaking. His eyes locked on mine. "No, but if it was someone whose son or daughter was tormented by Mark Schulman, I wouldn't blame them."

"Would you blame your dad?" I asked.

He stood and his tone became much harder. "You know what, Detective. All those nights I sat in my room crying because of how much I hated my life, how much I hated Mark Schulman, and even how much I hated what I was and I wanted to die, never once would I ever have considered killing him or any of that fucking discipline committee. However, now that they're all dead, I don't care. I feel nothing. I'm not sad. I'm not happy. I'm just numb."

Becky grabbed her son's hand. "Detective, I think we're done now."

"Nate, you did not answer my question. Would you blame your dad?" I asked again as they stepped toward the door.

He turned back to face me. "Detective, I would wonder how he could have done it, I would hug my dad and tell him thank you, and maybe I would even tell him it was wrong, but I would never blame him. Most likely, whoever did this, whether it was my dad or not, saved my life. I don't know that I would have made it through the school year if the bullying was left to continue. Mark Schulman may not have killed anyone himself, but he put the gun in everyone else's hands. I have sat in my room with a gun pointed directly into my brain because of that asshole." His mother's face dropped and she was about to speak but didn't as the boy continued. "And now I sit in my room wondering what tomorrow will bring. So don't ask me again if I would blame my dad or anyone else if they're the ones behind this whole thing. There's only one person guilty of murder, and that is Mark Schulman."

Becky rubbed her hand over her son's head and it was very clear to me the previous question would not be addressed further. No more words were spoken. Nate had said them all. I could not argue with the boy, but it was not my job to justify murder. It was my job to arrest murderers, and I now believed more than ever that Jack Kittleson would have handcuffs on him before the weekend was over, whether he was in Minnesota or not. Nate stood and reached out his hand to me. We shook and the boy and his mother left. They walked directly through the office never speaking or reacting to anyone. Their heads were held high. They did believe their father was behind these murders, and just like their father, they thought there was no way I could prove it.

19 OUR TEAM WATCHED the two leave and then all eyes stared at me through the window. I felt like a zoo animal. I rolled my eyes and motioned for them to come in. Huston and Halterman were in first while Franky headed over to Carter's office to get him. Shortly, all were around the table eager to hear the great information I was able to extract.

"I didn't get shit," I stated. "Other than I'm now sure Jack Kittleson is behind it, neither one of those two would give any evidence against him, even if they knew anything. I think they believe he's responsible, but there was no confiding in them in his actions."

"Plausible deniability," Halterman said. "If they don't know any facts, they don't have to lie to protect him."

"Well, is that it?" asked Carter. "He has left town. All the individuals he felt were responsible are dead. I would assume the killing is going to stop so there will be no new evidence. We would have to find something in the evidence we already have. What are the chances there's something there?"

I shook my head. "There's always something we missed in every case, but what do we have in this one? We have almost no evidence to work with. A shoe print that probably was planted, some stolen chemical taken from a former employer, a shot that only a handful of people could hope to make, and a burner phone used to talk a principal into suicide. There's nothing the district attorney will even consider for a warrant, much less an arrest."

"Then do we go back through everything again and see what turns up?" asked Halterman.

"Or do we just let this one go?" questioned Huston. "The kid was bad news. None of them deserved to die, I do agree, but nobody is really complaining either."

I was surprised at Huston's comments. "It's not our place to act as judge or make one murder less important because of the person killed. I know Mark's parents want this crime solved. I would guess all the other families do as well."

My tone came off more condescending than I would have preferred, but the message was still clear. We were homicide detectives, end of story. "I agree," she replied. "I just wanted to know where everyone stood."

Nice response, I thought.

Franky put his hands on the table. "Then I guess it's settled. Let's go back into the Royals room and go through every murder. Let's not leave one page unturned. Something has to be there. Maybe not enough to convict, but enough to keep this investigation going. We don't want this to turn into a cold case. We are the best department in the country for a reason. We don't allow cold cases."

Everyone seemed onboard with this. It was not the Jim Valvano "Never Give Up" speech, which by the way is the greatest speech of all time, but it was good enough to get everyone focused. We all collectively headed into the other conference room when my phone rang. I looked down and said the name out loud. "Zimm." I glanced to Franky. "Maybe he just found the missing evidence we need."

"Hello, Zimm," I answered.

There was a pause. It was short, but still a pause, as if he didn't know what he was going to say. This immediately put me on alert. "Hey, Tommy," he finally replied. "We got something up here."

"You found something in the tapes?" I asked, actually lifting my voice in excitement. All eyes in the room turned to me.

Again he paused. "No, not exactly. My team reviewed all the tapes and already sent you copies of any hits on the car. There are some overlaps but even our face recognition software couldn't make out the driver clearly. It is his car, but we can't confirm he's the driver." He paused again, took a breath, and continued. "But that's not why I'm calling."

I wanted to keep those around me included as best I could, but this call was different. There was something going on with Zimm that was not like previous discussions. "Okay, so the tapes are being sent to us here in Chicago for review, and there may be some evidence we can confirm but your initial work is inconclusive." The team around me understood. "But what else has you concerned? I can hear it in your voice."

"I think you need to come up here as soon as possible," he replied.

"You want me in Minnesota? Can I ask why?"

"Because I have a murder-suicide with your business card pinned under the knife that stabbed the first victim." My face went white, and I nearly dropped the phone. After what had to be a five to seven second pause, Zimm added, "Are you able to come up here?"

My voice was soft and slightly broken. "Yeah, buddy, I will send you my travel arrangements as soon as I have them."

Those in the room saw my change. "What is it?" asked Franky.

"I need to go to Minnesota, immediately. Zimm has a case with my business card at the scene."

Carter nodded. "I'll get you a flight set up. Head to Midway. Southwest has the most flights."

"Is this related to our case here?" asked Franky.

"I don't know yet, but this case is the only case I have ties to in Minnesota."

"That you know about," added Franky.

"Yeah," I replied. "That I know about."

I walked over to my desk and grabbed a few things. Halterman stuck her head out the door. "Do you want me to go with you, partner?"

"Normally I would say yes, but since I'm meeting Zimm there, I think I'll go alone. You keep working with the team here to find anything we might have missed. I will keep you guys informed on what I find up there."

She smiled. "Then aren't you forgetting something?"

"What?" I replied. "I can figure out clothes if I'm stuck overnight."

"Don't you have a girlfriend waiting at home for you that flew halfway across the country to surprise you?"

"Ah shit!" I said. "Thanks, I guess I need to call her."

"You guess?" she replied smiling. "I would say so."

•　　•　　•　　•　　•

I was in my car within five minutes and hit my speed dial for Tammi. She picked up on one ring. "Hi, Tommy. Please say you are on your way home. I have something special planned tonight."

My heart sank and I must have given the same slight pause that Zimm gave me because Tammi replied before I could even get a word out. "Jesus, you're not coming home, are you, Tommy?"

Like ripping a Band-Aid, I just needed to say it. "There's a dead body in Minnesota with my business card on it. I'm heading to Midway now and have to fly there."

"You're leaving the state!" she interrupted. "This is fucking bull..."

"Hey, Tammi," I now interrupted. "I have an idea if you are up for it. Why don't you meet me at Midway? I will get you a ticket and we can spend the time together. I will have to be on the case for an hour or two I'm sure, but after that, we can find a nice place to eat and spend the night. We can call it a mini vacation." This was a desperate move. I recognized the situation was going nowhere positive and had to make an immediate call. I took a shot. Either she would see through it and tell me to hit the road recognizing I really didn't want her to go but I was not ready to lose her completely, or fall for it as genuine.

"I can be at the airport in thirty minutes," she replied, actually sounding happy.

It was funny, this was what I wanted, but the minute I got it, I started to wonder why the hell I just invited her. "Great," I replied. Grab some clothes for me and some bathroom stuff and when I get my flight confirmed, I'll get you one as well. I'll meet you at security."

We both hung up and I imagined what her thoughts were. She was probably jumping around the room quickly gathering things excited I had invited her on a trip. Excited that I cared that much to not give up on us. Conversely, all I could think was, *shit, what did I just do*?

•　　•　　•　　•　　•

She walked down the ramp from the parking lot directly toward security. Midway was smaller and security was usually pretty smooth. I had already gotten clearance for my gun but it still would be an issue as I went through. There are several facts in the world that everyone accepts. Things like, the sky is blue, the grass is green, and TSA agents are assholes to cops because they can be. However, with all my misgivings about asking Tammi to join, when I saw her approaching, my heart moved–or maybe it wasn't my heart but about 18 inches below my heart—whatever it was, it definitely moved. Oh my God, she was gorgeous.

"That was the look I was hoping for," she said softly as she arrived.

"You were able to throw that ensemble together in thirty minutes, of which twenty was a drive?" I asked. "How can you do that?"

"I told you. I had a big night planned for us. I was going to take you to the Chicago Chop House and maybe see about my old job."

I froze and turned her to face me. "What?" I said astonished. "You're not moving to California?"

"Not if it means losing you, Tommy," she replied, taking both my hands in hers. "I love you."

"Keep the line moving, you two," stated a crabby TSA voice to my side.

She smiled broadly. I wanted to say I love you too. I had said it to her numerous times, but for some reason, it just didn't feel right. "I love you too, Tammi." What can I say? I'm a guy.

We continued walking much to the pleasure of the TSA agent who basically walked alongside us making sure we didn't stop again. We arrived at the screening area and I handed the agent my identification, badge, gun, and paperwork from the airline. I'm not sure, but I think the large man controlling the scanner actually smiled when he saw my information. "Come this way, Officer O'Malley," the big guy said, still grinning. He then gave Tammi the up-down and motioned her forward. "You may go through the scanner, honey."

"It's Detective O'Malley, and she is not your honey," I replied in my best *I'm not taking your bullshit* tone.

"Well, looks like I might have a live one today," he replied, not giving a care for my tough guy persona. "I hope you don't miss your flight because of an additional full cavity search."

"I hope I don't also," I replied. Clearly the "for your sake" I didn't say was still heard by the jackass.

All in all, the delay was minor and we were at the gate in plenty of time. I had forked out the additional forty dollars to board early so we had boarding numbers four and five. If you have never flown Southwest Airlines, they are by far the best airline in America but only if you want your planes to be on time, the flight attendants to be courteous and sometimes even funny, and the flight to be for the most part, enjoyable. If you wanted first class service with free drinks, you got the first class service on every flight, but the drinks cost you four or five dollars. I would take that every time. I took my traditional seat, the exit row with no seat in front of it. Tammi sat right next to me. The flight was not full so after everyone was on, she could have spread out one seat if she wanted to, but she stayed against me, tight. I liked it.

I had texted Zimm our flight info when I was waiting for Tammi. He was going to have a car there to pick me up but instead, since Tammi was with me, I had the department get me a rental. I had not had a chance to talk to him further. We had a few minutes before phones had to be turned off so I thought I would throw a call his direction. If I could find out what the hell had happened there, I could use the flight to think through it, although Tammi may have other things on her mind. I had always fantasized about the mile high club, I mean what boy hadn't. However, I was probably too old for such activities and the last thing I needed to explain was an indecent exposure issue–so for Detective Tomas O'Malley, that would have to remain a fantasy.

"What are you thinking about?" Tammi asked.

"Uh," I stammered. "The case. Yes, the case."

"Oh," she replied, because I was thinking about..." She leaned over and whispered in my ear.

"Bingo!" I said out loud, smiling.

She leaned back and closed her eyes placing one hand on my leg. "You sure you need to do this case thing in Minnesota?"

I was still smiling at the words she had whispered, but did still need to make this call. "Unfortunately, yes, but that does not rule out your suggestion."

She just remained with eyes closed leaning back as I grabbed my phone and hit my speed dial. "You on your plane yet?" Zimm asked, without even saying hello.

"Yep," I replied. "About ready to take off. I have a minute or so, can you fill me in?"

Zimm understood I had little time and went straight to what he knew. "I don't know much yet. I am headed to the scene right now. I got a call this morning because the detective on the scene knew I had a relation in the Chicago PD. Your card was there on the murder victim. It was actually pinned with a knife to his chest. It is my understanding the perpetrator who stabbed the man then pulled out a gun and shot himself. They didn't have the name at the time of my first call. I pulled the address and realized I was just there. It's the Kittleson house. I believe Jack Kittleson is dead."

"Jesus," I replied flatly.

Zimm continued. "Yeah, I thought you might say that. I put a call into my boss and the case is mine"—he paused—"and yours. The detectives on the scene are simply preserving the scene for us."

"Who is the other victim? Do you have an identification?"

"I don't even have a positive ID on the first victim yet, but I should have most of the preliminary information in hand by the time you arrive. Just come straight here when you can. Lakeville is twenty-five minutes or so from the airport."

"Will do," I replied. "Hey, Zimm, thanks for calling."

"No problem, partner. See you in a couple hours."

We hung up and Tammi looked over to me. "I can tell this is not good news. I will leave you be on the case. I know it's more important. I'm just glad you didn't shut me out. Thank you for bringing me with you."

I smiled and pressed my lips together, but didn't answer. My mind was on Jack Kittleson. I wondered who had killed him. This case was not dead yet, but my primary suspect was, so maybe the case would be closed after this flight. Maybe the final piece of evidence was in those videos or in the house. Regardless, I would know more shortly. I leaned back in my seat and Tammi laid her head on my shoulder. To both our surprises, we were asleep before takeoff.

•　　•　　•　　•　　•

The flight was perfect and when we walked into National to get our car, the young man behind the counter looked at Tammi and magically we were upgraded to a Ford Expedition. If I was hot, I would use it for everything, and I guarantee I would always get upgraded. Instead, the guys behind the counter usually looked at me and I got whatever was left.

I pulled into the neighborhood where Jack Kittleson and his new wife Kim lived.

It was a golf community called Brackets and the houses were large, but not obscene. Very nice, large trees, and family friendly. I liked the area. It reminded me of Naperville, but not as pretentious. I knew even when we were a block away which house was his. There was a wall of flashing lights, crime scene tape, and vehicles. It appeared most of the neighborhood was outside watching. When I pulled up in the rental car, I was immediately stopped. I rolled down my window and showed my Illinois badge. "I was called in to work with Eric Zimmerman. Is he available?"

"Yes, Detective O'Malley, he let us know you would be coming. Pull over there and park. Zimm is inside talking with the victim's wife." He looked over to Tammi and how she was dressed and questioned if she was a detective as well. "Is she..."

I cut him off. "Nope, she's going to take the car and get us checked into a nearby hotel." This statement seemed to please the officer.

I pulled the car over. "There's a Holiday Inn one exit up. We have a suite reserved there under both our names. Go check in. They recommended a restaurant called Porterhouse down the street but also said they have a nice place attached. I set us up at Porterhouse but you can scout around. I may be one to two hours and I'll have Zimm drop me off back at the hotel. Check things out and I'll call when I know something."

"I will take care of things, but don't forget what I whispered to you in the airplane. I don't want to lose those thoughts because it takes you too long." She was smiling and the dress she was wearing had slit up the side which she shifted to allow her long leg to show. "If you know what I'm saying..."

I could not take my eyes from her leg. "Yes, damn it, I know what you're saying." I opened the door and ran smack dab into a shorter, bald man in street clothes. The impact sent me back against the car and him to the ground.

"Jesus," I said. "What the hell?"

"Sorry," the man said as he picked himself up.

"Can I help you?" I asked, reaching my hand down to help him up.

"Mike," the man replied. "Mike Gerber." He reached out to shake my hand. "I'm Jack's neighbor. "We're just wondering if everything is okay."

"Well, Mike," I replied. "Slamming into me is probably not the best way to get information, if I could tell you anything anyway, which I can't. So therefore, excuse me as I need to go do my job." I stepped by him shaking my head. *Are you serious*? I thought.

I approached the crime scene tape and the officer I had met was waiting there but his eyes were locked behind me. I followed his gaze to see Tammi climbing into the driver's seat. I smiled. *Yep, she's with me*, I wanted to say, but instead I simply said, "Right through there?" I pointed toward the door.

The medical examiner was still on the scene. There was a body in the doorway with a knife through the chest and a body on the front patio with most of its head missing. However, my heart stopped when I recognized both bodies. I had spoken to both of them that day and even broke up a scuffle between them. Jack Kittleson had the knife through the chest and presumably the man who wielded that knife was laying on the ground beside him. That man was Mike Schulman.

The medical examiner was a man in what appeared to be his seventies but I'm sure he was not that old. Quincy came to mind as I looked down to him. "Can I help you?" he asked, clearly not recognizing me.

"I'm Detective Tomas O'Malley, Chicago Homicide. Detective Zimmerman called me in. I know both your victims."

"And that is your card permanently affixed to his chest then, Detective O'Malley," the ME said.

I looked closer to the knife and saw my card, now covered in blood, essentially stapled to Jack Kittleson's chest. "It is," I replied.

He stood and I wasn't sure, but I think I heard his back creak as he pushed himself up. He noticed my nonverbal response. "Yes, Detective, I am old. I should have retired two years ago but the cases keep pulling me back in." I started to protest that I didn't mean anything and he waved it off. "You are not the only one I get that crap from, but not usually from people I just met." He was smiling so he kept me at ease. "Now, you said you know both victims. We have a positive ID on Kittleson because his wife witnessed the crime, but she did not know the perpetrator. Who is this?" He motioned to the nearly defaced body of Mike Schulman.

"His name is Mike Schulman. His son was killed in a multiple homicide case in Chicago. Mr. Schulman, like me, thought Jack Kittleson committed those crimes, but we had nothing yet to tie directly to him. We were and are still building the case. Evidently he did not want to wait for the evidence to develop so he took things into his own hands. Now more are dead and two more families are without parents."

"It sounds like a tough case, Detective," he replied. "I will get my report done tonight so you have it. This portion looks pretty straightforward. Murder-suicide. We have a witness and the evidence confirms it."

Wow, I thought. Providing information before the investigation is complete. Doc G could learn a few things from...I didn't even catch his name. "Thank you, and I did not catch your name?"

"Grove, Doctor Alan Grove." He paused, took off his glove, and reached his hand out. "You know, you may know my daughter-in-law. She's been the medical examiner in Chicago forever. Elise..."

"Gerstenberger," I finished for him.

"Great, so you do know her. She married my son..."

"Alan Grove," again I completed. "The second, I presume."

"Well, he is the second but we don't call him that. We call him Doctor Grove the sellout." He smiled as he meant it in an endearing fashion. "He doesn't even practice medicine and works at that pharmaceutical giant in Chicago making ten times what we do and we're actually saving lives. Just doesn't seem right, but I couldn't be more proud."

"I can tell," I replied. "Now, I suppose I should speak to Zimm."

He pointed to the other side of a staircase to what I assume was a kitchen. "Through there. He's speaking to the wife."

"Thank you, Dr. Grove, and so you are aware, your daughter-in-law is pretty talented as well."

He smiled and I carefully made my way through the entry and into the house. I heard some talking coming from the kitchen and immediately recognized one of the voices as my friend, EZ Zimmerman. Before entering, however, I decided to look through the wall of pictures in the living room. Mrs. Kittleson had done an incredible job organizing four shelves that were deeper on the bottom and as the shelves went up, the depth got less giving it a nice dimension on the wall. On those shelves was their life. Pictures of their family, awards, mementos, and basically everything you would need to see to learn who this family was without knowing them. I looked through everything very carefully. I saw Jack with Nate, Nate winning some contests at school, photos of Kim with what I was guessing were kids from a previous marriage, and then my eyes rested on one picture. It was a photo of Kim standing next to her husband with the photo placed on a gold plaque. First place in the Horse and Hunt Club annual sharpshooter contest. If I still needed any proof the guy could have made that shot on the soccer field, I now had it.

I turned and walked into the kitchen where Kim Kittleson's eyes raised as she saw me. "I know who you are," she said. "You're that detective from Chicago. Jack described you to a tee."

"Hello, Tommy," stated Zimm. "Good to see you. This is Kim Kittleson, Jack Kittleson's wife. She witnessed the whole thing. Kim, this is Detective Tomas O'Malley. He's been handling the case back in Chicago."

"I am sorry for your loss, Mrs. Kittleson. I had been speaking with Jack quite a bit these past few days. I know he loved his family very much." I was trying to break the ice. I didn't know what to expect with Mrs. Kittleson yet. I found out quickly.

"Listen here, Detective O'Malley. Jack told me all about you. How you were trying to railroad him into jail. He had nothing to do with these murders and your constant bending of the events to tailor it to making him guilty. He told me about the altercation in the police station. He told me how that man blamed him for the murders and you did nothing about it. I don't want to talk to you, Detective. As far as I'm concerned, you put that knife in that man's hand and you killed my husband."

At least she wasn't going to mix words, I thought. "Mrs. Kittleson, I am not here to upset you. I am here to solve six murders. I am not going to lie, one of my suspects was your husband, but Detective Zimmerman and I were working very hard to clear him. All we needed was to confirm some times when he was in Minnesota. I am sure he would have been cleared by the end of the weekend." Yep, I was still lying, but I was on what I called "damage control" lying.

She turned her head as if to say, *I don't care what bullshit you're laying on me. I am not interested.* "You can say whatever you want, Detective. Jack did not like you, and now he's dead. Anything you want to say to me is not worth hearing."

I understood her anger, and really didn't have anything more to say. I did think Jack Kittleson was guilty. Did that cloud my judgement with Mike Schulman? Most likely, but nobody could have seen Schulman driving six hours to commit a murder. We had run a full background on him. There was nothing in his past that would have predicted this.

Zimm used the short silence to break in. "We will get the report from the medical examiner tomorrow; however, we do believe it will say what you've already told us. Jack's body will be released to you I would guess by noon or so tomorrow. Other than that, I'm not sure if there's anything else we need at this time. If something comes up that we don't expect in the report, Detective O'Malley and I will be back to discuss it. I know it seems like Jack was not dealt a fair hand, but I have reviewed the whole report, and the Chicago team, in particular Detective O'Malley, gave him every opportunity to clear himself. Between DVR cameras not functioning and the inability to account for his time, clearing him has just taken longer than we would have planned."

She seemed to accept that answer better than anything from me, but still there was no trust coming my way. I turned to exit the kitchen and then thought I would try one more time to find some common ground. "Before I came in, I was impressed with the shelving you put together on the wall. I love that picture of you and Jack and the shooting award."

"Thank you, Detective, but I guess there won't be any more shooting contests in our future, will there?"

Right back with a slap across my face. I wanted to reply but a glance to Zimm confirmed what I was feeling. I better just let this one go. The time was not right to find a bond. My investigation needed to end. The case may be dead. The murders were going to end for one of two reasons: Because the murderer was dead or because all the people involved are now dead and the plan was complete – or both. Either way, the easy solution to this case was to pin it on Jack Kittleson and close the case without charges being filed. Whether it was through the proper channels or not, he had faced the death penalty, and the case was over.

Zimm and I talked briefly outside. He confirmed that the passports and video had all been sent to my attention and would arrive tomorrow in Chicago. He offered to have me and Tammi join him for dinner so I took a few minutes to fill him in on the current events in our lives. After hearing every aspect of our story, Zimm simply said, "Good God, go to your own dinner. The last thing I want is to be around your mess tonight."

Zimm had a way with words. We bid each other farewell. We agreed that the case was most likely dead. At this point, we would need another murder to create some new steam around it and nobody wanted that to happen, or believed it would. The facts were, even if it was not Jack Kittleson, he was going to be labeled with it. We would inspect the tapes and determine if we could confirm it was not Jack, but assuming we could not, there would be no reason to continue without another viable suspect. My fear was simple. If it wasn't Jack, then someone got away with six murders by taking the law into their own hands. What would stop them from doing it again?

I showed up at the hotel about an hour after Tammi left me. She had the place fully organized. She had wine on ice, beer in the refrigerator, and had gotten a new room away from the water park that was loaded with kids and noise. This was a super hotel, and seeing what Tammi was wearing made me define it as incredible. We were not going to make our reservations, that much was clear. We spent an extra hour before dinner ensuring we still were compatible, then after having Porterhouse find us a table just before they closed, we had one of the best meals I have ever eaten, a meal that my beautiful date was equally impressed with. We then went back to the hotel and tested our compatibility two more times.

The next day we headed to the airport first thing in the morning and it seemed like things were the way they used to be, with one exception, since she mentioned possibly not moving to California, she had not mentioned it again. It was like a heavy weight was sitting on us but nobody wanted to talk about it because it would hamper all the progress we had gained. I didn't know what she was going to do. I didn't know what I wanted her to do. I was definitely under her control when we were together. She was beautiful and out of my league, but now I just wanted things back to the way they were, before California. However, my fear was even if she did stay, my feelings would never be the same. My feelings toward her were different now. She was still everything I dreamed about in looks, but her career was something that drove her, and with this recent offer in California, she would either blame me for not taking it or soon another offer would come and the situation would repeat itself. I was not going to leave Chicago, and I didn't think she would always stay. Knowing that, what were we really doing?

We landed just before noon on Saturday. The Kansas game was already on and

I stole a glance as I walked by Harry Carry's restaurant in the airport. I had heard they were going to close this location during the remodel of the airport. It was a great place to go with the limited options. In fact, the first day I saw Jamal Jackson after his father had been killed, we sat and had a meal here. Kansas was up by twelve only two minutes into the first half. I had no time to watch today so the highlights would have to be good enough.

"That's the boy from that murder," Tammi said as she followed my eyes to the television above the bar.

"Yep," I replied. "That's Jamal Jackson. He will probably go pro after this year. With everything that happened with his family, I think he wants to provide for them."

Nothing more was said. We continued to our cars. We both parked in the same lot and by chance were only five spaces apart. After a passionate kiss, we went our separate ways. I had already called the office and they were on the lookout for the packages from Minnesota. I was going to head straight there. I was going to close this case today if it took the rest of the day to do it. Franky and the team were going to meet me there and we would finalize the case. They had reviewed the file yesterday after I left for Minnesota. I was going to add in what I learned in Lakeville and end it there. A quick review of the video recovered from Zimm and we should be done. I felt horrible about where this case had gone. I had been a step or two behind every action and now, after six murders and two suicides, I had nothing conclusive to show for it. With multiple governors involved in this case, there would be fallout. I wondered how far it would reach. I remembered the exchange with Toose and Only regarding Carter. One case was going to change so much.

Just then my phone rang. "We just received two packages," Franky said through the speakerphone. "The videos all came in with labels, time stamps, and descriptions. I sent them to IT to break them down. They said it should only take a few hours. By the time you get here, we'll know if there's anything our guys can see that theirs did not. They said we have two things going for us. First, we know what we're looking for, and second, we have a..."

I was not sure if the phone went dead or if Franky just stopped speaking. "Franky?"

"I'm still here," he replied. "I don't know what the hell he called it but for our purposes, we have a Flux Capacitor and Minnesota does not so we might be able to add some clarity to the video."

"We have a Flux Capacitor?"

"Yes," he replied with emphasis. "We do, and it's a good thing."

"Okay then, let's hope it's fluxing today," I replied. "See you in twenty."

For the next two hours after I arrived, the team went through everything they came up with the day before. I had already contacted them yesterday with the events in Lakeville, and Franky actually was the detective who delivered the news to Runae Schulman. He said it didn't go well, but left it at that. As we reviewed everything, I think we all knew the results but nobody would say it until Carter finally closed it all down.

"Unless we find conclusive video support that Jack Kittleson was in Minnesota during any of these murders, my final report to the governor is going to list him as the primary suspect but with his death, we are suspending the investigation." This meant it would not be considered a closed case, but nobody would be actively working it either.

I was going to protest but realized there was nothing to say. There is no such thing as the perfect murder, but these were close. We reviewed everything and we had no evidence. Not a little evidence or a few pieces of evidence, we had nothing.

Just then Craig Swanson from the lab appeared in the doorway. "Swanny," I said. "Please say you found something."

He shook his head. "Sorry, guys. We were able to lighten the video significantly more than the Minneapolis guys did, but it still didn't give a confirmed facial recognition on your suspect. It is close, but only a 60% match. Not enough for even a warrant."

"But I thought you had the Flux Capacitor?" I asked.

"Flux Capacitor?" Swanny questioned in return.

Franky interjected. "You know, the thing you told me about that was better than what Minneapolis had."

"Oh," he replied. "IRMaCS–the Illinois Recognition Matrix Comparison System."

"Flux Capacitor?" I stated softly staring at Franky.

"What? If I had said IRMaCS you would have said, what is IRMaCS? I would have then said, a Flux Capacitor thing that helps identify people, and you would have said…"

"Enough," interrupted Patti. "You two are like kids." She turned to Swanny. "Go ahead."

Swanny smiled. "To answer the question, yes, we used IRMaCS and it did improve the results achieved in Minnesota, but not to an acceptable level. We do not have conclusive evidence that will confirm your guy was in the driver's seat."

"Then that's it, isn't it?" asked Patti.

Franky, Carter, and I all looked at each other, and we knew the answer. She was right. We were not going to keep the case open without a viable suspect. We would not close it. It would go into the cold case files for a later date. Truth is, I may put a reminder in my calendar to review it each year and maybe spend a few hours on it, but unless something else happened, another similar murder or something involving our other suspects or victims or maybe the school, this case would remain unanswered. That pain came to me. That pain in my gut that crept up every time I failed. I walked over to my desk, cleared off what I could in short order, and then stuffed the file from this case in my paper tray on the corner. I turned and headed to the door.

"What? You're just leaving?" Patti asked.

I stopped and turned back to see both ladies were looking at me but Franky and Carter had both started moving to their desk and office as well. "Folks, it's over for now. It's also Saturday and I have someone at home and I need to determine what direction our relationship is taking. I am not in a good place, so I'm going to go do something that I have let go for the last week. I am going to go to my dojo and train for two hours and then I'm going home. Do you want to join me, Franky?" Franky was not into martial arts, but he often would train with me simply to keep himself in shape. He was older than me and often used it as a form of meditation over an actual workout, but either way, it helped. I needed it today. That much was certain.

"I'll be right behind you," he replied.

The conversation ended the questions from everyone and the entire team slowly disbanded, each going to close down their computers and pick up their personal items to leave.

"So, that's all you need from me?" questioned Swanny.

I smiled at him. "Yes, Swanny, you can go too. Sorry, but your information was less than helpful."

I headed to the elevator without another comment. Franky was gathering a few items and was about to leave when Swanny came over. "Here are the passports from the Kittlesons. They came in a short while ago, and I thought I would bring them up when the results were finalized with the video."

Franky looked at the large envelope and motioned to his desk. "Drop them here. I will send them back next week. We don't need them now."

Swanny threw them down. "They really were not both needed. The wife's was expired for more than a month. I checked the system, and she had another on order but it wasn't sent out yet. I put a hold on it but will release it with an explanation before I head home today."

"Sounds good," Franky replied. "And Swanny, as always, thanks for your hard work. I know it's Saturday and sometimes we forget that you work as many hours as we do."

"No problem, Franky. You and Tommy are the good guys. Anything you need, just ask."

They nodded good-bye and left it at that. Franky gathered his stuff and the two women were walking out just as he left his desk so he joined them in the elevator. Before he left the office area, however, he hollered back to Carter who remained at his desk. "See ya, boss, don't stay too late. This case is done."

Carter nodded but said nothing. Huston leaned closer to Franky and asked, "Is he just going to stay here today?"

"Most likely," Franky replied. "Most likely."

20 MY WORKOUT WAS as hard as I had done in weeks. Even Master Yi was in disbelief on the extent to which I pushed myself. Master Yi was the highest ranking black belt in the United States. He had trained me since I moved to Chicago as a boy. He was now in his seventies and would not be training much longer; in fact, he did little training now, but always took time to spend with me. He also liked Franky. He called him Yujin, which literally translates from Japanese as "friend," but I always thought he meant it more along the lines of "nice guy." I don't think he ever saw the killer instinct in Franky, but Franky didn't need it.

When we finished, we were sitting on the floor with Master Yi, and even Franky had worked up an incredible sweat. "Thank you for joining me today, Franky. It was a good workout."

"No problem, partner, though maybe I can't call you that anymore."

We both smiled but no further comments were made. I slapped Master Yi on the back as I did every time. I don't know when or why I started doing it, but for whatever reason, he seemed to hang around until I did it. It was a signal that the workout was done. Master Yi got up, bowed, to which I returned, and then headed back to the main floor. He had a class of young boys there. They would not appreciate Master Yi visiting their training. They didn't know what they had available to them. Young and immature.

"Did anyone say anything after I left so abruptly?" I asked Franky. Then added, "I wasn't going to respond properly to questions if I stayed."

"Nope, I'm not sure I spoke other than a good-bye or two." He paused. "Oh, wait, I did have a brief conversation with Swanny. Basically told him we appreciated his work on a Saturday."

"Good call," I replied.

"He also dropped off the passports, not that we needed them anymore. Jack Kittleson is dead and Kim's was expired. No chance they were going anywhere now."

I nodded then froze on what he had just said. Instantly everything started swirling in my head. The crimes, the organization, the shooting ability, and alibis. It was a light coming on. It was full throttle jazz, that feeling I get when everything comes together. Just like when Hannibal on that old TV show from my childhood, *The A-Team*, was close to solving the crime, he always said he was on the jazz and he always loved it when a plan came together. Right then, with one comment, my plan had just come together.

"What is it, Tommy?" Franky asked.

"I need to go back to Minnesota, immediately." I replied.

I called Tammi and let her know. She was not happy. I knew we needed to talk more but this was not a time I would be taking her with me. I also called Carter because he would have to approve the flight. Once I told him what I knew, he had the flight set up in minutes. Franky went back to tell our partners, and I then placed a call to Zimm.

"What about Tammi?" he asked. "Is she with you this time?"

"Not this time, Zimm. I don't know what to expect tonight."

"Your guys going to be okay with you being gone? This will probably wait until tomorrow. We can watch the place."

"I know that," I replied. "But this has been too planned out. Who knows if there was an exit plan in place? It needs to happen tonight."

"Okay," stated Zimm. "I'll be at the airport when you arrive. We can head there together. I'll also have some backup just in case."

"Sounds good, partner. See you in two hours."

I can't believe I could have been so shortsighted. The simplest answer is always the easiest.

• • • • • •

Zimm and I arrived at the door, both with guns drawn. There were Minneapolis police around back, covering the garage and blocking off the road. No cars would be driving in front of the Kittleson's house until this visit was over. We stepped around the chalk line left from Mike Schulman's body. The crime tape was also still around but other than that, which was enough, the house appeared like a normal suburban family dwelling. I raised my hand to knock, then Zimm hit my shoulder and pointed to the doorbell. I smiled and we both moved to the side of the door out of habit. We didn't think anyone would open fire, but I had thought that before and been wrong.

We heard the bell ring inside and then a female voice echoed back in return. "Come on in, the door is open."

I recognized the voice although I had only heard it once before. Kim Kittleson was home. We opened the door slowly and peered inside. The room was exactly how we had left it. There was still blood on the floor left from Kim Kittleson's husband's murder and a slight bit of disarray. However, it was the figure of the wife, the person we were coming to see, that caught my attention. Standing in front of the display of shelves, the ones that included the picture of her and husband and the first place trophy in shooting, was Kim Kittleson, handgun in hand. Both Zimm and I turned our guns toward her.

"Kim, please drop the weapon. It's all over," I said, slowly and clearly.

She didn't move. The weapon was not pointing at us. Instead, it hung low, by her side. She reached her other hand to the shelves and pulled down the picture I had seen. "Is this what gave it away? When you mentioned it yesterday, I thought you might have figured it out."

I slowly took a step closer and started to answer but she raised her gun partway and cut me off. "Stay right where you are. We're just talking now. This will all be over soon enough but you don't need to rush it." A bead of sweat trickled down her cheek, or a tear, I couldn't tell which. "Now answer me, did the picture give it away?"

I held my gun on her. If she lifted her gun on either me or Zimm, I would fire. There was no doubt or hesitation in me. This is where Franky and I were different. I did not know Zimm well as far as the line of duty was concerned, but I believed he leaned more to my side. I held my position and replied to her previous question. "Not at first, but it was a final piece when I put it all together. If you're asking where your plan failed, it was your alibi."

"I never gave you an alibi," she replied. "In fact, you never even interviewed me."

Zimm seemed surprised at that comment. I was sure he was wondering what kind of detective I was. I couldn't believe it myself. "You're right. Your crime was almost perfect. Your husband gave you the best alibi ever because he believed it. He believed you were in Canada so he gave no impression of it not being true. Tie that with my stereotype that a stepmother could never feel as strongly about a hurting stepson than a father would for his own son. I took Jack Kittleson's word as gospel. He gave you the perfect alibi, but I guess you wish you had renewed your passport sooner. You could not have gone to Canada on an expired passport. It was after 9-11 that Canada and the United States began requiring passports to cross the border. You were never in Canada, were you, Mrs. Kittleson?"

She smiled and took a step away from the shelves to stand behind a recliner. It gave her a feeling of protection, though half her body was still exposed. She rested her hand with the gun on the back of the recliner but did not release it. "The passport. I never even thought about it. I thought I would have never been traced back to anything. To be honest, I was okay getting caught. I wasn't trying to bring harm to anyone but those responsible. When Nate called me several weeks ago, I knew he was close to suicide. I had heard those words before and replay them every day in my mind."

"I know, Kim," I replied. "I reviewed your file on my flight here. You lost your daughter to suicide before you met Jack. By what I could read, it brought about the end of your first marriage."

She scoffed. "The end of my first marriage. It brought about the end of my life. Until I met Jack, I was not going to make it. He taught me how life could go on, but I wasn't going to let Nate make the same choice and have it destroy Jack and Becky the same way it almost destroyed me. Nobody deserves that."

"Can you tell me about the murders? How did you do it? How did you leave no evidence?"

I thought by her expression that I was losing her. Her eyes were staring at me but really staring through me. I didn't know if she was going to speak again, until her voice cracked, breaking the silence. "I left you the shoe prints at every site. I was sure you would look into Jack, but I also knew he had numerous cameras at work that would provide him a solid alibi. But if I used his shoe size, it would focus your time on him. Further, there was no way a woman would wear a men's size eleven. Everything else was microbiology. I am a cellular biologist as an undergrad and I have my masters in microbiology. My first job was working in cleanrooms. Just like in a cleanroom, I wore Tyvek jumpsuits, I planned each event, and I even stole some chemical, gaining entry from the old programmed door opener in our SUV. The shot was still one of my best. When I saw you looking at the picture, I thought you realized that was a couple's award. Jack taught me how to shoot ten years ago. I was a natural, even beating him numerous times. We were the most famous couple at the Horse and Hunt Club. We won every year."

"How about the fire? How did you do that?"

"I actually thought I would have to stop after the shooting. There was too much police coverage. You guys were camped out at the houses. Then, when I was driving back to my room, I passed the lawn care place. They had trucks. I walked up to one of the trucks and the keys were right on the seat. That's how I came up with the idea. I printed a couple large posters at Fed Ex. They didn't look great but they looked good enough. My plan was to burn down all three houses, Principal Bales' and the two teachers, but I could never get Bales in his house alone. I actually put the accelerant down on all three houses. Then, when I watched, I learned both teachers were in one by themselves. I just got lucky."

I don't know if I was impressed or appalled that Kim said she was lucky to kill two people at once. I would be lying if I was not impressed with the murders. I remembered during the investigation when I said it was like these crimes were planned by a woman but performed by a man. That was because I was too full of male chauvinism to realize that the right woman could do both.

She took a short break in her story and wiped her eyes. She was starting to fade. I knew what this was. This was a confession. I knew how confessions usually ended. I needed to stop this now, while I still could.

"You know, Kim, I don't need to hear anymore. You acted out of love to save your stepson. Your husband would be proud." She ignored my comment. I glanced to Zimm and saw he had his gun fixed on her head. I lowered mine. "Kim, let's put an end to this now, before anyone else gets hurt."

"You know, I knew I had no shot at Bales, so I called him to tell him I would never let it end. I would let all this clear and then come and get him, when he least expected it. He would never be safe and always be looking over his shoulder. I didn't expect the depression. He truly felt as if he failed those kids, Nate, the Malecha girl, all of them. When Jack told me he had committed suicide, I felt so torn. I began to question everything I had done. I thought about the people beyond those responsible I was affecting. Then when that asshole came into my house and stabbed my husband, it all ended for me." She raised the gun and put it to her head.

"Mrs. Kittleson, leave the gun on the chair and let's talk about options," Zimm said. "It does not have to end this way." I liked the timing. She had responded well to him yesterday. Maybe he could save her today.

She turned to stare at him. "Yes," she said softly, "yes, it does."

•　•　•　•　•

I don't think I heard the shot, but I definitely know I saw the blood spatter on shelves. Police entered from every door. Several had already made it into the house during this conversation. Zimm had lowered his gun and taken my gun from my hand. Although I didn't fire, Zimm had. Kim Kittleson had removed her gun from her head and turned it toward me. In all my years, I had never hesitated. I don't know why I did today, but I did. Zimm did not and because of that, I was alive. Zimm's gun had been taken from him, as is standard in any police shooting. He was going to be taken in for a statement, as would I. The next five hours I do not remember. The case was closed, the guilty were dead, as were many of the innocent. Now was simply the time to put everything together for the final report.

I stayed at Zimm's that night. He owned a high-rise in downtown Minneapolis. I had no idea how he came across a multimillion dollar property, but I'm sure the story would come my way sometime. Tonight, I simply wanted to have a drink and sleep. As I knew from the first time we met, EZ Zimmerman was a reformed alcoholic. This meant he didn't have any alcohol in his house, but what he did have, was a bar called Runyan's on the main floor of his high-rise. I learned it was famous for wings, but they also kept two drinks always fully stocked, McNaughton's Canadian Whiskey and Wild Turkey. They had added Turkey ever since the night I met Zimm in Chicago. Although he didn't own the bar, he heavily influenced it.

Tonight was a Wild Turkey night.

"Thank you, Eric," I said to him.

"Hey now, only my mother and father call me that," Zimm replied.

"Tonight, you saved my life. I will say thank you to my friend, Eric Z. Zimmerman." I shook my head. "I don't know why I didn't fire."

"Because you cared about the woman," he replied.

"I did not care about her," I stated sternly, almost offended.

He smiled and took a sip of his water. He always ordered a McNaughton's as well, but left it in front of him. He told me before it was always a test, to keep him true to his control. Today that McNaughton's was further out of his reach than before, which I believe was intentional. "I don't mean it in a bad way," he said. "Think of it this way. When you have an ex-wife and if you ever were to remarry, you would want your new wife to care that much about your first kids, even though they were her step kids." He took another drink. "Maybe I am reaching, but I knew halfway through the conversation you were not going to shoot if the situation presented itself. Kim Kittleson was not going to walk out of there alive. The only question was whether I was going to shoot her or if she was going to shoot herself."

"I believed that also." This was true. I believed that right after she started confessing, everything except the part that only Zimm would shoot.

"What you may not have heard is, after Jack died, his rather large life insurance went to Kim. When Kim died, her life insurance and now his, all goes to Nate. I had my boss check before we left the station. In her final act, suicide by cop, she secured Nate's future. Nate was the one she was trying to protect all along."

I did not answer and simply finished my Turkey on the rocks.

"Have you called Tammi?" he asked after a few minutes.

"I have," I replied. "She'll be gone tomorrow before I get back."

He turned to me and actually placed his hand on my back. "This just isn't your day, partner. I thought she was talking about staying?"

I nodded. "She was, but when we talked through it, she knew inside she would always hold it against me if things didn't work out. She said she wants to give it six months. If we could remain together after six months apart, then we could do it for as long as needed."

"What did you say?"

"I told her good-bye."

21 I WAS SITTING in the Humphrey terminal of Minneapolis-St. Paul Airport late Sunday morning. I had had several calls the night before bringing everyone up to speed. Zimm had been a very gracious host and set me up in my own apartment in his high-rise building. The Wild Turkey and later McNaughton's was hitting me hard this morning, but not as hard as the Buffalo wings. Another trip to the bathroom was definitely in my future before my flight. ESPN was on in the background and I quickly got updated on all the basketball scores. I was glad to see Jamal was headed to the final four. I was sure his mom would be going to see the games in person.

My mind was still a bit of a blur. I was questioning how I handled the situation. I wondered if what Zimm had told me was true, or if there was something else going on with me. Did my relationship with Tammi and everything going on affect my judgement? I didn't know, but this was the first time in a twenty-plus year career that I was unsure. I did not like that feeling. I did not like that feeling at all.

Just then I felt a slight pressure on my shoulder. It felt like a gun barrel but my immediate instinct told me I was in an airport. I turned my head slowly and greeted the last smile I thought I would see at that moment.

I would have been slightly surprised if it had been Zimm or even Franky, to a slightly higher level had it been Tammi or even Halterman, but the eyes I saw were not the ones of any friend or a person who cared for my well-being. The eyes I saw were filled with hatred.

"So, Detective, I heard you wanted to see me."

I did not allow the shock to show on my face or reaction. I turned slowly and with my right hand, reached across my body and removed his fingers that were formed into the shape of a gun from pressing into the back of my shoulder. "Hello, Marco, it's been a while."

Marco Filini didn't move or show any signs of stepping back. In fact, he was in what would normally be called a person's space. He was not touching me and I was still sitting, but he had walked around the chairs and now stood to where his legs were within an inch or so of my knees. "Again, Detective, I heard you wanted to see me. I heard it was for my own good, but I seriously doubt that."

"Marco, why don't you take it down a notch? I solved the case and in turn, cleared you in the process." I stood which would normally have caused the person standing so close to move back. He did not which meant I in turn could not move away. We stood eye to eye, about four inches from each other. I felt like Sylvester Stallone and the big Russian guy before their fight in *Rocky IV*. I just wasn't sure if I was Ivan Drago or Rocky.

"You want to tell me how the woman from Lakeville killing a bunch of teachers and a student in Chicago has any tie to me?" Marco asked.

Ah, he did his research. A bit creepy actually. I remained equally as close and the few shots of spittle I received from him would absolutely be returned. "It was being painted as a professional hit. As I told Moretti, I didn't think it was you because I didn't think it was your style, but the feds were throwing your name around as a suspect. My point to meet with you was to ask if you knew who would be trying to set you up, either in the field or in the FBI office. In my opinion, there was no reason to tie you to the crimes, but someone was and I wanted to understand why."

He remained locked on me for another five to seven seconds, then he stepped back. When he did so, I noticed my entire body was locked, arms flexed, chest tight and pushed out. I was like a male turkey, feathers up, trying to put on a show for some ladies. What the hell was I doing?

Filini started to show a reduced level of intensity but still remained focused on me. "Detective, the last thing I need is you worrying if I'm being set up. You want to worry about me, then worry about what alley I'm going to find you in to finally square off. I told you before, we will meet sometime."

"Listen, Marco, I'm not sure why you have a hard-on for me, but you need to dial it down. If you and I ever meet, it will simply result in you being arrested. I don't have time to put on a show for your own ego."

"You owe me, O'Malley. You owe me that meeting."

That one caught me. "Why in the hell do I owe you anything? Why, because I put your boss through the ringer on a case? Get over yourself."

He looked stung and actually angry at my response. A couple of people in the terminal had taken notice of our small confrontation. My fear was security was going to be called and with Filini, you never knew what could happen. I needed to diffuse this before it went any further. Filini however, was already angry. "Are you fucking kidding me? You don't remember? You don't remember Vegas?"

What the hell was he talking about? Vegas. I hadn't been to Vegas since I was a teenager. "What the hell do you mean, Vegas? I haven't been to Vegas."

"1986–the Taekwondo Nationals. You were slated to be in Pool A and then the next thing I knew, you ducked me and got moved to Pool B. You were the one nobody wanted to face. Nobody but me. Then the only way we would meet was in the finals."

"1986?" I repeated slowly. "I was in the finals. In fact, I won the 1986 nationals, but I didn't end up against you."

"That's because I was disqualified for a bogus ruling. A ruling I heard Master Yi argued for so you wouldn't have to square up against me."

Marco was really starting to appear angry. His face was red and his arms angled out as if he were ready to attack. The people watching were increasing in number and now had to be at least eight. I was sure security was on its way. "Marco, I have no idea what you're talking about, but I guarantee you that neither Master Yi nor me had anything to do with any ruling. Until now, I didn't even know you, or anyone I should be concerned with, was at that tournament. I had planned to win that tourney from the start and I accomplished my goal."

"You owe me, O'Malley, and you will pay up eventually." Marco turned and began walking away.

I hollered back to him. "Hey, Marco, how did you know about the case I was on?"

"I make it my business to know, Detective," he replied. "And by the way, sorry to hear about you and Tammi."

Wow, I thought to myself, *the guy was good*. "Thanks, Marco, I appreciate the concern."

He smiled with the same bright white teeth I remembered seeing that first time at Polino's strip club. No teeth could be that perfect. I glanced around and the small group paying attention and snapping pictures and video of the prefight they thought would turn into something big all had begun disbanding. I wasn't sure what to think about that encounter. Marco Filini didn't scare me, because nobody scared me when it came to a physical altercation. However, Marco also was not like anyone else I had squared up against before. I had lost matches in the gym, but I lost them because of a strict list of rules we had to follow and a well-placed kick ended up with some points or a takedown that gained my opponent an advantage. On the street, those rules did not apply. I was usually better in an "anything goes" world, but I imagined Marco was as well. I guess time would tell. I would never go looking for Marco, but the truth was, I wanted him dead. He had killed a lot of people and was at least partially responsible for the suffering both Tammi Hutchins and Jessica Jackson received, not to mention the death of Vice Detectives Tom Clark and Diana Gallows, both killed while under cover. As I thought about those victims, the desire to meet with Marco began to grow. I turned back to where he had walked and saw him staring back at me smiling.

"Yes," Marco said to himself. "Now you want to meet too."

NOTE FROM THE AUTHOR

Word-of-mouth is crucial for any author to succeed. If you enjoyed the book, please leave a review online—anywhere you are able. Even if it's just a sentence or two. It would make all the difference and would be very much appreciated.

Thanks!
Kenneth

ABOUT THE AUTHOR

Kenneth S. Kappelmann is an award-winning author, including Fantasy Book of the Year (2013, *The Return of the Dragons*) and Best Sequel (2014, *The Dragon Unknown*). Driven with a fantasy background, the stories unfold in never foreseen fashion leaving the reader unable to guess who is truly behind the crimes.

Twitter: kappelmannbooks

E-mail: kappelmannbooks@yahoo.com

Facebook: HiddenMagicReturnoftheDragon

www.kappelmannbooks.com

Thank you so much for reading one of our **Crime Fiction** novels.
If you enjoyed the experience, please check out our
recommended title for your next great read!

Never Been Found by Kenneth S. Kappelmann

"This was a great murder mystery." –*Smashbomb*

View other Black Rose Writing titles at
<u>www.blackrosewriting.com/books</u> and use promo code
PRINT to receive a **20% discount** when purchasing.

www.ingramcontent.com/pod-product-compliance
Lightning Source LLC
Chambersburg PA
CBHW011135100726
47898CB00009B/2987